Someone softly kissed her cheek

Ginnie stirred, troubled, because she knew she hadn't dreamed the kiss. Something dangerous was happening to her, something real, and she had to fight it, if she could only struggle up through the depths of sleep.

A hand was touching her neck. Was it real? It seemed preternaturally strong, and it gripped her throat.

Wake up, some deep part of her mind screamed in alarm, and Ginnie fought to obey.

With great effort, she opened her eyes, but the hand on her throat tightened. Her eyelids fluttered and she caught the briefest glimmer of light. Then the light disappeared and all she saw was darkness.

ABOUT THE AUTHOR

Bethany Campbell, a former English teacher and textbook consultant, writes full-time for Harlequin. When she's not writing, Bethany enjoys travel and collecting cartoon art. She is married and the mother of one son.

Books by Bethany Campbell

Dead
Opposites
Bethany Campbell

Harlequin Books

TORONTO • NEW YORK • LONDON
AMSTERDAM • PARIS • SYDNEY • HAMBURG
STOCKHOLM • ATHENS • TOKYO • MILAN

To Bill and Kathy McFetridge

Harlequin Intrigue edition published December 1990

ISBN 0-373-22151-7

Printed in U.S.A.

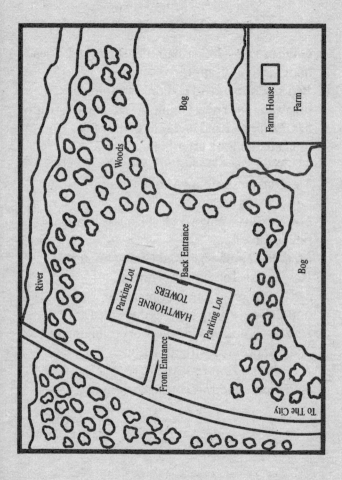

CAST OF CHARACTERS

Ginnie Price—In her bathtub, she found a dead body...that disappeared.

Wayne Priborski—He didn't want to get involved, but knew Ginnie was telling the truth.

Mr. Prouty—Kind and old, Ginnie felt obligated to look after him.

Mr. Swengler—He hid *things* in the woods.

Mr. Donner—A man who couldn't possibly hurt a living creature?

Mr. Fairfax—Why was he dismissed from the police force?

Mrs. Treat—She believed Ginnie because Hawthorne Towers *was* haunted.

Mr. Burbage—The superintendent whose building keys were supposedly stolen.

Robbie—A naive kid who worked maintenance and disappeared without a trace.

Hawthorne Towers—An apartment building whose past and present were connected.

Prologue

The apartment house stood at the edge of a woods outside a city in southern New Hampshire. Beyond the woods flowed the river, dark and twisting.

The exterior of the building was a monument to all that was excessive in Victorian architecture. Doors and windows arched sharply, like demonic eyebrows. Cornices, friezes, pilasters and iron cresting complicated the structure's already complex and ponderous lines. The red brick had weathered poorly through a century of New England winters, growing pitted, dark and streaked with black.

The building was rectangular with two towers rising from the third story, one on the east end and one on the west. It sat before the woods like the severed head of some huge beast with a pair of blunt horns.

It had been built as a dormitory for female mill workers drawn from their homes by the textile industry. The mill it served and the nineteenth century came to an end almost simultaneously, and the building began its myriad transformations.

It became, in turn, a school for rebellious boys, a tuberculosis sanatorium, a girls' academy, a private hospital and finally, in the 1970s, an apartment building.

Its exterior was now marred by an angular network of fire escapes that looked like rusty scaffolding and during the last six months, the interior had suffered through still another remodeling.

The apartment building, which was called Hawthorne Towers, was eight miles from the edge of one of New Hampshire's largest cities, but it seemed farther. It seemed, in fact, far from everything, hidden on an obscure and winding road where few had reason to travel.

The only nearby structures were a rotting cluster of wooden skeletons and fallen bricks a mile away—the remains of the burned-out mills. Little of the buildings remained except their fire-blackened foundations and charred ribs. Slowly the brambles and pines had reclaimed the ruins. The site, like many in New Hampshire, was said to be haunted.

No one had ever told Ginnie Prince that Hawthorne Towers itself was haunted, but no one had to—her imagination began to work overtime the moment she saw the place. Try as she might, she could not shake her conviction that the building was more than a collection of rented rooms. It seemed to her like an entity with a life and soul of its own, an uneasy soul that was both disturbed and disturbing.

Since Ginnie had come to New England from the midwest seven months ago, she had lived at Hawthorne Towers. She'd thought the place, isolated and ornate, looked like the setting for a Stephen King novel, but housing was hard to come by in southern New Hampshire.

She'd told herself that the building was quaint and that she shouldn't be silly about it. What did it matter if mists from the river sometimes wrapped around it like a ragged shroud? Or if people in the neighboring village jokingly called it "The Dungeon"? The rent was reasonable, the rooms spacious. Ginnie had swallowed her misgivings and leased the apartment in the east tower for one year.

Later, she realized she hadn't been thinking clearly when she rented the place. Her marriage had just broken up, and she'd left Indiana desperate for a change of scene. She'd taken the first job offer that would get her out of South Bend and, in the same headlong mood, she'd rented the first passable apartment.

Now she wished she had not been so hasty. Her new job, as legal council to a coalition of citizen's groups, was not as fulfilling as she'd hoped. The groups squabbled incessantly among themselves, and the big battles, against the nuclear reactor on the coast and the hazardous-waste dump, had been fought and won long before she'd come.

And, although she had never considered herself nervous, she found that Hawthorne Towers filled her with a nameless apprehension. Despite the old building's excellent upkeep, to Ginnie, it gave off an almost palpable aura of ruin. Elegant ruin, but ruin nevertheless. She sensed that beneath the layers of improvement and the shiny new fixtures, decay gnawed deep into the building's secret places.

At night in her tower bedroom, she could hear scuttling noises in the walls, noises that might have been the wind or simply the building settling. But the rustlings and creaks might just as easily be mice or even rats, and she could not fall back to sleep.

On bad nights, she tried not to envision that the sounds were made by the undead, scraping their bony fingers as they tried to get into her room. She tried to keep supernatural thoughts from her mind, but found that she could not. She kept imagining all sorts of horrors populating the shadows.

Many of Ginnie's least-pleasant fantasies centered on the third floor, which was being remodeled. On weekdays, it was an ordinary place smelling of sawdust and paint, noisy with sounds of construction. But when the work stopped, it changed. It became dark, deserted and somehow sinister to her.

By the seventh month Ginnie had lived there, she had come to dislike and distrust the place. Strange things kept happening. A picture that hung in the hall would not stay in place. It fell so repeatedly that she finally took it down permanently. Sometimes she had the feeling she was being watched. Her best nightgown, a sheer white one, disappeared. She tried to convince herself she'd lost it at the Laundromat. She could not.

Slowly she became convinced that she should move, even if it meant breaking her lease. To do so, however, she was going to have to find a different job, a better-paying one. That was fine with her. She was willing to leave both the job and Hawthorne Towers far behind to start a new life again.

Then, one Thursday night in December, her uneasiness about the third floor suddenly became justified. The manager of the apartments, Mr. Burbage, was struck down and robbed of his wallet and keys. He had been working alone and late on the third floor, changing some burned-out light bulbs. Someone had struck him from behind, knocking him unconscious, and he fell hard on his right arm, fracturing his wrist. The stolen keys unlocked every door in Hawthorne Towers, including Ginnie's.

Never easy in the building, she slept that night with an armchair pushed against the door. She intended to change her lock as soon as possible, but the next afternoon she had an interview for a better job in Maine and she didn't intend to miss it. It was an junior legal assistant to an action group representing the victims of hand guns. The organization was young, focused and vigorous.

In addition, she had made reservations to stay at a hotel in Kennebunkport. She wanted to do some last-minute Christmas shopping, and the town had wonderful shops. She would also be glad for the chance to spend even one night away from Hawthorne Towers. As soon as she got back, she told herself, she would change the lock and install a police lock, as well.

In the meantime, she tried to keep herself from imagining what might happen in the nooks and shadows of Hawthorne Towers now that the keys were stolen. She asked her next door neighbor, a kindly-seeming man named Mr. Prouty, to keep an eye on her apartment for her while she was gone. He promised he would.

But on Friday morning just before Ginnie left, the temperature dropped and snow began to fall. Mr. Prouty, walking his dog, slipped on the ice, hitting his head. He had to be taken to the hospital in an ambulance.

Mr. Burbage, the manager, was still recuperating from his own injuries. Robbie, the young man who helped with maintenance, would be busy keeping the walks and stairs clear and the lobby mopped up. And, of course, with the third floor empty, there was no one living anywhere near Ginnie to watch things for her.

In short, there was nobody left in Hawthorne Towers who could see that Ginnie Prince's apartment stayed safe.

Nobody at all.

Chapter One

Ginnie didn't reach her destination in Maine.

By afternoon, a violent blizzard had closed over the east coast. If she hadn't wanted a different job and a different apartment so badly, she wouldn't have set out. As it was, halfway to Kennebunkport, she was forced to turn around and start home.

The ice had put her badly behind schedule and the sky was already growing dark. She stopped at a gas station to phone and cancel her interview at the Justice for Victims office. There was no answer. The whole staff, wiser than she, must have gone home, where all sensible people should take shelter in such weather.

She tried to cancel her hotel reservation, but the call wouldn't go through. She glanced out the window at the driving snow, shook her head, and tried again. Nothing. A line must be down somewhere, a sign that the storm was, indeed, a major one.

The mechanic, a lean, weather-roughened man of about forty, watched her with an intensity that disturbed her. Ginnie, who had been divorced for little more than a year, still felt uncomfortable when men paid attention to her.

"Got far to go?" he asked. He wore a flannel shirt and sat in a swivel chair, his feet tilted up on the low counter. His teeth were bad, his hands were dirty and he was smoking a cigarette.

"About sixty miles," Ginnie said, watching the wind whip the snow against the station's big front window. Suddenly she didn't want to go back out into the storm. Cars wrecked in weather like this. People died.

"Wouldn't try it if I was you," the mechanic said. He stared at her with interest that was frank and sly at the same time. She was a tall young woman of twenty-seven, striking rather than pretty, and too thin since her divorce. She had long curly auburn hair and electric-blue eyes. Her normally fair skin was even paler from tension, and it made her eyes seem larger and her lashes darker than usual.

She pulled on her gloves and tried to act calmer than she felt. "Look," she said, "is there a motel around here?"

He kept staring at her. He blew out a stream of smoke. "Nope," he said at last. "All closed for the season."

Mentally she muttered a few swear words. She stared out the window again. Beyond the snow, the night already seemed to be falling, black as death.

"I wouldn't go out there, hon. You'll never make it," the mechanic said, not taking his eyes off her. "Me, I'm about ready to close up, go home, have a couple drinks, stay warm. I live two hundred yards up the road. You're welcome to join me. Like I say, I wouldn't drive in that." He nodded toward the whirling snow. "No, ma'am. I wouldn't be fool enough to chance that. You come home with me. I don't ask nothin' in return. Just tryin' to do you a favor."

Ginnie gave him a measured look. He sat farther back in his chair, trying to look jaunty. The self-satisfied smile on his face told her that he lied; he did hope for something in return, and the something would be sex.

She turned and headed for the door. She was not good at such scenes. Suggestions of casual morality always startled her. That's why divorce had taken her by surprise: it had never *occurred* to her that her husband would be unfaithful. She had naively believed he was too ethical for adultery.

"Hey, lady, wait!" the mechanic called as she opened the door and the cold air blasted in. "I mean it—you'd be a lot smarter to—"

She kept walking. The door shut behind her, cutting off his words. The wind lashed as she made her way back to her car and got in. Snow had already obscured the windshield again and she turned on the wipers to brush it away.

She started the car and began the torturous homeward route again. By five o'clock, the sky was as dark as if it were midnight.

Driving through the blowing veils of snow gave Ginnie a headache as sharp and evil as a devil's pitchfork. She wished once more that she'd never set out.

She should have known that the day was going to be nothing but a series of disasters, she told herself. She should have known as soon she walked outside and saw snow falling and the ambulance pulling up. A small crowd of tenants had gathered around Mr. Prouty, who lay on the sidewalk, groaning softly.

"Let me up," he was saying. "I have to go to work. They need me." Mr. Prouty's job was at the blood bank, and he was dedicated to public health work. It pained Ginnie to see a man so concerned with other's well-being in pain himself.

Robbie, the young maintenance man, squatted by Mr. Prouty, his hand beneath the older man's head. Robbie's face was pale. It was Robbie's job to put rock salt on the sidewalks and stairs to melt the ice, and he obviously hadn't done it yet that morning. He looked terrified that he'd be blamed for Mr. Prouty's accident. Robbie was a rather handsome young man, but he wasn't very bright and he was as sensitive of criticism as a shy child.

Mrs. Treat, the huge elderly woman who lived on the second floor, had also been among those gathered around Mr. Prouty. She stood holding Mr. Prouty's miniature dachshund, Alfy, against her coated bosom and staring down at Mr. Prouty with proprietary interest. Alfy, seeming distressed at his master's pain, had howled and struggled in vain to escape Mrs. Treat's embrace.

"I foresaw this," Mrs. Treat intoned, shaking her head so that her jowls wobbled. "I dreamed just the other night that not one, but *two* of the men in this building would soon be lying down in pain. I *knew* it."

Ginnie had looked into the old woman's green eyes and seen an expression that was almost gloating. She looked away again, not knowing what to say. Mrs. Treat liked to boast that she was psychic; little happened that she hadn't claimed to foresee, and Ginnie wasn't comfortable around the woman. She could only stand there feeling sorry for poor Mr. Prouty, who seemed disoriented and in pain.

Yes, Ginnie now thought darkly, if Mrs. Treat really had psychic powers, why hadn't she warned Mr. Prouty to stay off the ice? For that matter, why hadn't she told Ginnie not to bother to start out to Kennebunkport?

She's probably afraid to tell me my future, Ginnie thought, her head starting to hurt even worse. *After all, my past and present aren't exactly golden.*

She narrowed her eyes against the glare of her lights on the weaving snow and slowed the car's speed to a crawl. She could not see more than a few feet in front of her, and her tires kept sliding. Her hands were numb from gripping the steering wheel so tightly, and all the muscles in her neck and shoulders ached with tension.

It should have taken her an hour and a half to drive the winding roads back to Hawthorne Towers. In the snow and darkness, she saw that it would take almost five hours. She could move only at a creep, and she lost count of the other vehicles she saw that had slid off the road.

The car's heater wasn't working well and its radio broadcast nothing except warnings to stay off the highways. That and news of accidents and closing. Sometimes the grimness was punctuated by an equally grim commercial in which a man offered a reward for information about his missing twenty-two-year-old son, Jackie "Junior" Hopkins, who had last been seen a few months ago in southern New Hampshire.

"My son is not a bad boy. But he's confused, and my wife and I want him back. Please call this number if you have information on the whereabouts of Jackie 'Junior' Hopkins." The man's voice always ended sounding as if he were stifling a sob.

Ginnie felt deeply sorry for him, but she couldn't stand to hear either his sorrow or the highway warnings again. She switched off the radio and drove on in oppressive quiet. The only sound was the dull whump-whump as the windshield wipers fought the heavy snow.

She was no longer sure she could reach home in five hours. She'd had to slow her speed even more. It might now take her six. For the first time in months, Hawthorne Towers seemed like a refuge to her, a place of safety.

By the time she reached her parking space in the apartment lot, her stomach was full of knots and her shoulders were rigid with tension. Her knees felt shaky, as if they might not hold her up much longer.

Her hand on the bannister, she trudged upstairs, so exhausted that not even the darkness and silence of the third floor could shake her. She had fought the snow so long she still seemed to see it swirling before her eyes.

She opened the door of her apartment and switched on the lights. She hung up her hat and coat, kicked off her boots and went directly into the bathroom. She needed aspirin badly. Her eyes hurt, her ears rang, she was dizzy and she could feel the veins in her temples swelling and contracting.

She pushed open the bathroom door, turned on the light then stopped, her hand still on the switch.

Her headache fled, a forgotten trifle. A plunging sensation shook the pit of her stomach, as if the floor had given way beneath her.

She backed out of the bathroom, her mouth half open in horror. Snowflakes melted in her hair, but she didn't notice them. *This isn't happening,* she thought. *I must be hallucinating.*

She blinked to make the hallucination go away. It did not.

What she saw was not possible. She felt a terrified chill bloom in her bones. She squeezed her eyes shut once more, but when she opened them, the same sight greeted her.

A strange man sat slumped in her bathtub. There was no water in the tub. The man was dead.

His sport coat glistened with moisture, his shirt front was sodden and gray with it, but his trousers, brown tweed overcoat, gray fedora, shoes and woolen gloves looked dry. A bluish cast tinged his face and his expression was unspeakable. His eyes, half opened, were red with burst vessels. They seemed to look straight at Ginnie.

She took another step backward. The man looked shabby and needed a shave. He had a hole in the fingertip of one glove, and through it she saw that under his bluish fingernail there was a black line of dirt.

The man kept staring with his reddened eyes from under the brim of his hat. A fine trickle of dirty water crept from the corner of his mouth.

Ginnie tried to scream. She couldn't. The best she could accomplish was a small, breathless sound.

She didn't close the bathroom door. She was afraid to. Who knew what the dead man might do once the door was shut? She needed to keep an eye on him as long as possible; she had seen enough horror movies to know that.

She inched backward down the hall until she could just see the man, but his bloodshot stare was hidden by his hat brim. She tried to scream again and could only choke out the same ineffectual sound.

Shaking, she bent and tried to draw on one of the boots she had kicked off when she entered the apartment. It was difficult because her hands were trembling so violently. Keeping her gaze trained on the dead man's blue and shadowed face, she decided to go barefoot. The snow she had tracked in just moments before was cold beneath her stockinged feet.

Not daring to turn her back on the bathroom, she reached into the entry closet and pulled her coat off its hanger. She shrugged back into it. She reached for her muffler and draped it unevenly around her neck. Her throat felt extremely vulnerable, as if someone might suddenly put violent hands on it to strangle the life out of her.

She reached for her overstuffed leather purse sitting on the entry table. She opened the door of her apartment and backed out carefully. Somehow she managed to lock the door. It was reassuring to have a solidly locked door between her and the staring corpse.

She turned and stood at the top of the stairs. Without understanding why, she carefully buttoned the top button of her coat. She tried to scream again. She couldn't.

Her knees shaking worse, she walked down the stairs, holding the bannister. She paused at the third-floor landing. The hall stretched away before her, full of darkness and ladders and tarpaulins lying like crumpled ghosts on the floor. Still gripping the bannister, she descended to the second floor landing.

People lived on this floor, Mr. Fairfax and Mrs. Treat and a new tenant, a man she had not yet seen.

Ginnie opened her mouth, but her screaming mechanism still did not work. A knot in her throat blocked any sound she tried to make. Perhaps, she thought, it would be best to scream on the ground floor, where the most people lived.

Swallowing hard, she started down the stairs again. The marble stairs were cold as death beneath her feet. She leaned hard on the bannister, no longer trusting her legs to support her. At last she found herself standing on the icy tiles of the lobby.

A man stood in the lobby, staring at her. He wore neither hat nor coat. He was dressed in faded jeans and a black shirt with the sleeves rolled back. He looked at Ginnie, wariness in his eyes. She did not realize that her face was unnaturally pale and that her eyes looked wild.

She recognized the man. He was the dark, muscular man with the limp. He lived in the west tower of the apartment building. He was the one who walked around all the time, sometimes even late at night. Although he was handsome, he always looked somehow angry.

She tried to speak, tried to tell him about the dead man. But she could say nothing. She felt as if someone had hollowed out her mind and a dark wind blew through it.

The man frowned. He took a step toward her. He studied her bloodless face. "You all right, lady?"

Ginnie looked at him. He stood an inch taller than she did in her stocking feet. He had a blue tattoo of an anchor on his forearm, and the words U.S. Navy. How tacky, thought Ginnie, feeling dizzy and far away. He was a nice-looking man, she had always thought so, but skin art was definitely déclassé.

Suddenly, something came back to life in her. She opened her mouth again. At last she screamed.

The dark man looked at her, stunned. He took another step toward her. He grabbed her by the upper arms. "Lady?" he said. "Lady?"

Ginnie kept screaming. Now that she had recovered the ability, she intended to exercise it to the fullest.

The man shook her, his face stony. "Snap out of it." When Ginnie refused to stop, he shook her harder.

She could almost feel her brain rattling against her skull. Screaming did no good, she thought in fright and confusion. This man was hurting her. The louder she cried out, the angrier he looked and more forcibly he shook her.

But he made her stop screaming. She stared, still openmouthed, into his black eyes. Her own eyes grew wider and more terrified. She took three deep breaths so she could tell him: there was a blue man with red eyes sitting in her bathtub, and he was dead.

Instead something in her mind gave way. She fainted in the dark man's arms.

Chapter Two

The woman fell forward, her head against Wayne's chest. He caught her. His leg almost buckled, but he kept standing and held her.

He hadn't held a respectable woman in his arms since the accident, nor did he want to. Now he had one, whether he liked it or not, and it was a disturbing sensation.

Two years ago, Wayne Priborski had been a captain in the navy, an aviator with a healthy career and an ailing marriage. Then the accident had nearly killed him. Both the career and the marriage were washed up, and he had become a man who kept strictly to himself, looking neither forward nor backward. Suddenly having this woman in his arms sent a jolt through his whole system.

As he maneuvered her toward the stairs, she sagged against his chest and her curly auburn hair brushed his chin. She smelled like lilies of the valley. For her height, she was surprisingly delicate, and when his cheek came into accidental contact with hers, her skin felt cool and smooth as chilled satin.

He managed to sit her on the second step, her back against the balusters, her head nodding forward.

He knelt stiffly on the stair beside her, conscious that doors were opening, that people were staring at him and the woman. His leg pained him but he ignored it.

He took her face between his hands and shook her head slightly. Her red-brown curls bobbed. She had an oval face that was almost as pale as the snow swirling outside. She sighed softly.

He bent closer to her, pain shooting harder through his leg. "Lady?" he said gruffly. "Hey, lady!"

Ginnie's eyes fluttered open. She found herself staring into a square-jawed face with dark hair, dark eyebrows, dark eyes and an irritable expression. His hands were warm and powerful against her cold skin. She could feel her pulses leaping drunkenly under his fingers.

Her mouth was dry. She opened her mouth slightly and took another deep breath. She reached deeply inside herself for her voice.

He stared at her more intently, frowned even harder. She had the bluest eyes he had ever seen, and true terror shone from them. What in God's name had happened to her? he wondered.

"There's a dead man in my bathtub," she managed to say. "He's wearing an overcoat and hat. One of his gloves has a hole in it." The words brought the memory back too vividly. She fainted again, falling forward onto his chest.

Wayne sighed and held her cradled against him, smoothing her tumbled hair back from her forehead. People were stepping out into the lobby now, edging closer to the two of them. He unbuttoned the top button of her coat. His action conveyed more impatience than compassion.

"What's wrong?" a harsh voice asked. It was Fairfax, the wiry, middle-aged man from the second floor. Wayne knew Fairfax by sight and by name, but that was all. He'd heard that the man had once been with the police, but what he did now, Wayne didn't know. Fairfax had a craggy, suspicious face, and he stared down at Ginnie and Wayne as if they were guilty of some criminal act. Wayne stared back implacably, with a look that told Fairfax either to help or to mind his own damn business.

On the landing next to Fairfax stood the fat woman, Mrs. Treat, who lived next door to him. She wore thongs, a blue muumuu with lavender flowers, and pink hair curlers. Her florid face was mottled with distress.

A small white dog yapped excitedly. One of the first-floor tenants, Paul Donner, scurried up and knelt at Ginnie's feet. Under his short maroon robe, he had long, white, hairless legs. "What have we here?" Donner began to rub Ginnie's back with a rhythmic, motherly motion. His dog yapped jealously.

"Something in her apartment scared her," Wayne said without emotion.

"Poor baby," Donner cooed. He patted her back and took her pulse. "Poor, poor baby."

"I heard a scream. It sounded like death itself," Mrs. Treat said. She stared down at Ginnie ominously, as if she could read everyone's fortune crumpled there at the foot of the stairs.

"Is she all right?" asked Burbage, the manager, who stood in the entrance of his apartment, bracing himself against the doorframe. He was still far from recovered from his injuries.

Burbage was a short, squat man with thinning hair that had once been red. Now it was shot through with white, and he had a bandage patching the side of his skull. His right arm hung useless in a canvas sling. Mrs. Burbage, as usual, was nowhere to be seen. Burbage nodded toward Ginnie. "Is she all right?" he repeated.

"I don't know," Wayne muttered. The woman was an awkward bundle in his arms and once more her hair tickled his chin and got in his mouth. It was like having somebody brush silk against his face, a sensation too intimate for his liking.

Paul Donner's white toy poodle danced around on its hind feet, yapping even more loudly. Donner squatted before Ginnie's inert body, drew her from Wayne's arms and made her bend forward so her head rested between her knees.

Let Donner handle this, Wayne thought, rising, his fists clenched against the memory of touching the woman. Pain streaked through his leg. He took a step backward so that the poodle wouldn't do its hyperactive dance on his foot.

He looked down the hall. One door stood slightly ajar. A pair of pale eyes stared at them all. It was that creep, Swengler, Wayne thought. He gave the old man a sharp look. Something about Swengler made Wayne uneasy; the man was ancient, but large, almost hulking, and when he spoke, it was with an unidentifiable accent. He drove a late-model Cadillac, but he never seemed to bring anything home from the grocery store except twenty-five-pound bags of cat food. It was universally known he had no cat.

"What scared her?" Paul Donner asked, patting Ginnie's hand and chafing her wrist. "Gigi, be quiet," he told the yammering dog.

Wayne stared down at the woman. Once more he found his gaze resting on her full and parted lips. "She says there's a dead man in her bathtub."

"Well!" Donner said. "That *would* be a surprise, wouldn't it?"

Wayne stared at Swengler's wrinkled, peering face again. He kept his gaze as steady and cold as Swengler's. "Nothing surprises me anymore."

Slowly Mr. Swengler smiled at Wayne. Just as slowly, he closed the door.

"Somebody should check this out," said Burbage, the manager.

Ginnie moaned and began to stir.

Wayne looked at the other men. Burbage was in no shape to climb the stairs. Donner was no man to send on a reconnaissance mission; besides, he'd already made it his self-appointed task to flutter around the girl.

His eyes met Fairfax's. Fairfax made no offer to help. The older man swayed slightly and his eyes narrowed in an effort to stay focused. He was, Wayne realized, slightly drunk. He studied Fairfax's face. He thought it must be true that he had once been a cop. The expression in his eyes said he'd seen too much.

"Somebody should check this out," Burbage repeated.

Ginnie moaned again.

"Shh," soothed Paul Donner. "You're going to be just fine."

Fairfax said nothing at all. He turned his back and walked back into his apartment, closing the door. *What the hell?* thought Wayne.

The silence of the others weighed oppressively. Burbage started to hobble out the door toward the stairs. He didn't look too steady on his legs.

"I'll go," Wayne said between his teeth. He didn't know if the woman had seen a body or not, but something had dealt her a shock. He reached for Ginnie's purse, opened it and took out her keys.

Paul Donner and Mrs. Treat were hoisting a half-unconscious Ginnie Prince between them so they could take her into Donner's apartment to lie down. Burbage, looking slightly sick, went back inside his apartment.

Wayne gritted his teeth and started up the stairs. His leg was hurting badly tonight. Fairfax should be the one doing this, he thought, it was a cop's sort of job. He wondered why Fairfax had turned and walked away from the scene that way. The man had looked aloof, almost angry.

He reached the fourth floor. The hallway seemed deserted. It was silent, bathed in faint light from the overhead fixture and the wrought-iron sconce on the wall. He glanced at the number on Ginnie's key and unlocked her door.

He pushed it open. When he entered, the apartment was as cold as the inside of a refrigerator. The woman had left in such a hurry that she hadn't bothered to shut off the lights. He looked down the hall and into the opened bathroom.

The bathtub was empty.

He supposed he had expected as much. He walked down the hall to check more closely. He was certain the woman had seen something. Nothing she had merely imagined would put such fear into her eyes.

He stepped into the large bathroom. He frowned. There were black marks like the heel marks from a man's shoes on the tub's white bottom. A small puddle of dirty water lay pooled in the tub's center, and a patch of dead moss or pond scum floated in it. A spot of something like watery blood shimmered wetly on the tub's rim.

The shaggy pink rug beside the tub was slightly wet and stained with another spot that looked like pale and dirtied blood.

He examined the scene again with narrowed eyes. *Don't touch anything,* he thought. The place was so cold that his breath was visible.

He frowned. He turned and looked down the hall toward the bedroom. Lying on the blue carpeting was a man's gray hat, upside down. He walked to it. It was an ordinary man's hat with a dark blue band, but it looked the worse for wear. It seemed dry on the outside but damp inside.

He looked at the hat, resisting the impulse to pick it up. *What the hell,* he thought again. He remembered the woman's blue eyes, wide with fright.

Suddenly there was a rattle, a clatter and a soft rushing sound. The heat in the apartment had come back on.

He glanced in the other rooms, including the closets. Nothing. All he found was a homey clutter. She was the kind of woman who kept things.

He locked the place up and went back downstairs to tell Burbage. Burbage didn't answer his knock. Instead his wife spoke through the closed door. "Who is it? What do you want? He isn't well. He's lying down again."

Wayne scowled to himself. He knew she wouldn't open up. He'd been through this song and dance before. "Tell him I think somebody's been in the woman's apartment. I think he'd better call the police."

Only silence answered him.

"Mrs. Burbage? Did you hear me?"

Again there was no answer.

"Mrs. Burbage?"

He swore softly. *Now I'm standing talking to a door,* he thought. *Has everybody around here gone crazy?*

Paul Donner's door swung open and Donner peered out. "Well?" he said archly. "Does our pretty friend have a guest in her bathtub? Or not? What's the matter? Oh—Mrs. B. must be in charge tonight. Won't open the door?''

Wayne exhaled a harsh sigh. "She won't even talk." He nodded toward the stairs. "There's nobody up there, but something's funny. Somebody should call the police."

Donner rolled his eyes. "Ooh. The police. No wonder Mrs. B. won't talk." His voice dropped to a low whisper. "Has something to do with her daughter's death. Police upset her. Come on in. We'll call from here."

He pushed the door further open with a flourish.

Against his better judgment, Wayne entered. But he didn't intend to get any more involved in this thing, he vowed to himself. No way.

THE POLICEMAN ARRIVED and went upstairs to investigate. Wayne didn't offer to go with him, nor did the officer ask.

Ginnie sat on Paul Donner's powder-blue velvet couch, holding a glass of crème de menthe. She looked at Wayne Priborski's dark, unsmiling face. She was still shaken, but resentment was crowding out her fright. Neither he nor Paul Donner seemed to believe what had happened to her.

"There *was* a man," she said. "I saw him."

Paul Donner was bustling in the kitchen, making coffee.

"We'll see what the police say," Wayne said.

The patrolman had looked dubious at Ginnie's story and irritated at being made to drive to the city's outskirts through such an icy, stormy night. But, since the keys had been stolen only the night before, he grudgingly went upstairs to check things out.

Ginnie played nervously with her blue paisley neck scarf. She wore a blue-gray suit and white silk blouse, and would have looked dressed for success if she hadn't been barefoot and almost as pale as her blouse.

She was deeply embarrassed at having fainted, for she had never fainted before in her life. She tried now to seem calm, to compensate. She was not quite succeeding. She swallowed hard, raised her chin and forced herself to meet Wayne's questioning stare.

Paul Donner came into the front room bearing a silver tray. He set it down, centering it exactly on his expensive coffee table. "There." He put his hands on his hips and looked down at Ginnie. "Drink down that liqueur and have some coffee to brace you up."

Wayne eyed Donner coolly. The man seemed to be thriving on the excitement. "Tell me again what happened after I went upstairs."

Donner began to pour a cup of coffee. "That woman who looks like Godzilla in a muumuu—"

"Mrs. Treat?" Ginnie asked.

"Mrs. Trick or Treat." Donner tried to hand Wayne a white china cup ornamented with roses, but Wayne refused it. "She and I brought Miss Prince in here. Mrs. Treat did most of the carrying. The woman could carry a refrigerator if she wanted."

"And then?" Wayne watched Donner pour another cup of coffee.

Donner took this one himself. He crossed his legs daintily and set the saucer on his knee. "And then she went home, muttering dire things about curses and death. I think the old bat's a witch. I really do."

"And everybody else?" Wayne asked.

"Drink your liqueur, dear," Donner told Ginnie. She grimaced and obeyed.

"Burbage?" Donner said. "He's the only other one I saw. He went back inside while you were still there. The Malones—that nice young couple with the ugly cat—aren't here this week. They're gone for the holidays. The new man upstairs? He's gone, too. As for Swengler, I thought I saw him open his door long enough to give us all his famous evil eye."

"What about Fairfax?" Wayne asked. He still wondered why the man had turned his back on the whole scene.

"Oh, Fairfax." Donner shrugged. "There goes one whose name is writ in gin. He used to be with the police department. He's suspended. You know, that whole pay-off scandal. Plus, he has this problem controlling his quaffing. He climbs *on* the water wagon. He falls *off* the water wagon. With a thud. And then he's a sulky thing.''

Ginnie didn't see how anyone who had come when she'd fainted could have gone outside, climbed the fire escape, taken the body and beaten the Priborski man to her apartment. It was impossible. Yet he swore there was no body in her apartment. That was impossible, too. She pushed an auburn curl back from her brow. ''Look—there was a dead man in my apartment. I saw him. As clearly as I see you.''

Donner gave an elaborate shrug but said nothing. Wayne Priborski kept staring at her, as if she were a troublesome puzzle that interested him in spite of himself. Ginnie, embarrassed at the intensity of his gaze, glanced away.

Wayne kept watching her. ''All I saw was a hat. You can ask the officer when he comes down.''

''I'm not sure I'd trust the police in this town to tell me the time of day,'' Paul Donner observed. ''We were lucky to even get one over here. They're so shorthanded right now.''

Frustrated, Ginnie set down her coffee. ''I *saw* a man. Somebody must have moved him.'' She looked at Wayne in challenge. Could he have moved the man himself? She didn't think so, but if not, who had? Was the corpse still in the building somewhere? She was frozen by the thought.

Wayne saw the anxiety flash across her face. ''Maybe he wasn't dead,'' he offered.

She turned her eyes to his again. He had the steadiest gaze she'd ever encountered.

''He was dead,'' she insisted. ''He was blue. He wasn't breathing. He didn't blink. He was *dead*.''

Wayne studied her. She was shaken, but she knew her own mind, he'd give her that. ''You didn't recognize him?''

Ginnie made a hopeless gesture. Both men were watching her as if she were crazy, and she knew her story sounded insane. She didn't care so much about Donner's opinion, because he'd always struck her as a rather silly person. But the Priborski man had a solidity, a strength about him that made her instinctively trust him in a crisis. "I never saw him before. He was about forty. He had..."

She struggled to remember what the man looked like. All she could recall was the expression on his face, and it made her queasy. "He had blue eyes," she finished, swallowing hard again. "Bloodshot blue eyes."

Wayne nodded, encouraging her to go on. "What color hair?"

"He wore a hat."

"How tall was he?"

Ginnie made a face of exasperation. "I don't know—he was sitting in the bathtub. He had something like pond scum on his shirt. His jacket looked wet, his shirt was wet, but his overcoat and hat weren't. It was weird."

She looked almost pleadingly at Wayne. He had told her the hat in the hallway had looked damp inside. It was the one detail that he'd seen that seemed to match her story.

She was disappointed when he said nothing, only raised one black eyebrow. Silence weighed awkwardly on the air.

Wayne, watching the emotions cross her face, felt an unexpected twinge of sympathy. "What else do you remember?" He made the words gruff and kept his face emotionless. He didn't want to get drawn into this mess any further.

A knock rattled the door and she jumped involuntarily. Paul Donner, too, gave a little start. "It must be that policeman." He smoothed his thinning hair and adjusted his robe.

Donner marched to the door, the poodle bouncing and barking behind him. The dog kept yelping as he opened the door and at the sight of the uniformed patrolman, she barked herself into near frenzy.

"Gigi!" Paul Donner rose and swept the dog up, holding her to his bosom. "Well?" he asked the patrolman. "Did you tame the savage hat?"

The officer was middle-aged and overweight. Ginnie thought she saw distaste flicker over his face as he regarded

Donner. "It seems," he said, "everybody's getting cabin fever with all the snow. Here's your man's hat."

He held out a gray felt hat with a broad brim and a small red feather in the band. Ginnie tensed, recognizing it as her own.

Wayne looked at first dumbstruck, then angry. He rose and walked to the officer. Wayne took the hat. He stared down at it, then handed it wordlessly to Ginnie.

This is crazy. What's happening? Ginnie thought. She exchanged a charged glance with Wayne. His eyebrows drew together in a disbelieving frown.

"It was on the floor in the hall." The officer nodded at the hat. "And the bathtub's clean."

Ginnie shook her head, rejecting the statement, but she was overwhelmed by perplexity.

Wayne stared at the officer. Anger flashed deep in his eyes. "That isn't the hat I saw. The tub had a pool of dirty water in it. And marks, like heel marks. Don't tell me I didn't see it. I did." He turned and looked at Ginnie. She was still pale. "And the woman saw something. She didn't pass out from seeing a hat on the floor."

Ginnie took a deep breath and silently thanked Wayne. Dark and unsmiling as he was, he was on her side.

The officer only smiled sarcastically. He had a fat face, hard and self-satisfied. "You want me to take you up and show you, buddy? Hey, it's almost the full moon. You're snowed in. You're all nervous 'cause those keys got stole." He nodded at the decanter of crème de menthe. "You've had a few drinks. You imagine things. It happens."

Wayne's gaze went hard as onyx. "I'm not the nervous type. I haven't had a drink. And I don't give a damn about the full moon. So, yeah. Why don't you show me that apartment—buddy? Maybe you missed something."

His steeliness gave Ginnie's courage a badly needed boost. She stood, her knees still shaky. "I want to go, too."

The men looked at her. She clenched her jaw and spoke through her teeth. "I hadn't had anything to drink, either.

And I didn't imagine anything. I saw a dead man in my bathtub, officer.''

The patrolman allowed himself a smirk. "Suit yourself."

Paul Donner turned from the open door, cradling Gigi more firmly to his chest. "Well, *I'm* not going anywhere. Except to bed. This is going to give me nightmares, I'm sure. I've had enough excitement for one night. And this dog's poor little heart is beating like a trip-hammer. Yes-ums it is!" He wrinkled his nose at Gigi and scratched her ears. She yipped shrilly.

Ginnie reached an unsteady hand to the hall tree and took her coat and muffler. Wordlessly she followed the two men upstairs. Her heart banged in her chest like a drum. She didn't want to go back, but knew she had to.

Back on her floor, her whole chest ached as she watched the patrolman unlock the door. His left hand on the knob, he swung it open. Wayne stepped in first. Ginnie forced herself to enter and wondered if she were going to faint again. But the policeman was behind her. Nothing could happen to her with him there. Could it?

She found herself standing beside Wayne in the bath-room. The tub was clean. It was freshly scrubbed, a small pool of clear water in the bottom. Streaks of cleanser shone dully in the fluorescent light, signs of a hastily done job. Although Wayne had said the apartment had been cold, it was warm now.

Ginnie and Wayne stared at the tub and then at each other. Wayne's face was set in a mixture of disbelief and stubbornness.

"There's your body folks," the officer said. His expression clearly said he thought they both were crazy.

Wayne's lip curled and he pointed to the small bathroom rug. "There's still a spot. Something like blood."

The officer smiled unpleasantly. "A spot on a rug ain't a dead man, friend. I think I'll say good night. It's sure to be a busy night out there." He touched his left hand to the bill of his hat. He turned and left, a slight swagger in his step.

Wayne stared after him with dislike, then turned his gaze back to the tub. "There was dirty water. And marks. And something like blood."

Ginnie took a deep breath, trying to stay calm. "There was a dead man." The memory of it came flooding back in a sickening surge.

Wayne looked at her. She was shaking again. He remembered holding her in his arms, the feel of her hair against his skin. He pushed the thought away as roughly as if it had been an adversary. He was filled with the urge to get away from her and whatever peculiar trouble she was in.

"I should go, too," he said. "Will you be all right here?"

She drew herself up, held her chin high and took another deep breath. Then she shivered so hard she almost felt her teeth rattle. Her throat seemed to close up again. She tried to smile and say yes. She found she could not.

Her apartment had been invaded, and she felt violated, dirtied and menaced. She glanced down the hall and caught a glimpse of her tiny Christmas tree standing, lonely and spindly, in the living room. It made her realize how isolated she was in this place, how alone and far from Indiana and a life that seemed to make sense.

She bit her lip, not wanting to reveal any more emotion. Wayne Priborski had already seen her at her worst. She didn't want him to see her that way again; it was like being naked in front of somebody. *Get hold of yourself,* she thought fiercely. She bit her lip harder.

Oh, damn, thought Wayne and gritted his teeth.

She glanced at his emotionless face and shook her head. She kept control of her voice, but it sounded strangled. "I'm sorry. I just don't think I can stay here. I'll get a motel somewhere." She went into the hall and pulled her boots on, trying to keep her hands from trembling. They shook anyway.

Oh, damn, thought Wayne again. He could tell it was taking all her willpower to keep from losing control again. She shouldn't drive in this weather or in her emotional state, and she probably shouldn't be alone. He was going to have to do something. He didn't want to. He didn't want to get involved. He had troubles of his own.

He surprised himself, and unpleasantly. "You can stay with me," he said. "I'll sleep on the couch."

She asked no questions. She simply nodded and went with him. She was profoundly relieved to lock the door behind her once again.

When they reached the dimly lit third-floor landing, she looked into the darkness and suppressed a shudder. She had always felt something waiting in the darkness of these shadows, something evil. Tonight it had a shape and a face, the dead man's.

Wayne sensed her wave of anxiety. He was not used to comforting people. He wrestled down the impulse to put his arm around her.

He, too, looked into the blackness, listened to the silence. The woman edged closer to him. Once more he fought the desire to touch her, to give her the simple warmth of human contact.

He already regretted asking the woman to stay with him. He stared harder into the darkness. A man such as himself had no business with kindness. But death was a different matter. Death he knew well. Death was an old friend.

Chapter Three

Wayne Priborski's apartment was dead opposite from Ginnie's. He lived in the west tower, she in the east. A person could not go from her place to his without going downstairs and passing through the lobby.

She thought she had recovered her composure by the time they reached his rooms, but once inside, she found herself having another attack of the shakes.

Wayne's apartment seemed even more isolated than hers. The third floor on his side was in the final stages of renovation, awaiting carpet and paint. No one yet lived there.

No light shone from beneath the one neighboring door. Wayne must be the only person on the entire third and fourth floors on this side, Ginnie thought as she entered. She and he were completely secluded up here.

Her heart was beating almost as hard as when she'd found the dead man. She tried, nervously, to get her bearings as Wayne shot the deadbolt on his door. She was locked in with him now, far from any other human being.

She glanced uneasily around the living room. The layout of her apartment and his was nearly identical: oddly angled living room, large kitchen, smaller dining area and corner bedroom. And, of course, the bathroom. Ginnie found it difficult to keep from stealing furtive glances at the bathroom door.

Although the floor plans of the two apartments were similar, the atmosphere differed. Ginnie had worked hard to offset the age and eccentricity of the place, to make her rooms light and airy.

Her furniture was modern, her decorations carefully chosen. She had cleaned and waxed her paneled walls and hung framed prints of French impressionist painters on them.

Wayne Priborski, on the other hand, while scrupulously neat, seemed not to care much about possessions. He made a brusk gesture for her to sit and she did so, on a great, lumpy overstuffed couch of indeterminate color.

She looked at a wall and found herself staring at a tacked-up poster of Marilyn Monroe standing over a grate with her skirt flying up. Setting on a scarred table was a lava lamp with slowly shifting red liquid in it, and on one wall was a black clock shaped like a cat. When the clock ticked, the cat's eyes flicked back and forth. Ginnie wondered uneasily if Wayne had such things because he thought they were nice or because he thought they were funny. A set of weights was stacked in the corner.

Now that she was alone with him, he seemed far less comforting than before. For one thing, he had too many muscles. She was not used to muscular men. For another thing, he seemed too intense, almost brooding. She was not used to that, either. Her ex-husband, Del, had been tall, blond, lanky and boyishly charming.

She sat on the couch, her hands clenched tightly together, and he stood by his desk, silently going through a drawer. She swallowed nervously.

He sat down in an old blue easy chair. He didn't look at her. Instead he examined the black object in his hand, checking it, taking it apart. With a start Ginnie realized that what he held was a gun.

She had been cold before, but now she felt as if ice had been injected into her marrow. She went extremely still.

A corpse had appeared in her apartment, then disappeared. Now she was alone with a man she didn't know, a man who looked extremely strong, and he had a gun. She suppressed another shake.

She looked at him and then at the door, estimating how far she would have to run to escape him. *That's stupid,* she thought, trying to keep control of her fear, *you can't outrun a bullet. Steady. Steady.*

But he didn't look up or seem in the least concerned with her.

"That's a gun," she said at last. Her voice sounded far calmer than she felt.

He kept fiddling with it with a concentration so intense it unsettled her even more. "Right."

A dark mood had descended on Wayne. He didn't really want to talk to the woman. He shouldn't have asked her to come to his place; she was the first person he had even allowed inside since he'd moved in eight months ago. He went his own way, lived his own life, needed nobody else. He intended to keep it that way.

Well, he thought, he'd gotten her to a place where she should feel safe, and from here on out she could take care of herself. He didn't need to do anything else. He sensed her watching him, but he didn't look up.

"Why?" she asked. "Why a gun?"

He shrugged one shoulder. "Whatever you saw—or thought you saw—was gone when I went up there. I'd think you're crazy, but the same thing happened to me."

The silence throbbed between them. Ginnie sat stone still, watching him. She watched the expert way his hands moved over the automatic as he reassembled it. "That doesn't explain the gun."

He glanced up briefly. He read disapproval in her eyes. He shrugged again, turning his attention back to the gun.

"Somebody was in your apartment. For all I know, they did stash a dead guy there, then took him out. They must have come back between the time I was there and the cop came. The question is why? And how? It must have something to do with the keys being stolen."

Ginnie tensed as she watched him recheck the gun. His eyes rose and met hers again. She was unsettled by the blackness of his gaze. His lashes were long for a man's, but they added no softness to his face. Never had she seen eyes so dark or unwavering.

"Another question is, why your apartment? You have any ideas about that?" His eyes stayed fastened on hers, studying her.

She blinked in surprise, disconcerted. Surely he didn't think she had something to do with the man's death, did he? It suddenly occurred to her that perhaps he had as little reason to trust her as she did him. Was that why he had the gun out?

"I—" she started to say, then stopped.

"You what?"

"I—I wasn't supposed to be in my apartment this weekend. I had business in Maine. I had to cancel because of the snow."

His expression became even more alert than before. "Did anybody know you were going?"

She tried to think, but couldn't keep her eyes off the gun. She wished, fervently, that she hadn't come here with him. There was something about him that set him apart from other men she had known and it perturbed her. She made her reply as careful as possible. "I told Mr. Burbage. Or rather, I told his wife. She wouldn't open the door. I was worried—because of the stolen keys. I didn't want to bother them, but I thought I should leave word."

Wayne glanced up at her again, one straight eyebrow raised. Mrs. Burbage was a wild card, an unknown element. She stayed in the apartment most of the time and only went out in the company of her husband. Wayne had only seen her from a distance.

"So why didn't you change your lock?" he challenged. He had changed his immediately. He wasn't the type to wait on Burbage, or anybody else for that matter.

"I was going to. As soon as I got back. When I heard about Burbage being attacked, I didn't feel like going out alone. It was already night. I put the chair against the door."

She sighed and pushed her unruly hair back from her face. She was suddenly weary unto death. She was tired of the long dark New Hampshire winter, tired of Hawthorne Towers, tired of loneliness and fear.

She took a deep breath. "Look, if you've got that gun out because you think I had something to do with all this—"

"Anybody overhear you? When you told the Burbage woman?" He kept his eyes locked with hers. He put the gun carefully on the table beside the lava lamp.

Ginnie chewed at her lower lip, trying to remember. She kept her gaze on the gun because it made her nervous. "I thought—I thought that maybe that old man's door opened. That he might be listening. You know. That big old man."

"Swengler." Wayne nodded. "Yeah. I don't know the story on Swengler."

Ginnie gritted her teeth, feeling another involuntary shudder overtaking her. "He reminds me of that actor who used to be in all the horror movies. You know, Boris Karloff. Once, I met Paul Donner down in the basement, in the laundry room. He said he thinks Mr. Swengler was a war criminal. A Nazi in hiding."

Wayne's mouth took on a sardonic slant that wasn't a smile. "Yeah? He also thinks Mrs. Treat's a witch. God knows what he thinks I am. A werewolf probably."

His cool steadiness disconcerted her. She tossed her head. "Well, she's strange. She never misses a chance to tell me that she's psychic. I heard she makes her living as an astrologer or something." She stopped and frowned, remembering. "She was coming down the stairs with a basket of laundry last night when I was asking Mr. Burbage if he could keep an eye on my place."

He gave a short, mirthless laugh. "So half the people in the building knew you'd be gone. What about the guy next to you? Prouty, is it? Did he know?"

Ginnie nodded once. "I asked him to keep an eye on things for me. But then he fell. He's still in the hospital, Paul Donner said. He works in the lab there."

"And you didn't know who it was in the bathtub? You'd never seen him before?"

She shook her head. The memory of the dead man's staring eyes filled her with anxiety and more than a little nausea. "No. I never saw him before." She put her hand to her head, which was starting to ache again. "Listen, I don't think I'm going to be able to sleep. Do you have a drink around here?"

"I don't drink." His answer was so sharp she wondered if he'd once had a drinking problem, although he didn't look the sort. He seemed far too much in control of himself.

"A sleeping pill?"

"I don't do pills." The same edginess barbed his tone.

She sighed, pushed her hair from her eyes again. Her hand was still shaking slightly. "I don't suppose you've got a cigarette, either."

"I quit."

"So did I." She twisted a strand of hair. She'd never been a heavy smoker and hadn't had a cigarette for three years. Now she wished she had two in each hand.

Wayne didn't look even slightly sympathetic. A frown scored his brow. He hoisted himself from his chair and began to pace the room. His limp seemed more pronounced than earlier.

Ginnie watched him warily and wondered what had happened to him. He stopped by the windows and pulled open the drapes. He peered out. Ginnie could see nothing but blackness outside.

"Somebody could have used the fire escape to get into your place," he said. "But they'd have tracked snow all over." He shook his head. "They must have got in again after I was there. Unless the cop cleaned up the mess. But that makes no sense. Why would he get involved?"

His remark made Ginnie's muscles tense. She wondered if the policeman could have done away with any evidence lying about the apartment. She thought hard. "No. It wasn't the policeman." She remembered the stroke marks of cleanser in the tub. "He was left-handed. Whoever cleaned the tub used his right hand."

Wayne turned to study her again. He tried to keep his face impassive. If what the woman said was true, she was far sharper than he'd given her credit for. There was an extremely observant brain under the tousled auburn hair. "How do you know?"

Ginnie tried to pull the jacket of her suit more tightly around her and ended up hugging herself. She was cold all over and the Priborski man was about as easy to communicate with as a chunk of New Hampshire granite. "I don't know. I just notice stuff like that, that's all. Details."

He stared out the window again. "Details. Did you notice any others?"

She had, but at the moment none of them seemed relevant. It was more important to her to establish what he thought of her story. "Listen, do you believe I really saw that man?"

He shrugged, his back to her. "You saw something."

"And you saw the hat. And dirty water in the tub. So what happened? Did somebody slip something funny into the water supply? We couldn't both have been hallucinating—could we?"

He turned, leaning against the wall and crossing his arms. His arms were muscular, his shoulders broad. Ginnie glanced at the weights on the floor and decided he must be into bodybuilding. Ordinarily she would not be impressed, she would probably even be contemptuous, but tonight she found the idea of physical strength comforting.

"No. We both saw something." He stared at her without emotion. "Somebody got into your apartment."

She crossed her own arms and wriggled into the corner of the sofa so she could look at him more directly. "And just how," she asked, "did somebody get into my apartment?"

One corner of his mouth crooked thoughtfully. It was a nice mouth, she thought, or could be if he would ever let it smile. "Either from the fire escape—or they hid on the third floor. They might have still been inside the apartment when you came home. Took the body when you left."

The blood drained from Ginnie's face. The realization that someone might have been hiding in her apartment while she was in it made her feel sick. "They could still be in the building," she said softly. "And the body, too. He might still be here."

Wayne's expression didn't change by so much as a flicker. "Look. I don't like the idea any better than you. I think maybe I should go over to the third floor on your side and check things out."

Ginnie gripped the arm of the couch so hard that her fingers went numb. "Are you *crazy*? Go down there alone?"

"I'm not afraid. I've got a gun. I've got two. You can keep one. Just don't shoot me when I come back."

She stared at him in disbelief. "I've never held a gun in my life. I hate guns. My fondest wish is that they'd make guns illegal. My father preached a sermon every year against guns. I'm not going to touch a gun."

"Fine." He went to his bedroom and came out wearing a shoulder holster and carrying an extra clip of ammunition. He thrust it into the pocket of his jeans and picked up the automatic.

Ginnie bit her lip. If Wayne Priborski thought she was going to stay behind, he was wrong. "If you go, I'm going with you. I couldn't stand sitting here wondering if you were in trouble."

He put the gun in its holster. "Yeah? You'd be a big help. What happens if we find somebody? You faint on him?"

"It's the first time in my life I ever fainted. I wasn't exactly expecting this dead man in my tub, drooling dirty water," she said. "What would you do if it happened to you?"

Wayne shook his head. The woman was pretty in a coltish way, almost beautiful, but she made him uneasy. "I'd make sure he was dead. Then I'd call the police. I wouldn't wander around in my bare feet fainting on people."

She stood, putting her hand on her hip, hoping for a show of firmness of purpose. "I won't stay here. I won't let you go off alone, either, gun or no gun. I'm going with you."

He looked pointedly at her. He lifted an indifferent shoulder. If she wanted to get in a contest about stubbornness, she was going to lose. He sat down and crossed his left ankle over his right knee. "I'm not taking *you*," he said with perfect calm. "So I guess we'll never know what's down there. Satisfied?"

He stared at her and she stared back.

Ginnie was the first to look away. She sat, too, and fidgeted with one of the buttons on the arm of the couch. She truly didn't think he should go down there alone. It could be dangerous. And the gun bothered her, bothered her deeply.

"Go to bed," Wayne said at last. "You look tired."

"I'm not tired." She toyed with the button.

"Go to bed," he repeated, an edge in his voice.

She decided she didn't like his tone. She let her gaze rise, then rest on his tattooed forearm. "What were you? Some kind of drill sergeant?"

"The navy doesn't have sergeants."

Ginnie shrugged as if she didn't care what the navy had. "Excuse me. What were you? A drill ensign?"

"Captain. What's the matter? You got some objection?"

Ginnie tried to look unimpressed. She had grown up in a small midwestern town, attended a small college, and married a fellow student who became an English professor. She had never known anyone in the military. She had been raised to disapprove of people like Wayne Priborski. And she still disliked the idea of a gun.

"Were you on a boat?" she asked, trying to steer the conversation back toward politeness.

"A ship," he corrected. "In the navy, they have ships. No. I was an aviator."

"Well, that's interesting." She was determined to remain civilized and genial. "What did you fly? A helicopter? A cargo plane?"

"Jets. I flew jets."

Ginnie frowned slightly. "You mean a fighter plane?"

"Yes."

"Oh," she said. Uncomfortable, she stared at him again. He had been trained to kill people.

He didn't like the way she was looking at him. She had a kind of sadness in her expression that needled him. "What's wrong? You don't approve?"

She looked away again. She supposed he was too young to have ever been in a war. He would have never really shot anyone down, although that, of course, was what he'd been prepared to do. It seemed even more incomprehensible to her that he would train for such a thing, make it his life's work. She tried to understand. "Why? Why'd you become a—that?"

"I wanted to."

"Oh." An awkward silence settled. She supposed she could never comprehend such a man. It was as if he came from some malign planet where the warrior class reigned supreme. Ginnie's father had been a Unitarian minister and a conscientious objector, a man committed to the principles of peace. Her mother, the kindest, gentlest woman she had ever known, had been raised a Quaker. Ginnie had rebelled against them in small ways but never large ones. She had always believed in the principles they'd taught her.

Wayne seemed to read her mind. "You said your father preached? You're a *minister's* daughter?"

She nodded, but said nothing.

The set of his jaw was sardonic. "And Daddy doesn't like guns and Daddy doesn't approve of the military or the people in it."

Ginnie didn't answer. It was far more complex than that, and she didn't want to think about her father or try to defend his ideals. He had died shortly before her divorce, and she missed him painfully. The whole conversation suddenly seemed futile to her. She didn't want to argue.

"And what do you do that's so great?" he challenged. "Are you Mother Teresa?"

"I'm a lawyer," she said. "For the Human and Environmental Rights Coalition."

"A lawyer? No wonder you ask so many questions. For HERC? Jeez, no wonder you look down your nose at everything." He didn't much like lawyers. He didn't like the group, either. A decent organization once, it had deteriorated into a bunch of irritable, in-fighting cranks.

The scorn in his voice was the final straw for Ginnie. She didn't like HERC herself, but she wouldn't denigrate it, and she refused to apologize for being a lawyer.

She sat, twisting the sofa button and feeling his eyes on her. "Maybe you're right," she said, at last. "Maybe I should go to bed."

He said nothing. He watched as she rose and made her way into the bedroom. She closed the door behind her.

He waited an hour. Then he rose and opened the door slightly.

He could see her form in his bed, see the regular rise and fall of her breathing. He thought he could smell her perfume in the cool air. Her hair made a dark pool on the pillow. He flexed his hand, remembering how that hair had felt, spilling against his fingers.

He closed the door again. He went out, locking the apartment door behind him. He intended to check the third floor.

He found nothing there, only sawdust and paint cloths and spiders. Emptiness. Silence. Nothing.

He went back to his apartment and unlocked the door. He checked once more on the woman. He stood in the doorway for a moment, watching her still shape. Once more he thought he smelled the ghost of her scent. It tingled in his nostrils like the phantom scent of spring.

Then he closed the door, took a blanket from the hall closet, took off his shirt, switched off the light and lay on the couch.

He stared up into the darkness and told himself not to think of her. *No,* he told himself. *Some minister's daughter who's into gun control? A lawyer for a bunch of crazy activists? No way.*

He closed his eyes. He and the woman had nothing in common. Nothing. They were dead opposites.

Chapter Four

Ginnie didn't sleep well and woke slightly before six in the morning. She sat up, blinking away wisps of nightmare. She looked around the room. The furnishings were sparse. The only ornaments were two posters on the walls, tacked up with geometric precision. One was of Groucho Marx. The other was, once more, of Marilyn Monroe.

She hugged herself. She was stiff and cold. Wayne's bed was hard, and he kept his apartment chilly. She had slept in only her slip and she was freezing; last night she had been too rattled even to think of packing a suitcase. She tried not to think about going back to her own apartment. But she had to. There was nowhere else to go.

She buttoned her blouse with shaking fingers. Her teeth chattered. She knotted the blue scarf around her throat, pulled on her jacket and put on her boots. Then she rose and pulled aside the bedroom curtain. Frost blocked any view.

Quietly she made her way into the living room, not wanting to wake Wayne. He was a discomfiting man and she didn't know how to react to him.

Under ordinary circumstances, she would have had nothing in common with him. Nothing to do with him. But, she thought, the circumstances of last night had been anything but ordinary. She would try to thank him later somehow. Perhaps send him a picture for his walls that wasn't of a dead movie star, she thought wryly.

She was startled to find he was already up, sitting at the kitchen table. He had his familiar angry look. He sat with his elbows on the table, frowning at the most complicated link puzzle Ginnie had ever seen. He gave her an unfriendly glance, although his greeting was friendly enough. "Sleep all right?"

"Okay," Ginnie said, lying slightly for the sake of politeness. "I kept waking up, remembering. Did you sleep all right?"

Wayne was not the sort of man to lie for any reason, least of all politeness. "No."

He looked up and saw the guilt on her face. She had a striking face, he thought, but it showed all her emotions. He wasn't comfortable with emotions and kept them exiled as best he could from his life. He had become adept at it.

"I'm sorry," she said. "It was very—very kind of you to let me stay here."

He lifted one shoulder. He wore a heavy dark blue sweater and pressed but well-faded jeans. "It wasn't your fault." He slapped his leg contemptuously.

She clutched her purse in front of her in an awkward gesture. "Oh! Your leg? You should have taken the bed."

This time she looked so guilty he found it comical. She must have a conscience as big as a house, he thought, and it must make her life hell, trying to live up to its standards. Slowly, in spite of himself, he smiled.

Ginnie's heart did a funny little backflip that she hadn't expected. He was one of those men whose face was transformed by a smile, and he suddenly looked so handsome that it gave her a start.

She clutched her purse more tightly and tried to keep her mind on the conversation. She nodded at his leg. "What happened to you?"

His smile vanished as quickly as it appeared. "Accident." He turned his attention back to the puzzle.

She was embarrassed. She hadn't meant to pry, but his reaction had bordered on rudeness; she was used to men who discussed things freely. *He's so damned tight-lipped, he never gives anything of himself,* she thought. All she was trying to do was fill the silence, to understand him a bit better. She pushed on because she really did want to know about him. "What kind of accident? Flying?"

He allowed no feeling to register on his face. "Hunting."

She sighed and shook her head. She was sorry he'd been hurt, deeply sorry, but that was exactly the sort of thing that happened to people who fooled with guns. "You shot yourself?"

He didn't look at her. "No. I got shot. In the back. The spine."

She paled. "The spine? You're lucky to be walking."

"Tell me about it." He threw down the puzzle. "You hungry? Want something to eat? Drink? Sit down."

She suddenly realized that she was ravenous. She had been so busy fighting the snow last night that she hadn't stopped for supper. She hadn't eaten since noon yesterday.

In her heart, she knew, too, that she wasn't quite ready to return to the apartment. She tried hard not to think about the dead man. She sat down, grateful for any delay in facing reality.

Wayne rose and turned on the fire under a teakettle. He rummaged through a cupboard and set a box of herbal tea bags on the table. Ginnie winced. She would have liked coffee, a long, pure black jolt of it.

He opened the refrigerator and took out a container of orange juice and a carton of skim milk. He set everything before her. Lastly he put an unpleasant-looking box of breakfast cereal on the table. "Help yourself."

Ginnie sighed and lowered one of the evil-looking tea bags into the mug. She would have liked sugar with her cereal, and toast slathered with butter and jam. She knew better than to ask. His food was as Spartan as his rooms. She tried to keep from sounding disappointed or critical. "You must be into health food."

He nodded and sat down, folding his arms across his chest. However he ate, it worked for him, she thought; he didn't carry an ounce of fat and his chest looked hard enough to crack walnuts on.

She poured milk on the cereal, took a bite and tried to keep from grimacing. It tasted like straw. Her appetite fled. She pushed the bowl away and decided to content herself with orange juice.

He pushed the bowl back in front of her. "Eat. You're pale. And you're too thin. No wonder you fainted."

Ginnie swallowed a sip of juice. "I fainted because there was a dead man in my bathtub."

"Yeah?" He got up, took another mug from the cupboard and made himself a cup of tea. "That whole thing kept me awake, too. I've got questions. Like why was your place so cold? The heat was off. Then it went on again, while I was there. Like magic. Strange."

Ginnie pushed her hand through her hair. "I remember the place was cold, but I had a headache. That's what was on my mind. Then the man in the tub kind of eclipsed everything. But things keep bothering me, too."

He leaned his elbow on the table and his chin on his fist, studying her. Just what had those jewel-blue eyes seen last night? he wondered. What had registered on that quirky brain of hers? "Like what?"

She frowned and pulled her jacket more tightly around herself. His attention was so intent it disconcerted her. "Like why were his overcoat and hat dry—but his shirt wet? I mean, I never saw anybody drowned, but that's what he looked like to me, a drowned person. But how do you drown yourself and then put on a dry coat?"

Wayne lifted one wide shoulder. "Because he probably didn't drown himself. Somebody did it for him. Why else hide the body?"

"But he didn't have a mark on him, at least that I could see," Ginnie objected. "He seemed like a fair-sized man— wouldn't he struggle? Besides, if you drown somebody in the bathtub, wouldn't the water be clean? The water looked filthy. It'd made his shirt gray. And there were little things—

like pond scum or something—sticking to him, even his face.''

Wayne's mouth took on a grim crook. He studied the woman, the alert eyes, the pale face. Her story was unbelievable. Yet he was starting to believe her. He remembered the dirty water in the tub. It teased him like an ache that wouldn't go away. "Maybe he drowned outside."

"Then why bring him in to my apartment?"

He shook his head again. She was right; there was no answer that made sense. He looked into her eyes, challenging her to think harder still. "Listen. We saw a lot of people from your side of the building, right? But not everybody. Mrs. Burbage never showed up. Anybody else?"

Wayne's dark gaze was too disconcerting. Ginnie turned away and stared at her tea. "Hardly anybody sees Mrs. Burbage. Paul Donner says her daughter, her only child, was killed in a car accident ten years ago. By a drunk driver. Mrs. Burbage never really got over it. He says she got extremely upset when the police came the last night. It reminded her of the night her daughter died."

Wayne watched the emotions crossing her face as she talked about the other woman. "Why does Donner always know all the gossip?"

"He *likes* gossip." She glanced up, meeting Wayne's eyes again. "But who wasn't around? The new man, I guess. On the second floor. The name on his mailbox is Kingsley, I think. But Donner says he's gone, too."

"So you think Kingsley's gone, but you don't know for a fact. Right?" He picked up the puzzle again, began to manipulate it.

"Look, is everybody under suspicion? I've never even seen the man," Ginnie said, frustrated. She hated thinking sinister things about her neighbors. "All right, I *don't* know for a fact that he's gone. But why just bring up the people on my side? Let's suspect *everybody* in the building. Couldn't it have been somebody from your side?"

"No." He twiddled the puzzle.

"Why not?"

"Almost everybody on this side is a student. They all go to Saint Aaron's. And they're all home, or someplace, for Christmas. I'm alone over here. Have been for a week."

Ginnie sighed, realizing what he said was true; the apartments had been preternaturally quiet this week. The first two floors of the west side of the building were populated primarily by college students. She often encountered them in the lobby, talking animatedly and laughing. They made her homesick for her college days and for more innocent times.

She looked at Wayne's lean fingers toying with the puzzle and remembered how he'd phrased his answer. "You said *almost* everybody over here's a student. You, too?"

"No. Not me."

"Then what do you do?" she probed. He looked around thirty-one or thirty-two. He didn't seem like the sort of man who'd bother doing tame things.

"Business," he said vaguely.

"Business?" She was surprised.

He shrugged, as if it were of little consequence what he did for a living. "I just bought into a new firm."

Ginnie looked at his implacable face, frustrated again. He wouldn't give an iota of himself. "What kind of firm?"

"Aeronautical engineering." His tone warned her that he was tired of questions.

Ginnie pushed on, anyway. "I—I guess the navy discharged you after your accident?"

He looked up briefly. The dark eyes snapped. "I quit." He focused his attention on the puzzle again.

"You quit," she repeated. "You mean you didn't have to, but you quit?"

"I was an aviator. They were going to ground me. They wanted me to jockey a desk or teach somewhere or some damn thing. I said, 'Thanks, but no thanks.'"

She found she was biting her lip again. He told the story with such brevity and bitterness that she sensed he had loved flying, that its loss had cost him more than he would ever tell.

She had an irrational impulse to stretch out her hand and put it on his. An equally strong instinct told her he would hate and reject such a gesture.

Instead, she found herself asking another question, although she knew he wouldn't like that, either. "So you ended up here. Why the tower?" She looked around the apartment and pulled her jacket tight again. The place was isolated, cold and bare.

"I wanted the tower."

Such a perplexing man, she thought, studying him. He was as much a loner as it was possible to be. Yet she sensed the accident had made him shut out others to an unnatural degree. "Why? I hate mine. It's creepy—especially with the third floor empty."

"Exercise."

"That's why you're always walking around at night? To exercise?"

He gave the now-familiar curt nod. He had slipped into a totally uncommunicative mood. His silence said he was tired of her curiosity. His hands moved swiftly and surely over the puzzle, adjusting this, manipulating that.

Why, Ginnie wondered, did he have to keep playing with that infernal thing? Couldn't he talk like a civilized person? He had been kind enough to help her last night. Why was he so reluctant to tell her anything about himself? "Why do you keep doing that?" she asked, patience fraying.

He shot her a cold black look. "My hand. The accident affected my hand. I need to keep using it. You've got an objection?"

She turned away, chagrined. The man had been badly hurt and he was trying to fight his way to recovery. He showed an impressive ability to tolerate pain and an almost ferocious discipline. "I'm sorry. I didn't mean anything by it. I'm still upset. I'm not used to seeing dead men or guns—"

"Guns?" He raised one black eyebrow. "You're putting my gun on the same level as seeing a dead guy in your apartment?"

"Look, I didn't mean it that way. I'm sorry, but that's the way it is. I just don't believe in guns. Or force or violence."

"Sometimes you can't avoid them."

"Well," she said earnestly, "people should try."

"People do try. They just can't succeed."

"Handguns are dangerous."

"Yeah? Well, when they outlaw guns, only outlaws will have guns," he said.

"That's not an argument, it's a bumper sticker," Ginnie said in distaste. "Don't you have any original arguments?"

He gave her a withering look. "Yeah. Last night after you were asleep, I went down to the third floor to check things. If I met somebody with a gun down there, what was I supposed to do? Pitch a dove of peace at him?"

Ginnie stiffened. "You went down there? Alone?"

"Who'm I supposed to take? My fairy godmother?"

"But—weren't you scared?"

"No. I wasn't *scared*." He injected the maximum of mockery into the word. As a pilot he'd faced death often enough. It was part of his business. It didn't bother him.

She looked at his stony face. She knew he was partly right about the gun, but so was she. He of all people, injured as badly as he had been, should understand the folly of guns. He was living testimony to the damage they could do.

She sighed. It was useless to argue. The two of them were so different, they would probably never agree on anything.

She stood. "Listen. You really have been kind. I should go back. Thanks for everything."

He threw down the puzzle. He, too, stood, favoring his left leg. "I'm going with you."

She stared at him in surprise.

He was careful to keep any emotion from his face and voice. "I don't think you should go back alone. I don't think you should stay there. Have Burbage give you another apartment. I'll help you figure a way to move your stuff.''

She kept staring at him. She could think of nothing to say. What an unlikely knight he was, standing there with his bad leg and his tattoo, his link puzzle, lava lamp and herb tea and his frowning, handsome face. He could not force himself to be friendly, yet he couldn't stop being gallant, either. A choking filled her throat. This man, determined not to be emotional, had made her more emotional than she cared to be.

He stared back a moment, then looked away, half-angry, half-embarrassed. He'd sworn from the beginning not to get involved, and he was getting more involved all the time. He didn't even know why. Every time he started to tell her goodbye, he ended up keeping her around or letting her go with him or staying by her side. He didn't want to. But he did it.

Oh, hell, he thought.

"Let's go," he said. *She's too tall. She's too thin. Her hair's too curly. She's always asking questions. I've got no room in my life for her.*

At the same time, he was oddly impressed by her. She was sharp in her way, she had bounced back from last night with remarkable strength, and she wasn't afraid to say what she thought. Yet, she seemed kind of wide-eyed and untested to him, like somebody who'd always lived in an ivory tower. He wondered what her story was, why she wasn't married. She seemed like the kind of woman who ought to be married. She should have a house, kids, stuff like that. But he asked no questions.

Instead, as they descended the stairs, she kept asking things of him. "Doesn't anybody live next door to you?"

"He died. About two weeks ago."

"Died?" Her eyes widened in horror. "Was he a student?"

"No. He was about fifty. A social worker."

"How'd he die?"

"Heart attack, I heard."

"Here? In the building?"

"No. Upstate. He was visiting somebody or something. Nobody's come for his things yet. I guess he didn't have any family."

"That's terrible," Ginnie said. This was a bad, building, an evil building, she thought with a superstitious surge. She eyed the steep stairs, the thick walls. It was full of too much darkness, too much loneliness, too much misfortune. It was an untypically pessimistic thought for Ginnie to have in the daytime, and it caused her to lapse into silence.

In the lobby they encountered Paul Donner, who was looking frantically for his poodle. "I haven't been able to walk her with all this snow," he said. Distraction and worry etched his soft face. "Sometimes, when she's restless, I'll open the door for something or other and she'll just bolt. Gigi—come *here*. Gigi?" He started down the basement stairs calling for her.

As Donner disappeared down the steps, Wayne almost smiled again. When the corners of his mouth twitched, Ginnie's heart once more did a funny little maneuver in her chest. Difficult, uncommunicative and different from her as this man was, she would miss him when she was alone again. She told herself that was silly and tried to shake the thought away.

As they climbed the steps to the fourth floor, she saw that sometimes he tried to suppress a wince. "Don't you ever take anything for the pain?"

His glance was brief. "No."

No she thought. *You wouldn't, would you?* She had an uncomfortable memory of her husband, Del. He couldn't get through the day without a tranquilizer, and had once taken a pain pill for a deep shaving cut. At the time, she had thought his sensitivity endearing. In retrospect, it seemed merely embarrassing.

When they reached the tower, all thoughts of Del fled. As she opened the door to her apartment, she felt a flutter of fear in the pit of her stomach. The nightmarish thought that the dead man was back in the tub, open-mouthed and red-eyed, seized her mind. But the apartment was warm and silent, the bathtub empty.

Wayne stayed by her side. As if to reassure her, he stepped a bit closer as she moved to the bathroom and looked in. She exhaled with relief. Everything was exactly as it had been last night. She started to turn to Wayne to smile her gratitude. She stopped, standing as if paralyzed.

No, Ginnie thought with a start. Everything was *not* the same. She stared down at the floor and a chill clasped the back of her neck.

Instinctively she reached for Wayne and laid a hand on the hardness of his sweatered biceps. He looked down, following her gaze.

The little rug beside the bathtub was gone, the one that had been spotted with something remarkably like a drop of dirty blood. "Oh, no," Ginnie said. Somebody had been in her apartment again. *It's a sort of defilement, a despoiling, a kind of a rape.*

Wayne looked around the room angrily, like a man looking for someone to fight. Then his eyes settled on the little bathroom window. The curtains had been parted. He couldn't remember if they had been closed last night or not. The window was covered with frost, a thick pattern of ice flowers.

There was a snapshot lying on the windowsill. It was an old snapshot, slightly dog-eared. He didn't remember that, either. But he could see how upset the woman was.

Without thinking, he reached out and put his arm around her. He drew her closer to him and she did not resist.

"Look at the window," he said quietly. "Were those curtains open last night? Did you do that? What about the picture?"

Ginnie's neck prickled at the warm of his breath so close to her ear, and she had gone so cold that his arm around her felt like a circle of fire.

The curtains had been closed last night, she was almost certain. And the snapshot had not been on the windowsill. Of that she was sure.

Wayne pulled her tighter, but she could not look away from the windowsill. She reached out and her fingers poised over the photo, which lay face up. "Should I touch it?" she asked, her hand going still.

"Wait." He reached into his pocket and dug out a clean handkerchief. "Use this."

She took the handkerchief. It made it awkward to pick up the photo, but she managed. She held it and looked down at it, feeling queasy. She was grateful for Wayne's arm around her.

The snapshot was an old one, of her, her mother and father. It had been her favorite photo of the three of them together. It was one of the last photos taken of Ginnie's mother before she died. When it started to become worn, Ginnie had put it in a rather expensive frame. It normally sat on her bedroom dresser.

Someone had taken it from the frame and put it on the sill. The snapshot was once more naked, an unprotected picture that had seen better days. Except one thing was different, she realized: the faces.

Their eyes were stabbed out, gone.

Chapter Five

For a few seconds, Ginnie felt sick. She sagged slightly against the strength of Wayne's arm. When she tried to swallow, she could not. Neither could she speak for a long, terrible moment.

"It was my favorite picture," she managed to say at last. Her voice broke slightly. She felt tears smarting in her eyes and blinked them back angrily. What was happening to her? And why? Resentment warred with fright within her.

"Are you all right?" Wayne's voice was low in her ear.

She realized, to her dismay, that she was depending on him again. She straightened her back and tried to brush his arm away. He would not allow it.

"Damn!" she said, pulling herself together. With determination, she blinked back the tears. "Why's this happening? Who's doing it?"

Her hands shook with both rage and fear, but she forced herself to wrap the photograph carefully in Wayne's handkerchief. Just as carefully she tucked it into her purse. Once more she tried to shrug his arm away.

"Ginnie—"

"Damn!" she said again. "This is it. I'm going to the police. I'll *make* them listen—"

"Ginnie—"

"There's no reason for this—I haven't done anything to anybody. I hardly even know anybody in this whole state.

This is just . . . terrorism. I mean it—I'm going to the police.''

Wayne drew her back into the hall, then pulled her closer to him again, his hands on her shoulders. "Stop shaking. Talk to me. You're *sure* you don't know who could be doing this.''

"No," she cried. "I don't have enemies!"

"Steady," he ordered. She was badly shaken and couldn't hide it no matter how hard she tried. He knew that she wasn't going to faint again and that she was in a fighting mood, which was good. But she had a kind of wild air about her, angry and anxious and desperate.

Once more she tried to squirm away from him, but he knew she had no idea of where she intended to go.

"Steady," he hissed between his teeth, pulling her closer, so that she was pressed against his chest. As she tried to twist away again, she tossed her head, tousling her thick mane of hair.

"Let go!"

He pulled her tighter still. "The truth—is there *anybody* who'd want to hurt you, scare you? Somebody that HERC is hassling, maybe?"

"No." Her voice was choked. "I work in the background. I'm practically the invisible woman.''

"An old boyfriend, somebody like that?"

She shook her head, agitated. "I don't have any old boyfriends. I haven't been divorced that long. I've been keeping to myself.''

Divorced, Wayne thought, that explained some things. Keeping to herself; he could understand that. But he sensed she couldn't be a real loner, not at heart. He tried to keep his voice kind, but it came out harsher than he'd intended. "You're attractive—has somebody tried to get close to you? Somebody you turned down? Who could carry a grudge?"

"No," she insisted. "Nobody's noticed I'm alive. Let go of me. I want out of here."

"You'll get out. But we should search this place. To see if anything else's been disturbed. And this time, pack. What about your ex-husband? Could he be behind this?"

At the mention of Del, she went still. "He's a thousand miles away. He doesn't have any grudge. He's glad I'm gone."

Then he's a damn fool, Wayne thought. At the mention of her husband, she looked stricken, emotionally stripped. Her face was even paler than before.

For the first time he noticed that she had the faintest spattering of freckles across her cheekbones. They gave her an aura of innocence and freshness that awakened something a bit frightening within him. He didn't allow his face to change expressions, but something flickered deep within his black eyes.

Ginnie was too upset to read what his look might mean. She thought only that he didn't believe her. "Look, my husband found somebody else. He's glad I'm out of the way. He'd never do anything like this."

She looked at Wayne, the emotion naked in her eyes. She had been cosy and content in her marriage and had never suspected that Del was not. She had come to New England to forget the unhappiness and make a meaningful new life, but now life had turned a nightmare with neither purpose nor pattern.

"All right," Wayne said, keeping his tone calm. "All right. Don't cry."

"I'm not crying," she countered, almost angrily. "I'm all cried out. The tears are pretty well gone."

Almost without his volition, one of his hands moved up to lightly frame her face. His forefinger touched the skin just beneath the corner of her eye, as if to tell her that had there been a tear, he would have brushed it away.

She blinked in surprise. The movement had been so gentle she never would have imagined it from him.

"Right," he said, calm and encouragement in his tone. "So if this isn't happening because of anybody you know or anything you've done, it must be happening because of what you saw.''

She stared at him, her lips slightly parted. "You mean—the dead man?"

"The dead man. Somebody's trying to scare you out of here. Because you saw something you weren't supposed to."

"But the police didn't believe me."

"No. Face it—they probably won't believe you this time, either."

Her expression was at first frustrated, then grim with determination. "This time I have proof, that picture—"

His hand was on her jaw now, holding it gently so that she was forced to look at him. "The picture doesn't prove anything except that somebody was here again. The police may not even believe that. What could they do, anyway? One mutilated picture isn't going to make them act. It's not a major crime. It's not even a specific threat."

His words sank in and she looked at him in dismay. He was right, of course. "Then what?"

He nodded to reassure her. "We'll try. That's all we can do. In the meantime, let's go through your apartment, check it out. Then pack."

"Pack," Ginnie said numbly. Of course, she should pack. She never wanted to spend another day or night in this apartment.

But she had nowhere to go. Nor could she afford to rent a second place while paying rent on this one. She had, after all, a lease.

Wayne nodded again, as if reading her thoughts. "Look, you've got a lease, but somebody's getting in. Ask Burbage to put you in a different apartment. Ask for the one next to me. It's empty. That way, I could, well—you know."

For the first time Ginnie became aware of how close he was and how securely his one hand held her shoulder, how lightly the other framed her jaw. He smelled very nice, she noted irrelevantly, of something that hinted vaguely of saddle leather, autumn leaves and good brandy. His eyes, which seemed black from even a rather short distance, were actually the deepest brown she had ever seen. She experienced an unexpected tightness in her chest.

"Next to you?" She tried hard to think clearly and not to be so conscious of him. She knew about law. Burbage had an obligation to take steps to ensure her safety. He would have to let her move into another apartment. It was as simple as that. But it meant she would be close, extremely close, to this dark and paradoxical man.

He nodded. His gaze had fallen to her mouth and it remained there. He knew he should take his hand away from her face, but he did not. He liked the feel of her skin and how fair it looked against the bronze of his fingers. He knew he shouldn't make the offer he was making, and the words didn't want to leave his throat. When he did summon them up they came out husky, almost rough. "Like I said, I could—you know..."

She tried to take a deep breath but managed only a shallow, ragged one. "You could—what?"

His hand had moved to rest lightly against her throat, and her pulse leaped beneath his thumb. His gaze stayed fastened on her mouth but he kept himself from touching it, although he wanted to know if it felt as soft as it looked. He reached deep inside for the words again. "You know. I'd—be there. If anything happened. I'd be there."

He looked into her eyes. *My God, she's got a nice face, but why get into this?* he thought. *I should leave her alone, dammit. Am I crazy?* He suddenly became aware that he all but had her in his arms.

His expression grew guarded, self-conscious. Ginnie, too, felt an unexpected mixture of emotions and looked away.

He cleared his throat and let his hands fall from her. He took a step backward. He made a brief gesture that told her she was free to move; he would interfere with her no further. His expression said he already regretted what had passed between them, any tenderness on his part.

She tried to smile in reassurance that everything was all right, that nothing was changed, but she couldn't. She tried to think of some way to start a different, safer conversation, but couldn't.

He shrugged again and seemed to have nothing to say, either. They were saved from the awkward silence by a timid knocking from the direction of the front door. Startled, Ginnie turned, her heart beating fast. Wayne whirled toward the sound like a gunslinger ready to draw.

There, peeking in the doorway, stood Ginnie's neighbor, Mr. Prouty. She had not pushed the door shut when she and Wayne had entered. She hadn't liked the thought of being shut in, trapped with memories of the dead man.

Mr. Prouty waggled his fingers in shy greeting and gave her a hesitant smile. He was a round little man, several inches shorter than Ginnie, with sagging jowls and slicked down white hair. Today his usually ruddy face was pale.

"Miss Prince?" he said, then waggled his fingers again. "Are you all right? Mr. Burbage said you had a scare last night. Has everything been set straight?"

"Mr. Prouty," Ginnie said, brightening to see him on his feet and at home, "how are *you*?" She went to the door and opened it more widely, stretching her hand to him in welcome. "The last time I saw you, they were loading you onto a stretcher."

Mr. Prouty took her hand and pumped it, although not too energetically. He still looked a bit weak. "I'm fine," he said gamely. "Just a little conk on the noggin. A slight concussion. I guess they wanted to make sure I hadn't knocked any brains loose. Oh, my, I saw stars, I did for a fact—it's not something that people made up. Pink and green stars! It wasn't a pleasant experience. No, it wasn't."

Ginnie smiled in sympathy. Mr. Prouty was a rather fussy person, far too plump for his own good, and she could not tell if he were closer to fifty or seventy. He wore oversize horn-rimmed glasses that looked as if they belonged to a comic-strip owl, and he always spoke loudly rapidly, and with a slight lisp. He was a bit eccentric and occasionally nosy, but he had always shown her more friendliness than anyone else in the apartments. Ginnie suspected he was lonely.

"I don't *like* hospitals," he said emphatically. "I'm glad to be home. I tossed and turned all night long, worrying about my loved ones."

"Oh, Mr. Prouty," Ginnie said. She had forgotten all about his beloved dachshund, Alfy, and his two parakeets. "Your animals—how are they? How did they get along without you? You must have been worried sick."

"Oh, they seem fine," he answered, darting a look of critical curiosity at Wayne. "I guess that Mrs. Treat woman looked after them. I was not particularly happy about that. I tell you frankly, I don't like the idea of that woman in my apartment. Alfy's fine, although he was starved, poor thing. She didn't mix his kibble with canned food the way he likes. Alfy's a very picky eater. But I guess she didn't put a spell on him or anything—let's hope. And the birds seem their usual perky selves."

He paused, eyeing Wayne again. "I don't think I've met your friend," he said to Ginnie. "Although we've nodded in the lobby."

Ginnie blushed slightly. She wondered if Mr. Prouty had seen her and Wayne standing so closely together, gazing so warily into each other's eyes. Mr. Prouty didn't look as if he quite approved of Wayne, but then there was a great deal of the modern world that Mr. Prouty didn't approve of.

"Oh," she said, embarrassed. "This is Wayne Priborski. He lives in the other tower. He was just helping me to—" She stopped, uncertain exactly what to say. "He was just—helping me," she finished lamely.

Wayne stepped forward and shook Prouty's hand, but neither man looked truly friendly. They seemed to be taking each other's measure.

"Edward Lawson Prouty," Mr. Prouty said. He winced at the strength of Wayne's handshake and gave him another long, suspicious look. "Glad to make your acquaintance."

Wayne only nodded.

Prouty released Wayne's hand and returned his attention to Ginnie. His expression grew concerned. "What's this business about your fainting, Miss Prince? Mr. Burbage said you thought you saw something last night. What happened?"

Ginnie did not answer immediately. She wasn't sure how much of the story she should tell him yet. It might alarm him, and he was, after all, freshly out of the hospital. But, she thought, something sinister was happening on their floor, and she had a moral duty to tell him, to warn him. She didn't know how to begin.

Wayne spoke instead. He stood squarely before Mr. Prouty, feet slightly apart, his arms crossed. "She saw something, all right. She came home unexpectedly and somebody was here. Whoever it was disappeared by the time I came up to check it out. You said Mrs. Treat took care of your pets. She has a key to your place?"

Mr. Prouty stared at Wayne open-mouthed in surprise. His gaze turned once more to Ginnie, his eyes so round behind his glasses that he looked more like an owl than usual. "Mrs. Treat was in your apartment? How extraordinary!"

"No," Ginnie said, still unsure how much of the story to reveal. "She wasn't the one—it was a man—a strange man."

"But," Wayne said, scrutinizing Prouty's reaction, "you said she was up here. Did you give her a key?"

"Well, no," Prouty answered, looking embarrassed. "Certainly not. I wouldn't give her a key. Never."

"Then how'd she get in to feed your dog?" Wayne asked.

Mr. Prouty cast about for words, then shrugged helplessly. "The fact is that she *took* the keys."

"Took them?" Ginnie's brow crinkled in a frown.

The older man tried to look dignified but didn't quite succeed. He plucked ineffectually at the buttons of his well-worn cardigan sweater. "Well, I don't even remember too clearly. And I was certainly in no condition to object. There I was, lying flat on my back, actually seeing stars, and she was fumbling in my coat, saying, 'Don't worry! I'll take care of your puppy and your birdies! I'll pack a little case to send you at the hospital.' "

"You mean she just appointed herself caretaker?" Ginnie asked. She didn't know if she should applaud Mrs. Treat's foresight or abhor her boldness.

"I think she just wanted to see my apartment," Mr. Prouty stated unhappily. "I'm sure she was ecstatic for the chance to go through my dresser and rummage in my medicine cabinet. The next time I see her, she'll go into a psychic fit and try to amaze me by revealing how many pairs of socks I have and what brand of aspirin I take."

"Was anything disturbed in your place?" Wayne asked.

"Only Alfy. He *hates* his kibble plain, it puts him in a terrible snit, it really does. He likes a little bit of a can of Cheese 'n' Chicken Goodies mixed in. But this person that you saw in your place, Miss Prince—he didn't menace you, did he?"

"No," Ginnie said carefully. "He didn't menace me. But it was a strange experience, Mr. Prouty, and frankly, more bizarre things have happened since. I don't think I want to stay up here."

"But my dear, we've talked of your leaving before. You have a lease. You can't leave. Where will you go?"

"Not out of the building. Just out of this place," Ginnie nodded to indicate her apartment.

"The place next to me's empty," Wayne said. "I don't see any reason she can't use it. And I'll be there to watch out for her."

"Watch out for her. Oh. I see." Mr. Prouty's tone clearly implied that he found Wayne's motives suspect. Perhaps he felt insulted at the thought that he couldn't watch out for Ginnie. He gave the younger man a stern look, but, when Wayne's returning gaze didn't waver, he at last turned back to Ginnie.

"Miss Prince." Mr. Prouty's lips were pursed with care. "I wouldn't go running off so precipitously if I were you. I know you're not happy with your apartment. But this is something that has to be thought out. Weren't you going to be systematic and hunt for another job first? Whatever do you think you saw last night? To make you move out of your place on a moment's notice and in next door to this—gentleman?"

Ginnie tried to be honest. "I *am* hunting for another job. I had an interview yesterday in Maine, but I had to turn back. I'd intended to be gone all weekend—remember? But when I got home, I found a dead man in my bathtub. Dressed, but dead. When other people came to investigate, he'd vanished. And things in my apartment have been disturbed. I don't mean to alarm you, but something's going on up here. And I don't want to stay."

Mr. Prouty's expression had changed from disapproval to disbelief. "Miss Prince, you've always been so imaginative—a dead man in your *bathtub*?"

"I didn't imagine it," Ginnie said with conviction. "I saw him. And I know somebody's been in my apartment since he disappeared. Somebody has a key. I refuse to stay here. The management has to provide better protection. I can't live like this."

"My dear, my dear," said Mr. Prouty, shaking his head. "I remember now that you were going away—you were driving in that terrible storm? For how long? Why, they said a person couldn't see a hand in front of his face."

Ginnie nodded. "I drove in it for hours—probably five or six."

"Then no wonder you thought you saw something—a dressed-up man in your bathtub, you say? If you stare into the snow that way—well, it makes the eyes play tricks. Any sort of intense driving can do it. Once I drove all night when I was going to see my mother in the hospital. I swore I saw a huge fallen tree blocking the road—as real as you standing there before me—but when I got out to move it, there was no tree at all. It was only tired eyes and a tired mind playing tricks. Really, Miss Prince, please don't go dashing off because you thought you saw something."

Although Ginnie knew that he was well-intentioned, she hated the look on his face. It was half-amused and half-pitying. Although his argument seemed logical, she could not bear to listen to it. "Mr. Prouty, really—"

"It's that Treat woman," Mr. Prouty said darkly. "She's got your nerves on edge. Every time the plumbing rattles, she swears it's a spook. She wants you to believe in ghosts and vampires, when there are no such things."

Ginnie drew in her breath slightly. It was true that Mrs. Treat was strange and that she never missed a chance to buttonhole Ginnie to tell her of some strange psychic or paranormal happening. By doing so, she had given Ginnie's dislike of the building an extra twist of intensity, another degree of strength. But Ginnie truly did not believe that seeing the dead man had anything to do with anything Mrs. Treat had ever said.

She shook her head. "It's not because of Mrs. Treat. I know what I saw. It was *real*."

Mr. Prouty began to say something, then clamped his lips together, as if he thought the better of it. He looked at Ginnie sadly. "I wish I'd been here last night, my dear, to help you. And I'd talk to you more now...but I'm really starting to feel a bit under the weather." He passed his hand over his forehead, which had begun to shine with a fine film of sweat.

Ginnie looked at him with alarm. He seemed to have weakened before her eyes. "Mr. Prouty, are you sure you're all right? Perhaps you should lie down."

"Yes. Perhaps I should," He shook his head as if to clear it. "I didn't mean to argue, my dear. It's just that I hate to see you act in haste."

"I know," Ginnie said, walking with him from her door to his. Wayne stayed behind, watching after her.

Mr. Prouty was obviously trying to act more chipper than he felt. He forced a smile, but Ginnie could tell he didn't feel well. "I hope you're wrong as much for my sake as your own," he said kindly. "If what you say is true, I certainly don't want to be up here by myself. And besides, if you go, I'll miss you. I've grown used to having you nearby. It's always been more cheerful somehow, knowing you were here. No hard feelings?''

Ginnie smiled down at him, guilty at having caused him distress, guiltier still for being about to leave him. She watched as he fumbled with his doorknob and let himself in. He moved inside with the small, halting steps of the convalescent. "Down, Alfy, down," she heard him say. "I can't play today, little friend."

She swallowed hard, then went back to her own apartment. She glanced at Wayne's somber face, then looked away. "I've been thinking of nothing but myself. I feel terrible about leaving him alone up here. He's not nearly as well as he pretends. He looks weak as a cat."

"He's an adult," Wayne said without sympathy. "He makes his own choices."

"Still," Ginnie objected, "he's an old man, he's alone and he's been hurt. There's nobody to look out for him."

Wayne's face went stonier. He crossed his arms again. "You warned him. What else can you do? Don't start attaching morals to everything you do. Or you'll never get anything done."

"But I don't feel right about leaving him."

Wayne gave her a look of ill-disguised impatience. "You want to stay here? Fine. Stay."

Ginnie paused, wondering if she were wrong to leave. But then she had an all-too-sharp recollection of the dead man staring through her with his sightless eyes. She could see again the blue-gray skin, the water dribbling from the corner of the slack mouth, the terrible stillness of his face.

Her gaze once more met Wayne's. "No," she said softly. "I don't want to stay."

NOTHING ELSE seemed disturbed in Ginnie's apartment except for the empty frame that had held the photograph. It lay facedown on her bureau. Careful not to touch it with her naked fingers, she wrapped it in one of her own handkerchiefs and put it in her purse alongside the snapshot. Then she packed. Wayne took the largest piece of luggage, a sort of duffle bag, and slung the strap over his shoulder, telling her he'd come back for the rest later.

On the second floor, he stopped at George Fairfax's door.

"What are you doing?" Ginnie asked.

"Fairfax used to be a cop. He might tell us the best person to go see. Somebody who'd listen." He knocked on the door.

"I don't know," Ginnie said, shaking her head. "He doesn't look very friendly. He never speaks or anything."

No one answered the door. Wayne knocked again, more loudly. They waited. Nobody appeared. Wayne tried a third time, Fairfax still didn't answer.

"He must be gone," Ginnie said.

Wayne hoisted the bag back to his shoulder. "Must be."

On the ground floor they stopped at the manager's apartment. Burbage was not happy when Ginnie asked to move, at least temporarily, into the apartment next to Wayne's.

"Miss Prince, you're nervous, I'm nervous, we're all nervous," Burbage said tiredly. He had a cigarette in his hand. "I know you had a scare, but it turned out to be nothing. Donner told me what the police found. I suggest you relax and stay where you are. I can't go moving everybody around."

Burbage did not ask them inside. Ginnie could hear the sound of a television turned up too loudly. She sensed that Burbage was protecting both the privacy of his apartment and his reclusive wife, and that he had stood guard against the world for so many years that it was habitual with him.

"Mr. Burbage," Ginnie said earnestly, "I'm not imagining things. The keys were stolen and since then somebody's been in my apartment—more than once. It's not safe."

Burbage exhaled a cloud of smoke. It drifted around him like a miasma. "I can't put you in the other tower. The place is already leased."

"To a dead man." Wayne's tone was sarcastic.

Burbage wasn't about to back down. "To a dead man whose estate isn't settled. His rent's paid till the end of the month. He's got possessions in there. I don't even know who to contact about them."

"I won't disturb his possessions," Ginnie promised. "I'm a responsible person. But I don't feel safe in my apartment."

Burbage looked unmoved.

"Look," Wayne said. "She's got a lease. She pays her rent, you're supposed to provide a safe place. Keep up your end of the deal. Or she can move out and not owe you a cent."

Burbage threw Wayne a displeased glance. His expression was even more sour and weary than before. "No. *You* look. You think the place isn't safe? Change the locks. I can't get to it before next week. I've got a bum wrist and Robbie's run ragged. First he's got to change the locks on the apartments where people are gone. They could be stolen blind. You other people got to take some responsibility for yourselves."

"Mr. Burbage," Ginnie said, "I will *not* go back to that apartment. Something strange is going on there."

Burbage gave a humorless laugh. "You'll feel safer in the dead man's place? Whoever took the keys could get in there, too. Sorry, Miss Prince, nobody's been in the place since he died. I can't let you have it."

"I'll call a locksmith," Ginnie said. "I'll pay to have the lock changed. Just let me use the apartment."

"Impossible."

"Come on, Ginnie," Wayne said in disgust. "You can stay with me. I'll sleep on the couch. You can start looking for another place tomorrow."

"She can't break her lease," Burbage said flatly. "She's leased the east tower, that's where she has to stay, that's it, that's the bottom line, amen."

Something snapped within Ginnie. She was tired of begging Burbage and she was tired of depending on Wayne's charity. She felt she'd been backed against the wall and she had no choice but to fight. She straightened to her full height and looked Burbage in the eye. Deep in her gaze, a blue fire sparked.

"I don't want to drag this to court. But I will. I'd do it just for the principle. Somebody's been getting into my place. I have a witness—Mr. Priborski—who can testify things have been tampered with. Things have been taken. That's criminal trespass, Mr. Burbage. It's happened repeatedly and I've informed you. If you don't afford me better protection, you're violating a covenant of the law. I've got a right to protection—you've got a duty to provide it. That's the law. Obey it or go to court."

"Hold on, hold on," Burbage said, frowning with disgust. "What are you talking about? Court? Just because you're a lawyer—"

"Just because I'm a lawyer doesn't mean I can't fight for my own rights," Ginnie answered, setting her jaw, "I'm not threatening you and I'm not bluffing. I'm stating a fact. Give me my rights or I'll get them in court. And it'll cost you plenty before it's over, because I'll ask for damages, as well."

She spoke with such force and conviction that Burbage looked at her with a displeased surprise. Wayne gave her a lingering sidelong look. What had happened to the wide-eyed, quiet, coltish girl who'd fainted in his arms last night? She wasn't being pushy, but she wasn't backing down an inch from Burbage, either. She was a strange one, Wayne thought, full of surprises.

Ginnie looked at Burbage in challenge. He said nothing. The television blared in the background. It was beginning to give her a headache.

"You don't want to answer me?" she asked. "Fine. You can answer to a judge."

She wheeled and started toward the front entrance of the lobby. Wayne looked after her, half-amused, half-impressed.

"Hold it, hold it," Burbage called after her irritably. "Come back. We'll talk. All right, you can use the other apartment. But you've got to sign papers. Any claims that anybody makes on the place, any problems, they're *yours*, you got me?"

Ginnie, profoundly relieved, stood looking at him, hoping that he wouldn't change his mind.

"You got it?" Burbage repeated.

She nodded.

Yeah, Wayne thought, *and she got you.* He walked to her side and took her arm. "Come on. We'll call the locksmith."

He gave Burbage a satisfied glance and drew Ginnie toward the stairs to the west tower. The sound of the television was stifled as Burbage shut his door. An announcer had been droning on about Junior Hopkins, and his smooth voice was cut off roughly in midsentence. "There's still no trace of Junior Hopkins, who was last seen two months ago in downtown—"

Ginnie hardly heard the words. Her blood was pounding in her ears from the confrontation. When she and Wayne reached the foot of the stairs, he paused and looked down at her. He let go of her arm but he still stood close. "I didn't think you had it in you," he said. "You've got a tough streak. I think, deep down, every pacifist likes a good fight."

He smiled. Once more she was aware of how his smile, so rare and so fleeting, transformed his face. It was the kind of smile that breaks hearts, incites fantasies and haunts dreams, and it always took her aback.

"I'm not usually like that," she said, embarrassed. She worried now if she had been too aggressive with Burbage. "I just felt I should stand up for the principle. But I shouldn't have been as sharp as I was. That wasn't necessary. I keep doing all these stupid things lately. Like fainting," she said in disgust.

One of Wayne's eyebrows came down in a measuring frown. "You're ashamed of passing out? I've seen guys pass out from looking at a hypodermic needle. Are you ashamed of anything you don't do on principle? Do you ever have fun, for instance?''

His tone sounded so harsh that a flush of resentment warmed her cheeks. She had always wanted to be a moral, rational person who stayed in control of herself, but Burbage had pushed her to the edge of her tolerance, and now Wayne pushed her beyond. Not only did his criticism sting, but he had confused and perplexed her ever since she had met him.

She did precisely what she most disliked; she struck out. ''You're not exactly Mr. Wild Exuberant Fun yourself,'' she countered. ''I just try to solve problems in a civilized way. We don't all need guns and muscles and—and tattoos.''

Now both his eyebrows drew down into a frown. ''Lighten up. If you don't like what you see here, you can go back upstairs with Prouty. If somebody comes in your place, scream to him to help. He can pelt them with a parakeet—if he doesn't faint before you do. You want your stuff? Come or go, it makes no difference to me.''

He pulled the duffle bag from his shoulder and held it out to her, anger and challenge in his face. ''I mean it,'' he said. He had known from the beginning it was a mistake to get involved with her. ''Come or go. It's the same to me.''

Suddenly, Ginnie was overwhelmed by regret. She shouldn't have bristled at his remarks; she had no right to snap at him. He was not, by nature, a gregarious man, but he had gone out of his way to be kind to her.

''I'm sorry.'' She looked away so she wouldn't have to meet his eyes. Then he would see precisely how sorry she was. ''Forget I said that, please. The last twenty-four hours have been crazy. I'm not myself, I'm upset. And what upsets me as much as anything is that nobody seems to believe me except you.''

''Forget it,'' he said gruffly, shouldering her bag again. He was uncharacteristically sorry about the flare-up himself. He did not usually indulge his anger, and he had no right to provoke Ginnie after what she'd been through. The problem was that he was on edge himself, and she unsettled him in ways he didn't even want to understand. He'd get her to a safe place, he told himself, then put her out of his mind.

"Come on," he said. "Let's call a locksmith." He kept his expression under stern control as he started up the stairs.

Ginnie nodded, glad of the truce. She spoke, more to fill the silence than anything else. "I just hope somebody else believes me one of these days."

An unseen hand seized her by the elbow and a gasp ripped from between her teeth. She whirled, startled.

She stared down into the small green eyes of Mrs. Treat. The woman looked up at her, a self-satisfied smile on her moonlike face. Her lips parted, showing tiny white teeth, which reminded Ginnie of those of a small carnivorous animal.

"I believe you," Mrs. Treat said, nodding so that her chins folded and unfolded like fat pleats. "I believe you saw someone dead." She smiled more widely and kept her hold on Ginnie's arm. "And," she said, "I know who that dead person was."

Chapter Six

"What?" Ginnie's heart thudded so hard that she could hardly speak. Wayne, on the first step, stopped and turned, staring at the two women.

Mrs. Treat squeezed Ginnie's elbow harder and smiled more serenely. Her eyelids sank a fraction lower, making her look as if she were falling into a trance. "I believe you. I believe you saw a dead man. And I know who he was."

Wayne moved to Ginnie's side now, glaring down at the overweight woman. His face was dark with distrust.

"What—how do you know about it?" Ginnie managed to say.

"Mr. Donner told me. But more than that, I see things." Mrs. Treat raised a plump forefinger and touched the center of her own forehead reverently. "I feel them. Things other people don't."

"Yeah, yeah, lady, the Force is with you," Wayne said impatiently. "But what do you *know*?" He could tell Ginnie's nerves had already been stretched to the limit, and the old lady creeping up like that had startled her badly. Mrs. Treat wore felt slippers that cushioned any sound her footsteps might make, despite her bulk. She was bundled into a flowered housedress and a shapeless gray cardigan sweater.

Mrs. Treat's smile faded. "You, young man, were born under a star that cursed you with irreverence. It will do you no good. Rashness will be your undoing one of these days."

"Mrs. Treat," Ginnie said uneasily, "if you know something about that body, please tell us. Please don't keep it to yourself."

The pale green gaze shifted back to Ginnie. The woman kept her tight grip on Ginnie's elbow as if to make sure she wouldn't escape. "There's no mystery about who was in your bathtub, Miss Prince. The explanation is quite simple." She smiled again.

Ginnie resisted the urge to pry Mrs. Treat's fingers off her sleeve. As always, the woman filled her with a nameless dread. She forced herself to stay calm. "Who was he?"

Mrs. Treat laughed, a deep gurgling sound. "As I say, it's simple. And it's obvious. He's a ghost."

Wayne swore, quietly but eloquently.

Ginnie flinched slightly, in spite of herself. "Mrs. Treat, I try to respect other people's beliefs, but that man was not a ghost. He was as real as you or I."

Mrs. Treat reached up and adjusted Ginnie's collar. It was an intimate gesture, almost a loving one, and it repelled Ginnie. "Sweetheart, a ghost *is* as real as you or I. It doesn't matter if you believe in him. He believes in *you*."

Ginnie's eyes met Wayne's for a tense moment. He looked as doubtful and displeased as she felt. She turned back to Mrs. Treat. "What do you mean, he believes in me?"

Mrs. Treat kept smiling her maddeningly benign smile. "He *likes* you, sweetheart. That's why he materialized in your place. Because he trusts you. You have the air of a gentle soul. You would never hurt anything. Spirits sense such things."

Mrs. Treat glanced at Wayne again, and her voice grew harsher. "They can tell those who aren't gentle, too. And pay them in their own violent coin. I'd be careful, young man. You're the sort who attracts bad vibrations."

"Obviously," Wayne muttered.

Ginnie tried to draw away from Mrs. Treat's grasp, but the old woman was surprisingly strong. Ginnie could not break free from her unless she struggled, and, after last night, she didn't want to create another scene.

"Mrs. Treat, frankly I don't understand. If this ghost *liked* me, he'd do me a favor and stay out of my bathtub."

This time Mrs. Treat smiled so widely that her eyes turned its slits. "You're only frightened, sweetheart, because you don't understand. He wants you to set him free, that's all. That's why he appeared to *you*. Actually, you've been granted a rare privilege."

"It's a privilege I could do without." Ginnie's voice rang with bitter sincerity.

Wayne eyed Mrs. Treat's grip on Ginnie's elbow. "Lady, you don't have to hang on to her like that. She's not trying to run away."

Mrs. Treat relaxed her grasp but did not relinquish it. "You have to understand, dear. It's a happening of major import. You," she said, nodding at Ginnie, "are special. Because of your greatly spiritual nature. And I can teach you. I want you to come to my apartment. I have so many things to share with you. This ghost has come to open a psychic door for you. I can guide you through."

"I—it's a bit soon. I don't think I'm ready to go through any psychic doors right now."

"Look," said Wayne, shifting the duffle bag with impatience, "you're so sure the guy was a ghost, tell me this—whose ghost?"

Mrs. Treat stiffened at his challenge. "He was a former resident, of course. That's why his spirit still clings to this place. There are the vibrations of many spirits here."

"Great," Wayne said sarcastically. "Only about ten thousand people've lived here. Care to be more specific?"

Mrs. Treat seemed to be trying hard to transcend Wayne's contentiousness. She smiled again. "I often have the sense, very strongly, of a teacher. A schoolmaster, perhaps. A gentleman, but a troubled soul." She gave Ginnie's arm a squeeze. "He intuits in you, my dear, a kindness he finds soothing. If you'd come with me—"

"I'm sorry," Ginnie said, shaking her head, "but I don't feel very soothing right now. I'm really not in a frame of mind to discuss ghosts."

"This 'schoolmaster,' Mrs. Treat," Wayne cut in, "can you tell us more about him than that? That he was a troubled soul? That's pretty vague."

"Do you mean can I name names?" Mrs. Treat asked, with a slight sniff of contempt. "No. Names mean little to spirits. They're on a plane where such details are meaningless."

Wayne's expression was dubious. "Can you tell *anything* about him? Or are all the details conveniently vague?"

Mrs. Treat looked haughty. "He was an educated man. Outwardly refined, but inwardly tormented. I sense that he loved music. I can't tell you his name, but sometimes I have an impression of certain words that were important to him— *Hilton* or *Hilson* is one. *Loraine* is another. And I have the sense that he died during the depression—years of darkness, years of want—and that he died suddenly. That's why he's still here with us. His death was so sudden that his spirit is confused. It needs guidance. And for guidance—" she paused dramatically and stared into Ginnie's eyes "—for guidance, he's come to you. You must help him. And let me help you."

"Mrs. Treat," Ginnie said firmly, "I have to go."

Mrs. Treat cast a suspicious look at Ginnie's overnight case and the duffle bag slung over Wayne's wide shoulder. "Do you think you can run away from this? From him?"

Ginnie's skin went cold. "You mean the dead man?"

Mrs. Treat nodded, her disturbingly peaceful smile back in place. "You can't escape him, you know. Now that he's chosen you. No lock can keep him out. He'll keep coming to you. Until you help."

Ginnie couldn't help herself. She jerked her arm away and took a step backward. "I told you, I don't want to talk about this anymore. Not now. *Please.*"

Mrs. Treat looked hurt, but somehow she kept smiling. "You're just frightened, sweetheart. I can help you."

"I understand what I can see and hear and touch," Ginnie replied, "not what people say they 'sense' or 'intuit.'

You were on my floor yesterday. You were in Mr. Prouty's rooms. Didn't you see or hear anything *real*?"

"I saw a dog. I saw two birds. I listened to the silence. I listened to the wind. I saw the rooms of a lonely man. I saw the emptiness of his life. He needs companionship, that one. He needs someone to care for him."

Ginnie cringed slightly, feeling fresh pangs of guilt for leaving Mr. Prouty behind. Mrs. Treat, she realized, had designs on him and there was probably nothing spiritual about them.

Wayne regarded Mrs. Treat with skepticism. "That's all you saw or heard?"

"In the stillness, I heard the echoes of the past. It echoes most loudly in the tower, you know. This building likes to talk about its past. If you're sensitive, you've heard it whisper, especially at night."

Ginnie resisted taking another step backward. She rubbed her arm where Mrs. Treat had gripped her. What the woman said was true—Ginnie had lain awake all too many nights, listening to the building rustling and creaking as if it were whispering secrets to itself.

"And," said Wayne between his teeth, "how many times did you say you went up there?"

"Four," said Mrs. Treat. "I went four times. I packed a case for the hospital. I tended the dog. Mr. Burbage came for the key this morning when he heard Mr. Prouty was coming home. I try to be a good neighbor."

"Right now, I think we're good-neighbored out," Wayne said. "Come on, Ginnie. We've got to call the locksmith."

"Young man," Mrs. Treat said, "you'll learn you can't lock out destiny."

She turned her attention once more to Ginnie. "You'll learn, too. But I'll be there when you need me. And you *will* need me, my dear. You can count on it."

"Come on," Wayne said again. He put his hand on the small of Ginnie's back. She was grateful for the contact, the closeness. Most of all, she was grateful finally to be making an escape.

She started up the stairs, Wayne's hand still at her back. She thought she heard the closing of a door and turned to look. So did Wayne. Beneath them, at the bottom of the stairs, so did Mrs. Treat.

Someone, Ginnie realized, must have been listening to them. Questioningly, her eyes met Wayne's. His dark eyebrows were drawn together in a frown. He nodded. He understood what she meant.

When they reached the second-floor landing, out of Mrs. Treat's sight, Ginnie paused. Wayne let his hand drop away from her, as if touching her had been merely a courtesy he had provided for a few tense moments.

Her heart was beating altogether too fast. She did not know if it were in reaction to Mrs. Treat or to Wayne. Trying to concentrate on what had just happened, she turned to look down toward the lobby. "Was somebody listening?"

"Maybe. I thought it was Burbage's door. Did you see?"

Ginnie, doubtful, shook her head. "I thought it was that man's. You know, that big old man. Mr. Swengler."

Swengler, thought Wayne. In his mind's eye he saw the old man as he had been last night, peering from his doorway, cryptically smiling. Ginnie had been terrified, and Swengler, damn him, had stood there and smiled.

But he decided not to mention that detail to Ginnie. She had enough to contend with. She needed things to lighten up, not become murkier.

He raised one eyebrow and his mouth turned down at the corner, an expression of ironic resignation. "I'm starting to think we could have picked a better neighborhood. What do you think?"

Ginnie's finely boned face was solemn. "I just hope Mrs. Treat is wrong."

"About what?"

"About locks not stopping the dead man from coming back."

Wayne shook his head. "She's crazy," he said. "There's no such thing as ghosts."

For the first time that day, Ginnie smiled. She gave him a wry, sidelong look. "Famous last words," she said.

BURBAGE SENT ROBBIE UP with the extra key to the vacant apartment. He was a bland-faced young man of twenty-one or twenty-two, with rosy cheeks and a shy manner. He had a slight stutter. He had worked full-time as a maintenance man in the apartments since he had dropped out of school at sixteen. All winter long, it seemed to Ginnie, he had worn the same outfit: faded jeans that emphasized his bandy legs, a plaid flannel shirt over a long-sleeved undershirt and an old Boston Red Sox baseball cap.

He opened the apartment for Ginnie and checked the lights, water and heat. "We're having t-trouble with the heat," he said. Usually friendly, today Robbie was quiet.

"This place is almost like mine," Ginnie said, glancing around the apartment. Unlike hers, it was thickly cluttered with possessions.

Robbie was fixing a blind that had fallen halfway down. He stood on a chair. "Are you sure you want t-to stay here?" he asked.

She looked up at him in surprise. "Why?"

He screwed a bracket back into the paneled wall. "Because this is a dead man's place. I wouldn't stay in a dead man's place." He gave a brief, furtive look around the room. "All this stuff is dead guy's stuff."

It was, Ginnie thought, a morbid thing to say. "I'll try not to think of it."

"Mr. Donner says you think you saw a dead man in your bath-t-tub," Robbie said, putting the roller of the blind back in its bracket.

Mr. Donner talks too much, Ginnie thought, crossing her arms to warm herself. The apartment was chilly.

"If I thought I saw a dead man in my place, I'd move out," Robbie said. "I wouldn't st-stick around."

He stepped down from the chair and put it back in the kitchen. He came back into the living room. The expression on his face, Ginnie thought, was odd. He looked nervous. "If that happened t-to me," he said, "I'd leave. T-too many strange things happen around here."

Ginnie gave him a piercing look. She'd always liked Robbie, but he didn't seem himself today. "What do you mean, 'strange things'?"

"You know. Like Mr. Burbage getting hit. Only more. You know. People say this place is ha-haunted. Even my father says that. Since years ago. He says *he* wouldn't live here."

Ginnie frowned. "Did your father ever say anything about dead men appearing or disappearing?"

Robbie shoved his hands deep into his pockets. "He said there's ghosts here."

She looked at him as if she'd never seen him before. He was small, shorter than she, but powerfully built. He was strong enough, she imagined, to lift the dead man if he had to. "Robbie," she said carefully, "if I didn't know better, I'd say you were trying to scare me."

He shook his head, but his face was full of confusion. "No. I'm just t-telling you. This can be a bad place. After what happened t-to Mr. Burbage, I'm not going to stay. I'm leaving. Going on to better things."

That was Robbie's constant refrain. The day she had moved in, he had come up to fix a badly leaking faucet and told her he was going on to better things. Sometimes he went into the city, ostensibly to look for a better job. Sometimes he even left for a day or two at a time. But he always came back and he never moved on.

The front door of the apartment was open. Wayne knocked on the doorframe and walked in. He carried Ginnie's large suitcase and her garment bag. "Fairfax doesn't answer his phone, either," he said.

"He won't answer anything," Robbie said.

Both Wayne and Ginnie looked at him.

"He's gone," Robbie said. "He t-took a suitcase."

A beat of silence throbbed in the air. "His car's still here. It's in the parking lot," Wayne said.

"Somebody picked him up," Robbie explained.

Ginnie and Wayne exchanged glances. The boy seemed more nervous than before.

"Why?" Ginnie asked. "How long will he be gone?"

Robbie took a deep breath. "I think something scared him. I don't know how long he'll be gone."

"Scared him?" Wayne said. "What?"

Robbie shrugged. "I don't know. Like I say, strange things happen around here. I gotta go. I gotta change the furnace filters." Ducking his head, he walked out the door, as fast as his bandy legs could take him.

Ginnie looked after him, then at Wayne. "He's nervous."

"He knows something," Wayne said.

"It was almost like he was warning me to get out of here." She closed the door and for good measure, locked it. She turned and looked at Wayne. "Could he have moved the body?"

"He's not supposed to be here at night."

Ginnie leaned against the door, her face worried. "He can come in through the back door of the basement and nobody'd ever see him. That's how he goes home sometimes when he doesn't drive. He goes through the woods and past the bog and back to the farm."

"Robbie wouldn't have to steal keys," Wayne said. "Burbage keeps an extra set for when Robbie needs them. That's what he sent up for you. One of the keys of Robbie's set."

Ginnie shook her head. "But why would he hide a drowned man in my apartment? What would he be doing with a drowned man at all?"

Robbie had always impressed her as a gentle soul. Last summer he had fed a cat that had taken refuge in the basement to have her kittens. He watched over both cat and kittens faithfully until Mr. Burbage made him get rid of them.

Wayne stepped next to her. She looked so pensive that he reached out and tipped her chin up higher. "Let's let the police ask him," he said.

"You want to go with me?" Ginnie asked. The hand that touched her face was strong and warm. She felt a rush of emotion for this man who seemed so determined to help her. She didn't know if it was affection or desire or both. It rather frightened her.

His hand dropped away. He looked into her eyes. "I should. You alone, they won't believe. Two of us—maybe. We don't have Fairfax to give us any hints. We'll just have to take our chances. As soon as the locksmith is through, we'll go."

Ginnie nodded. "I wonder where Fairfax went. And why."

"Hey," Wayne said. "It's Christmas. People have places to go."

IN THE LOBBY, they met Paul Donner again. He was wearing white wool slacks and a blue sweater with white reindeer marching across his chest. He looked irritable. "Where *is* that Robbie?" he asked. "He's supposed to help me move my microwave. I have company coming for dinner tonight, and here I stand, my kitchen half-rearranged and everything at sixes and sevens."

"He said he was going to change the furnace filters," Ginnie said.

"Well, *I* was just downstairs and he's not there. I wish he *would* fix the furnace. My place is like ice," Donner said acidly. "My guests are going to say, 'What a lovely igloo. Whoever did your hoarfrost?'"

"He's not down there?" Wayne asked, cocking a dark eyebrow.

"That boy," Donner said impatiently. "He's off on some kind of rampage today. He was trying to convince me earlier that this place has ghosts. Ghosts! Would someone *please* repeal the New Age?"

"Ghosts?" Ginnie asked. She suddenly wondered if the explanation for Robbie's behavior was simply that he was frightened.

"I'm tired of ghost stories about this place," Donner complained, his hands on his hips. "Mill girls preyed on by phantoms. School girls stalked by specters. Things that go bump in the night. My God, the way some people talk, you'd think ectoplasm would be dripping off the walls."

"Mill girls?" Ginnie asked. "School girls?"

Donner waved his hand, as if banishing the thought of them. "Yes. Way back when. There was some kind of uproar when this place was a girls' school. There was an article in the paper last year. If somebody hasn't pinned you down and droned out the whole story to you, be grateful. It's a crashing bore."

"But what happened?" Ginnie asked.

"Oh, I don't remember," Donner said. "Where is that boy? I can't wait around for him all day. I *have* to get to the store and pray they have a ripe avocado. If you see him, tell him to get himself over here, will you?"

He went into his apartment. "Everybody has ghosts on the brain," Ginnie marveled.

GINNIE SAT, looking at the detective. The detective sat behind his battered desk, looking down at the mutilated snapshot. Wayne sat, keeping his face expressionless, looking at both Ginnie and the detective.

Morrie Sternberg was a lean, good-looking man with close-cropped black hair and eyes almost as dark as Wayne's. He glanced up and met Wayne's steady gaze.

He set down the snapshot, which he'd held with the handkerchief. "I'm sorry," he said. "It's not much to go on."

"If you could find who stole the keys," Ginnie said, "you'd know who's been in my apartment. Have you any idea who took them? Are you working on it?"

Sternberg did not look her in the eyes. He turned his attention back to his legal pad on which he'd taken notes. "We're working on it."

"Well, are you getting anywhere?" Ginnie demanded in exasperation. "Somebody's walking around with keys to every apartment in that place. What are you doing to find them?''

"Everything we can," Sternberg said mechanically. "Officers talked to all the residents the night it happened. You know that. There were no leads."

Ginnie ran her hand through her hair. She remembered a sour-faced officer had come to her door, asked a few brusk questions, scratched some words on a report, told her be careful and then left. She and Mr. Prouty agreed that he had done little more than alarm them both, and probably the rest of the residents, as well.

Wayne shifted irritably in his chair. "It's been over two days. You haven't got a single lead?"

Sternberg sighed again and didn't look up. He doodled a staring eye on his legal pad. "Burbage claims he can't remember anything. Nobody else saw anything. We've got nothing to go on. Burbage decided he didn't even want us to pursue the investigation. He thinks it was just a drifter, somebody who's long gone."

"He didn't want an investigation?" Wayne said. "You mean you've stopped looking into this?"

Sternberg kept his face professionally expressionless. "Of course, we're pursuing it. It's just that he's turned into an unwilling witness. He doesn't like being involved with the police because they upset his wife. Don't ask me why."

"The police are upsetting *me*," Wayne said between his teeth. "What's going to have to happen before you make any progress? Somebody gets robbed? Raped? Killed?"

Sternberg shrugged again. "We're hoping—of course—that nothing happens. Maybe Burbage is right. Whoever did it drifted on. Who knows?"

"*I* know," Wayne shot back. He pointed at Ginnie. "She knows. She's sitting there telling you somebody's been in her apartment, dammit. But you don't listen."

A vein jumped in Sternberg's temple. He clenched his fist on the desktop, but his voice stayed calm. "Making holes in a snapshot isn't a crime. Moving a hat isn't a crime. Stealing a bathmat is a misdemeanor, but it's hardly a major crime."

"Jeez," muttered Wayne. He looked at the ceiling in exasperation. "Jeez. You people amaze me."

"Look," Sternberg said, as if explaining the obvious, "I send people milling all over there, it's going to scare away whoever's doing this. We sit tight, maybe they'll get cocky, do something concrete, something we can get a hold on. Then we can make some progress."

"Until then, what's she supposed to do? Be *bait*? That picture was a threat, dammit. You should stake out a man in that apartment. You should keep the whole place under surveillance."

"We're extremely shorthanded," Sternberg said icily.

Nervously, Ginnie cleared her throat. There was an edge to the conversation, a sense of growing anger, and she wanted to bring reason back to the situation. But she also wanted Morrie Sternberg to act. If he wouldn't act out of duty, perhaps he would if pressure were applied.

"I'll do whatever it takes to get you to do something about this," she said. She took a deep breath. "If it's not looked into immediately, I'll complain to the mayor. I'll complain to the city council. I'll write letters to the newspaper. I work for HERC. If a person learns anything from that organization, it's how to complain—loudly."

Sternberg blanched slightly. The newspapers had been almost viciously critical of the police lately. The department did not need more negative publicity.

"It takes a policeman to make you happy?" he asked, resignation in his voice, "I'll send a policeman. Fine. Fine. I was *going* to send somebody over in any case. It just may take a little time, all right? Like I say, we're shorthanded. And every criminal in Merrimack County seems to know it—we got crimes up the wazoo." He slapped a stack of reports. "A Dunkin' Donuts robbed on the Daniel Webster highway. A gas station held up. Houses broken into. Cars burgled. But we'll get to you and your snapshot and your bathmat. All right?"

WHEN GINNIE AND WAYNE LEFT, Ginnie was uncertain that the police would be of any help at all. Wayne pushed his way out the front door of the police station and held it for her. He swore under his breath. "I can't believe these bozos."

"Maybe he's right," Ginnie said, dispirited. "If people are holding up filling stations and breaking into houses all over town, nobody's going to care if somebody ruins one old snapshot."

"Jerks," muttered Wayne.

Ginnie sighed. The cold air cut as sharply as a blade. The city seemed incongruously cheerful to her. Streets were bright with Christmas decorations, stores shone with colored lights.

Snow still fell, thick and steady. Across the street, before the entrance of a department store, a Salvation Army lassie stood, ringing her bell and looking chilled to the bone in spite of her wool cape and winter bonnet.

Wayne stopped and took a deep breath. The sky was already turning dark, although it was only half-past three. He stared up, over the tops of the buildings, as if he were looking at something far in the distance that nobody else could see. The lines of his face were so rigid, so taut, that Ginnie wondered if he were in more pain than usual.

"Are you all right?" she asked, uneasy because she knew he must hate such questions. Sometimes he worried her. She knew he suffered more than he let anyone know.

Hesitantly, she put her hand on his leather sleeve again. "Wayne? Are you all right?"

He made a slight grimace, then turned and gave her a lopsided smile. As usual, it made her heart begin to tumble in her chest. "I'm fine. Where do you want to go?"

He put his gloved hand over hers and patted it, twice, then held it in place against his arm. Ginnie was stunned by the friendliness of the gesture. She found, to her chagrin, that she liked touching him and being touched by him. She tried to quell the emotions coming to life within her. There was nobody, she told herself, who could be more wrong for her than Wayne Priborski.

She drew her hand away from his arm and turned up the collar of her coat against the icy breeze that cut the air. Once more she realized how handsome he was in his own dark, slightly dangerous way. Uneasy, she no longer trusted herself to look at him. Instead, she stared across the street at the Salvation Army lassie, red-faced but stalwart.

"I think I'd like to go to the newspaper office," she said, putting her hands deep into her pockets.

"Why? You really going to complain about the police?"

She shook her head. "No. I want to see if I can find anything about the building, that article Paul Donner mentioned. You can drop me off. I'll take a cab back."

"I'm not leaving you alone. Too much funny stuff has happened lately. I'll help you look."

It was a considerate offer, a friendly one, but his voice had been harsh when he made it, and his face was anything but friendly. He had a stubborn, almost ferocious set to his mouth.

"Thanks," she managed to say, but it came out so softly she wasn't sure if the wind hadn't carried it away unheard.

He said nothing, only nodded. They began to walk toward Wayne's car, a black Corvette that was parked down the block. Overhead, the Christmas garlands that lined the street swayed in the wind.

She kept her head down, trying to protect her face from the frigid sweep of the cold. They walked in silence. From one of the stores came the music of recorded carols, sounding patchy as the wind whipped parts of them away.

To save us all from Satan's power
When we were gone astray.
Oh, tidings . . .
. . . Tidings . . .

Neither of them spoke until they had almost reached the car. A stony calm had settled over his face.

"Wayne," she said, almost shyly, "what happened when you got shot? I wish you'd tell me."

Wayne shrugged. It was something he never talked about. But he supposed it wouldn't kill him to tell her. It was ancient history anyway.

A carol rang out with tinny merriment: "Fa la la la la, la la la la."

He glanced up again at the darkening sky. "Maybe I'm the ghost everybody keeps talking about." His voice was edged with bitter humor. "I'm the one that came back from the dead."

Chapter Seven

Ginnie stopped and stared at him. The snow fell harder now. Flakes rested on her gray wool cap and settled in her auburn hair. "They thought you'd die?"

He nodded impatiently, signaling her to keep moving. "They said I'd die. They said I'd never walk again. They were wrong. Come on. It's cold out here." He reached the car and opened the door on her side.

She didn't move. Instead, she looked into his eyes, trying to read the expression hidden in their darkness. She could not. "How did it happen?"

"Get in—you're going to freeze."

She got into the passenger seat and he closed the door. He moved to the front of the car, cleaned off the windshield and got in. He turned on the engine and let it idle.

She watched him from beneath lowered lashes. He seemed completely self-contained to her, independent, private and solitary. "How did it happen?" she repeated.

He tossed her a noncommittal glance. He wished now that he hadn't said anything. "You're a woman who asks a lot of questions, know that?"

"You're a man who raises questions. You never want to talk about yourself. Look, you've done a lot for me, and I'd like to know something about you in return. I'm just—interested, that's all."

He studied the instruments on the dashboard and turned on the windshield wipers. He had never talked about the accident with anyone. Yet now he felt compelled to give her some kind of answer, not just to shut her out. She was, after all, a nice woman, a little maddening sometimes, but basically a nice, decent, warm-hearted person. Besides, her eyes were always asking questions even when her mouth wasn't. They were hard eyes to ignore.

"It was—just an accident," he said. "We were hunting. Three of us. We were climbing through a barbed wire fence. My friend, Clooney, dropped his rifle, tried to grab it. He'd forgotten to unload it. It went off."

"My God," said Ginnie, appalled. "He should have known better."

"Yeah. He should have known better." Wayne put the car in gear and concentrated on maneuvering it into the creeping afternoon traffic.

"How long were you in the hospital?"

"Twelve weeks." He didn't like to think about that, either. He hadn't opened his eyes for six days. He'd just lain there, tubes in his nose, tubes in his arm, a tube down his throat to keep him breathing. Traction weights and pulleys holding him in place like an insect pinned to a board. When he'd gotten out of the hospital, he'd lost so much weight. They said he might never walk again, but he'd showed them, and he intended to keep on showing them.

"And how long before you walked?" she asked, wondering how he had stood it. He was not the kind of man who could adapt to inactivity.

He stopped at a red light and watched the hunched-over shoppers making their ways down the sidewalks, their arms laden with packages. "A year. It took about a year."

"And you quit when they said you couldn't fly?"

"Hell, they'll ground a guy for flat feet. You think they'd let me up there with forty tons of pricey metal? No. It was over. It was finished."

"So you just—quit?"

"I can still fly as a civilian. The company's got a plane. Not much of a plane. I take it up sometimes."

"And what about engineering? Do you like it?"

He shrugged. "It's what I studied in school." But it wasn't, he thought, the same as doing a thousand miles an hour in an F-18, high above the blue Pacific Ocean. It wasn't the same at all.

Ginnie shook her head sadly at the needlessness and waste of it. Wayne's body had been shattered, his career ended, his life permanently wrenched off course because of a stupid accident. Guns, she thought, feeling slightly sick. Why couldn't he have just stayed away from them?

He glanced over at her, his face impassive. "Let's end this discussion, okay? It's not my favorite topic. And I know you well enough to guess what you're thinking. I shouldn't have been out hunting in the first place. I got what I deserved. Chase Bambi and die for your sins."

Ginnie raised her shoulders in a gesture that suggested her own guilt. She didn't blame him, but she didn't understand him, either. "I get extremely upset when anything has to die, that's all. Or gets hurt."

He gave her the half smile that always caused her to feel as if she'd just stepped off a carousel that had made her giddy to the marrow of her bones.

"Even an old war horse like me?"

Especially you she wanted to say, and to say it perhaps even with passion.

But passion of any sort, she knew, was inappropriate, uncalled for. She stared out the window at the falling snow and kept her voice calm, even and cool.

"Even you," she said.

THEY SAT IN THE NEWSPAPER'S dark little microfilm viewing room with two old-fashioned projectors before them on the small table. On the dingy wall wavered images of pages of two separate back issues of the *Republican-Guardian*.

Ginnie wasn't even sure what it was that she hunted for so obsessively, except that it was some link to whatever "strange things" Donner said had happened at Hawthorne Towers. He had mentioned something about a fairly recent newspaper story. The only answer seemed to be to comb the microfilms of the last year or so day by day, column by column, looking for the significant headline, the odd event, the name of Hawthorne Towers itself.

She was grateful that Wayne had offered to help, for the job proved to be more cumbersome and more tedious than she'd thought. Unsmiling, he concentrated on reading as swiftly, yet as carefully as possible. She wondered if he were humoring her, if he thought she was foolish, acting merely out of an excess of nervous energy.

The room was so small that every time one of them moved, the other got jostled in the elbow, brushed along the thigh, nudged in the ribs. They accidentally touched each other so often that their apologies became mechanical, then finally stopped altogether.

Ginnie could not, however, stop herself from being conscious of the contact. It was impossible not to remember how hard and well knit his arms were beneath the blue sweater, how firmly the muscles of his legs worked beneath his tightly-fitting jeans. She rebuked herself for remembering such things, and she reproved herself for shivering pleasurably when his leg pressed next to hers or his breath tickled her neck.

She told herself that Wayne's nearness distracted her only because the job itself was so wearisome. The microfilms were of the most primitive sort and hard to read. No more than long strips of negatives, when they were projected on the wall, their print glared a fuzzy white against the black background.

"Why don't they index these things?" Wayne asked, bending his head and massaging his eyes with his thumb and forefinger. He had proven himself an impressively fast and disciplined reader, but his eyes were beginning to rebel.

"I guess it's too big a job." She wound the reel of microfilm so another page appeared, slightly distorted, on the wall. "At least they could get some projectors that didn't used to belong to Fred Flintstone. Wait—I think I've got something."

She adjusted the focus of the machine minutely. Wayne squinted. The image from her machine seemed to flicker slightly. Ginnie pointed to the lower left-hand side of the page.

The story was almost two years old.

The Hawthorne Towers apartment building on North Cumberland Turnpike has been sold to Puritan Property Management of Lowell, Mass., which owns a number of multiple-dwelling rental properties throughout New England.

Martin Forenza, vice president of Puritan Properties, said that the Kurtz Corporation has sold its interest in the building. The Kurtz Corporation, based in Utica, New York, acquired Hawthorne Towers building in 1961.

Forenza said both parties are pleased with the transaction. Puritan plans to renovate the structure, floor by floor, Forenza added, in order to disturb the tenants as little as possible.

Hawthorne Towers was opened as a dormitory for women mill workers in 1867 by General Malachi Hawthorne. In the 1930s and 1940s, it was the site of the highly respected Merrimack Academy, which was attended by the Pulitzer Prize-winning playwright, Louisa Anne Newsome. Newsome described life at Merrimack Academy in her 1972 book *Passing Through*.

Wayne stared at the story with a bemused frown while Ginnie hurried to copy it down in her small notebook.

"A lot of absentee landlords," he mused. "Out-of-town owners for almost forty years. That's weird."

"At least it gives us some dates," Ginnie said, underlining them in her notebook. "Maybe we should skip to one of them. What do you think? Maybe Donner was wrong about when the story was printed. We've gone through two full years. Should we try 1961? The thirties? The forties? Or 1867? He said whatever it was, it happened years ago."

Wayne's frown deepened. "I'd try the thirties. Or the forties. The 1960s may not be far enough, and the 1860s is probably too far. Who's Louisa Anne Newsome? Where've I heard of her before?"

"I have no idea," Ginnie answered. "Let's try the forties. Anything for a change." She rose and opened the door that led into the newspaper's reference room and morgue. A bored-looking girl sat behind the desk. She had a piece of plastic holly pinned in her hair, but it didn't make her look merry or bright. Ginnie asked her for the microfilm for the years 1940 to 1949.

The girl's broad face grew sulky. "It's late. You'll never get through all that. This place closes at five. Besides, I can't give you over four years' worth at a time. You only got—" she glanced at the watch on her plump wrist "—fifteen minutes. You wouldn't even be able to get through one year. You should come back Monday."

The girl looked past Ginnie and up at the wall clock, checking it against her watch. Her desk was clean, her coat draped over the back of the chair and her fingers drummed impatiently on the desktop. She was a young woman obviously ready for her freedom.

Ginnie squared her shoulders. "We can at least start another set of years. Give me 1948 and '49."

The girl opened her drawer, took out a nailfile and began to repair a ragged thumbnail. "I can't do that. The microfilm for those years is gone."

"Gone? You mean checked out already?" Ginnie glanced dubiously around the room. It was empty except for herself and this cheerless girl.

"Gone. Somebody walked off with it. Swiped it." The girl shrugged. She glanced up at Ginnie. "I could start closing up this place. It's almost time to go, you know?"

"You mean somebody *stole* it?" Ginnie asked, all her senses going on alert.

"I guess." The girl shrugged again and examined a hangnail. She brought it to her mouth and tried to bite it off.

"Why would anybody steal it?"

"I dunno." The girl's voice was muffled by the finger between her front teeth.

Ginnie frowned. "Well, who do they think stole it?"

Another shrug, another mumble. "I dunno."

"I had to sign out for the rolls I took. Isn't there a record of who had the film last?"

"I dunno."

Frustrated, Ginnie put her hands on the desk and leaned across it. She stared directly into the girl's face, which was wide, fleshy and distinctly bovine. "Well, why do you *think* somebody would take it?"

The girl successfully severed the hangnail, removed it daintily from her teeth and wiped it on a tissue. She examined her fingertip with interest. "Kids. Some kid doing a research paper for school. Doesn't want to sit in here and go through all the old papers. So he takes the ones he needs."

Ginnie frowned. She'd heard of students stealing journals and books for research projects, but never microfilm. How could they read it without the projector? "So where can I find records of those years? Do they have the old papers themselves stored anywhere?"

"I dunno."

"Does the city library keep copies of the same microfilms? They should."

The girl stood and took her coat from the back of the chair. "I dunno. Hey, I'd like to go home, you know? I got a personal life outside this place. And it's almost Christmas. I got things to do."

Ginnie straightened up, disgusted. She glanced at the clock. Only twelve minutes were left until five o'clock. "I've got things to do, too. And one of them is go through these microfilms. Give me 1947."

The girl already had one arm in the sleeve of her coat. Now she glowered at Ginnie. She rolled her eyes heavenward. With great melodrama she took the coat off again and hung it over the back of her chair. Putting a maximum amount of disgust into her step, she thudded her way to the microfilm cabinet and pulled out the box containing the spool for 1947.

She thrust it at Ginnie. "Sign here," she snapped, pushing a clipboard across the desk. Then she sat down heavily at her desk to stare at the clock and to brood upon the many wrongs done to her.

Ginnie went back into the cramped little room and sat down, accidentally jostling Wayne's shoulder. "This isn't going to be easy. Somebody's walked off with part of the microfilm for the forties."

She put the spool on its spindle and began to play with the focus. She glanced over at Wayne, who sat, his elbow on the table, his fingers resting thoughtfully against his chin. In the shadows, his face looked more angular than usual and his concentration seemed intense. She wasn't sure he had even heard what she'd said about the stolen microfilm.

"What are you doing?" she asked, turning her attention to the first edition of the *Republican-Guardian* for the year 1947. "I thought you'd been through that year once already."

"I have," he muttered, never taking his eyes from the image on the wall. "I'm going through it again. I want to know why I recognized the name Louisa Ann Newsome. I must have seen it in here somewhere."

Hurriedly Ginnie read the headlines of January 1, 1947. The biggest stories were the birth of the New Hampshire New Year baby at 12:02 a.m. in Nashua and the continuing rumors that the city's leading textile mill would soon close down.

January 2 was little different, except, of course, there was no New Year baby, January 3 less different still, and Ginnie was halfway through January 4 when she heard Wayne breathe a satisfied exhalation. "Here it is."

She looked, her forehead creasing with concentration. He pointed at the upper half of the page, next to the obituary listings. Ginnie tried to read quickly, for she knew their time at the newspaper was running out.

Ogunquit, Maine. New Hampshire playwright and essayist Louisa Ann Newsome died of a heart attack yesterday evening in her Ogunquit home. She was 59.

Newsome, a native of Sugar Hill, New Hampshire, was best known for her 1957 Pulitzer Prize-winning play, *The Summer People*. The play chronicles the unlikely love story of the ghost of a World War II flyer and a woman summering in a New England resort.

"Newsome's work often dealt with the supernatural. In her 1972 autobiography *Passing Through*, she gave a firsthand account of her own experience, including the so-called Haunting of Hawthorne Towers, a series of unexplained thefts and assaults that plagued Merrimack Academy in 1948 and 1949. The incidents were similar, Newsome noted, to those plaguing the women mill workers who lived in the building at the turn of the century. Newsome graduated from the academy in 1948 and attended Swathmore for two years.

The Summer People was Newsome's first produced play and her most successful. Her subsequent work never attained the same popularity or critical acclaim, which embittered her. "In America," she said in one of her rare interviews, "early success is the same as early death."

She is survived by one sister, Mary Katherine Cheswick, of Ogunquit, and a brother, Paul Newsome, of rural New Hampshire. The funeral service will be private.

Ginnie reread the notice, then turned, looking into Wayne's shadowy face. "The Haunting of Hawthorne Towers?" she said. "Thefts and assaults?"

"That's got to be what he meant," Wayne said, his eyes never leaving the story. "It's got to be part of it, at least."

Ginnie scribbled madly in her notebook.

1972, *Passing Through*
1957, *The Summer People*—ghost
1948-49—"Haunting"
died, Ogunquit, Maine, February 4, 1989
survived by—

An impatient knock shook the door. Ginnie glanced frantically at her watch. Only five minutes left until five o'clock.

"Hey, you in there," came the girl's voice. "It's time for me to put the files away. Come on. I'm not going to stay late on a Saturday night."

"Miss Congeniality," Ginnie said between her teeth. She scrawled ". . . survived by sister Mary Katherine Cheswick, Ogunquit, and bro. Paul N., rural N.H. . . ."

The door opened and a shaft of light temporarily blinded Ginnie. Narrowing her eyes, she could make out the shape of the girl from the desk. The girl had her coat on again.

"It's five to five," the girl said. "Time to turn in all materials. You can come back Monday." She switched on the room's lights, which made both Wayne and Ginnie blink.

"Okay, okay," Wayne said, holding up a hand to shield his eyes. "Give us a minute to rewind these things."

"Now. You gotta rewind 'em *now*." The voice had a smug whine that Ginnie was learning to hate. The girl flounced into the already crowded room, bent over Wayne's microfilm projector and shut it off. She began to rewind the tape, none too gently.

Wayne gave her a pointed look. He stood and started to draw back Ginnie's chair, but she was staring transfixed at the one image remaining on the wall. Her lips parted slightly in surprise.

"Let's go," Wayne said more gently, putting a hand on her shoulder. He paused, feeling how hard her muscles had bunched up beneath the silky material of her blouse. She kept staring at the words on the wall. He looked, too. *What in God's name does she see that has her clenched up like a fist?*

"This thing should be turned *off*," the girl said irritably. She reached over and switched off Ginnie's machine.

The ghost of the page on the wall died into nothingness. The projected words fled, and once more the wall became only a wall.

Ginnie reached for the switch and turned the projector on again.

"Hey!" said the girl, angered.

But Ginnie held her hand up in warning and something in her taut face kept the girl from trying to touch the machine again. Wayne, his hand still on Ginnie's shoulder, sensed the tension in her body rise another notch. His eyes followed her gaze.

The story that had caught her attention was brief. It was from the January 4, 1947 *Republican-Guardian* and it appeared in the society section. It seemed, on the surface, wholly unremarkable.

Last evening a surprise tenth anniversary party was held at Merrimack School for Girls in honor of Dr. and Mrs. W. E. Pilsner. The couple joined the staff second semester in 1937, when the institution was known as the Hilyard Academy for Young Ladies. Mrs. Loretta Pilsner is the school's music mistress. Her husband, Dr. William Earnest Pilsner, originally joined the faculty as history master and one year later became headmaster.

In attendance were Chief of Police Joseph O'Donohue and Mrs. O'Donohue, Dr. and Mrs. Lawrence Sternberg, Judge and Mrs. Walter Besain, and members of the Merrimack School staff. The Pilsners' daughters and son were also among the honored guests.

"Look, you people," the girl complained, "you may have all night, but *I* don't. And I still have to put all this stuff away."

Ginnie started to write down the date of the article and copy the names it contained. The girl, having rewound Wayne's microfilm now stood sulkily staring at Ginnie's machine. Her displeasure seemed to swell, filling the little room, crowding all the air out. Her lower lip thrust out and she made a show of crossing her arms in impatience. Even the sound of her breathing sounded accusatory.

Ginnie felt Wayne give her shoulder the slightest pressure, a signal that it was, indeed, time to go. She glanced once more at the words on the wall. She had been inordinately excited to find mention of the building, but the story, after all, said little. But the unexpected appearance of the name Sternberg intrigued her.

The girl sighed loudly, staring pointedly at Ginnie's projector.

Ginnie hastily wrote down the date of the article so she could look it up again on Monday. She switched off the projector, stood and let Wayne help her into her coat. The girl pounced on the projector avidly and rapidly wound up the few feet of microfilm Ginnie had managed to peruse.

Wayne ushered Ginnie out of the crowded little room and glanced significantly at the clock over the desk. It said two minutes to five o'clock. "Happy weekend," he called back to the girl sarcastically. "Enjoy every minute."

Ginnie said nothing until they were once more outside the newspaper office. The sky was dark, the sidewalk slippery and white, but the wind had died. There was an eerie peace in the air.

"Why'd you get so excited?" Wayne asked, taking her arm to help guide her over the ice. "Why tense up over a story about some old party? That's all it was about, right? A party?"

Ginnie stopped beside the car and turned to him, her eyes troubled. "Did you have time to read it all?"

He nodded as he reached over and turned up the collar of her coat. "Was it the name Sternberg? Here, get in before you freeze. You always want to stand out in the cold and talk."

He unlocked the door and swung it open, but she didn't get inside yet. A slight breeze, almost warm, came up. It stirred the ends of her muffler, tousled her hair. "Doesn't it strike you as a pretty big coincidence?" she asked.

He shrugged, his eyes narrowed against the wind. "No. There are a thousand Sternbergs in Merrimack County. It's no big deal. Get in. I'll buy you something to eat. It's been a long day. You're pushing yourself too hard."

Ginnie slipped inside the shelter of the Corvette. She waited for Wayne to get in, as well. "There's more, though," she said as soon as he had closed the door. "If I just hadn't felt so rushed. I mean, at first I was excited just to find a story on the building, but there was something about it that gave me a chill. It reminded me of something, but I don't know what. It's like having a dream you know is important, then waking up and not being able to remember it. Do you know the feeling?"

He looked at her. Behind her, through the frosty window, the lights of some business's Christmas display blinked off and on. It gave a fugitive red glow to her hair, intermittently cast a phantom pink aura around her.

He found he hadn't been listening to what she was saying. He had been caught up in watching the way the shadows played around her lips. He'd spent a lot of time around this woman, more than he should have. He was beginning to think he was going to have to do something to get her out of his system. He only knew one way to accomplish that, and it usually worked without fail. "What?" he said.

She paused, wondering uneasily why he examined her with such intensity. Was she being foolish and obsessive? Did he think she was imagining significance where there was none? She tried to pull her thoughts away from how near he suddenly seemed, his arm along the back of her seat. "What did you say?" he asked, his voice low.

She shook her head and looked away. She swallowed, feeling confused and foolish. If the name Sternberg was a common one, then the article had contained nothing of note. There was certainly nothing of such import that it couldn't wait until Monday.

"Nothing." Her voice was little more than a whisper. "For a moment in there, it gave me a strange sensation, that's all. I wondered if you'd ever had such a feeling."

He leaned toward her. "Usually," he said, "I try not to have feelings."

He took her face between his hands and kissed her. He didn't think of it as an act of affection. He thought of it as an act of survival. Maybe after this, he could stop wanting her.

Chapter Eight

Ginnie was not surprised that he kissed her. In some wise, shadowy part of her mind she had known that sooner or later, they would have to kiss.

What stunned her, even shocked her, was the intensity with which he did it. It was almost as if he were punishing himself or her or both of them for an attraction that should not exist. She could taste danger in that kiss. The problem was how sweet danger tasted.

The arms around her were too strong, too sure to resist. He pulled her against him so tightly that she was momentarily breathless. The feeling jolted her that her own body had no choice but to merge and become part of his. It was a frightening sensation, yet alluring.

At first his face was so cold against hers that her skin burned at his touch. Then his lips warmed hers and her flesh burned in a different way, stung by sparks of desire leaping into life. His mouth, which usually said little in the way of words, was now eloquent with a passion neither of them wanted or trusted.

Somehow—she was unsure when or how—he had stripped the glove from his right hand and pulled her hat away from her curls. His fingers were in her hair, gathering it at the base of her neck, drawing her more deeply into his kiss.

The leather of his jacket creaked as he shifted his position to bring her against him more tightly still. Then he drew back slightly, his mouth still hungry against hers. His right hand moved to unbutton her coat.

She realized that she had her arms wrapped tightly around his neck, yet she didn't remember reaching toward him. Then his hands were beneath her coat. His fingertips felt like points of flame against her back. He pulled her against him almost fiercely. Dazed, she clung to him harder.

He let her mouth escape from his for a cooling second. Then he bent and captured her lips again, this time with a hunger and determination that made her heart leap. She was rent by equal parts of yearning and alarm.

She had never wanted to desire a man again. Against her better judgment, and perhaps against his own, he was sweeping her away, taking her away from reason and self-control. Wave after wave of feeling surged through her, each more powerful than the last, each more beguiling, and each more disquieting.

What am I doing? she asked herself in dismay. *I'm in a parked car, necking like a teenager with a tattooed ex-sailor I hardly know. I'm not this kind of woman. I don't want to be.*

Desperately she withdrew her arms from around his neck and tried to thrust her hands against his chest. She tried to pull away from his arms, to get her bearings, physical and emotional. He held her fast.

He kissed her again and she realized that one of the things frightening her most was the frankness of his desire. She was not used to such powerful drives, in herself or in others. He knew exactly what he was doing. She did not.

She tried to push away again. This time he sensed her growing desperation and let her draw back, although he held her so she could not break away from him completely.

He saw the need in her eyes, but he saw the confusion and the newborn fear, as well. *No,* he thought, *this isn't a woman who takes things lightly. I'd be a fool to get involved with her.* Still, he did not let her go, not yet.

"What's the matter?" he asked gruffly. "Nobody ever kiss you before?"

"Not like that," Ginnie answered with honesty. She could hardly remember anyone's kisses except Del's. His were carefully orchestrated: a friendly peck on the cheek, a friendly nibble on the ear, an arm slipped snugly around her, a pair of lips softly waiting for hers. She shook her head, dazed. Eight years of making love to Del hadn't prepared her for so much as a kiss from Wayne Priborski.

Wayne lowered one eyebrow in a frown. He studied her face critically. "What do you mean, 'Not like that'? You know a better way? You want to show me?"

Once more she pushed her hands against his chest to extricate herself from his embrace. This time he let her. Nervously she brushed her hair back from her face. "It's just that you don't have to be a caveman," she said. "I was expecting a nice, friendly little kiss that didn't mean anything."

He gave a short bitter laugh. "That *was* a friendly little kiss that didn't mean anything. Why should it mean anything?"

"It shouldn't," she said coolly, although in truth, his reply hurt. She ducked her head and picked something dark off the floor of the car. "Here's your glove. Look, don't take this little incident wrong. I'm not usually this kind of person."

He pulled his glove on as he shot her a quelling look. "*What* kind of person?"

She straightened her coat and buttoned it back up with as much dignity as possible. "I usually don't sit in parked cars *groping* with strange men. This isn't going to lead to anything. Even if we are alone in that tower together. I'm not *that* kind of person."

"Oh," he said, turning the key in the ignition. "A human-type person. Excuse me. I'm a man, you're a woman. We're both unattached. This may be new to your experience, Miss Priss, but these things are known to happen. Yeah, once you get out of the Midwest, all sorts of things can happen."

Ginnie had been sitting, chin up, staring through her somewhat foggy window. Now her head snapped around and she glared at him. "I'm *not* a priss. Being from the Midwest has nothing to do with it. I'm just not some lusty wench driven only by my sizzling desires. I have—morals."

He put the car into gear and headed toward the street, which glittered icily beneath the street lamps. He shook his head in disgust. "You've got morals the way some people've got measles. Lighten up. I just kissed you to get it out of the way. Now we know what it's like and that it's no big deal. You and your morals are safe from me."

"Morals aren't a joke."

"Hey, look at me. Am I laughing? How'd you ever manage to get married, anyway? What was he? A preacher?"

"A preacher? Why?" Ginnie demanded. "Because I'm so prissy? No. He's a professor. A-an intellectual. Something you wouldn't understand."

"Right," he said, swinging the car onto a nearly deserted sidestreet. "Me Tarzan. Me Conan the Barbarian. Just your friendly neighborhood Neanderthal war monger. Excuse my hormones. Tell me, if this guy was so smart, why'd you leave him?"

Ginnie sat back rigidly against the seat, feeling as if she had been slapped. Her face, which had been flushed, paled. "I told you. I didn't leave him. He left me."

Her honesty, bitter as it was, defused some of his anger. In truth, he was more angry at himself than at her. She was all wrong for him, but he had given into the temptation to see what she was like. He would not do it again. He had no business with such a woman. No business at all.

Now her mouth was naked of lipstick and her lips had a stung, swollen look. He was to blame for that, as well as for the haunted look that had come into her eyes. Wayne, who had sworn never again to be sorry for anything, found that he was sorry for causing that look.

He drove on in silence. He wanted to say, "If he left you, he couldn't have been too smart." Instead he said nothing. It was better that way.

She rubbed a clear spot on her window and stared out, unseeing. She took off her glove and gingerly touched her lips. They still throbbed. Had she been insane to let him kiss her that way? To respond to him as she had?

Had divorce reduced her to this? Was she desperate enough to try to find excitement in the arms of a man who was practically a stranger and with whom she had nothing in common? Or had she simply wanted comfort, then been frightened when Wayne offered something different? Her head ached and she put her fingertips to her forehead.

He gave her a brief sidelong glance. "Hey. Are you all right?"

"I'm tired. That's all."

He looked at her again, this time letting his gaze linger. "You need food. I'll take you to eat."

"I'm not hungry. Let's just go back."

"No. You need to eat. I know a place where we can get you a good, healthy meal."

"No. If you show me a plate of bean sprouts and tofu, I'll die. I've had all the adversity I can take today."

"So I'll take you where you can get something unhealthy. A steak and a martini. Espresso. Pie and ice cream. A whole gravy boat full of cholesterol."

She shook her head stubbornly. "No."

"Yes," he said.

In the end, he won.

GINNIE HAD TWO GLASSES of wine and an after-dinner liqueur that left her feeling warm and mellow. She had eaten prime rib, a baked potato and a wedge of dark-chocolate cake. She sighed with satisfaction.

Wayne sipped his ice water. He studied her over the rim of his glass. "All right. You're refueled. Are you going to be able to relax and get a good night's sleep?"

She shrugged, giving him a tentative smile. "What I want most is to get back in those newspaper files."

"They're closed till Monday."

"I know. What I'd like after that is to get to a library and find Louisa Anne Newsome's book. I want to know more about this 'haunting.' The assaults and thefts."

"The library's not open till Monday, either."

"I'll try the used bookstores. I think some are open."

He set down his water glass. "You won't like this, but maybe you should ask Mrs. Treat. She's the resident expert on haunting. If anybody knows, she should."

Ginnie shuddered slightly. "I hate to get involved with her. But you know..." She paused, wondering if she should tell him the thought she had been toying with.

"But what?" he urged. He signaled the waiter to bring her another glass of liqueur. She was starting to look more relaxed. He wanted to see her finally get some rest.

Her mouth took on a speculative slant. "That story I found? About the party at Hawthorne Towers when it was a school?"

He sat with his arms crossed. He nodded.

"The names," she said thoughtfully. "The names and the—well, the situation."

"What about them?"

"Remember what Mrs. Treat said about her ghost? That he had something to do with the words *Hilson* or *Hilton* and *Loraine*? That he loved music and that he'd lived there during the depression."

Wayne nodded again, watching the way the candlelight played on her face.

Ginnie squared her shoulders. What she was about to say might not make sense to him. "Well, when Pilsner originally went to the school, it was named Hilyard. His wife's name was Loretta. She was a music teacher and they went there in 1937—during the height of the depression."

He raised one eyebrow dubiously. "Sorry. Sounds flimsy to me."

"But she was so *close*," Ginnie said. "Isn't that how psychics work? They get an impression, not precise information. It can't be a coincidence, can it, her being that close on all four points?"

His mouth quirked, as if he were trying not to smile at her foolishness. "You're asking me to believe that the ghost of this guy—"

"The headmaster. William Pilsner."

"That Pilsner's ghost still hangs around the building and has conversations with Mrs. Treat? Sorry. If she takes enough guesses, she's bound to get a few things almost right. Coincidence. I don't believe in psychics."

"I don't know if I do or not," Ginnie said. "But coincidence can't explain everything. I'm still bothered that there were people named Sternberg at that party. A Sternberg involved with the Towers—all those years ago."

"Ginnie," he said as patiently as possible, "I told you, the Sternbergs are a big family. They've been in this county a long time. There's even a street named Sternberg. The town used to have an assistant mayor named Sternberg. If you looked in the phone book, you'd find fifteen or twenty Sternbergs. It means nothing. Trust me."

The waiter set another glass of Tia Maria before Ginnie, removed the empty one, then sped off so swiftly, he seemed to dematerialize. She looked ruefully at the new glass.

"I don't need this. I'm already talking nonsense."

"Drink it. You can use it. It'll help you sleep."

"Another thing," she said, frowning slightly. "There are a lot of police involved in this. Or not involved, however you want to look at it."

This time his interest was piqued. He gave her a penetrating look, but it was questioning, as well. "What do you mean?"

"The police haven't done anything about Mr. Burbage being hit or the keys being stolen. That seems odd. A policeman came when I saw the body in the tub. He denied seeing anything at all. But what if he did? What if he's the one who cleaned things up?"

Wayne shook his head, playing devil's advocate. "Makes no sense. Besides, you said you were sure he hadn't."

"Maybe he helped somebody else. And you said Fairfax just walked away when I fainted, and later he disappeared. *He* used to be a policeman," Ginnie said.

Wayne's eyebrow arched even more sardonically. "Right now, a lot of guys in this town used to be policemen. How many got suspended? Ten? A dozen?"

Ginnie sipped her liqueur and sighed again. Its warmth spread through her, making her feel vague and dreamy. "And then these policemen from long ago get all caught up in it."

"What policemen from long ago?"

"That article about the party," she said. "It said one of the guests was the chief of police. And that other Sternberg person—"

"You're getting tangled up. The other Sternberg wasn't a policeman. He was a judge or something. None of them were 'caught up' in anything. They went to a party, that's all."

"But," Ginnie insisted, "there were crimes then, too, at Hawthorne Towers. And those crimes never got solved, either. Maybe it's all connected somehow."

He gave her the ghost of a smile. She was a smart woman, but her imagination ran wild. "How?"

Her feeble confidence in the theory faltered. "I don't know." She shook her head again, trying to clear it. "I shouldn't have had the liqueur. I can't think straight."

"You're tired. You need to go to bed."

The sensation of warmth vanished. Her body went tense and still, as if she were being stalked. The thought of being alone in a strange apartment, a dead man's apartment at that, suddenly filled her with apprehension.

He saw her wariness and misunderstood. The twist of his mouth became sarcastic. "I'm not plying you with liquor to get around your famous morals. I don't want to take you to bed. You're obviously the kind of woman who's only interested in sex if it involves a relationship. I don't have the patience for involvement. Life's too short."

Ginnie lifted her chin at a defiant angle. "I didn't accuse you of plying me with liquor. And I didn't bring up sex. You did."

He gritted his teeth. "Excuse me. We cavemen are like that."

She crumpled up her napkin in frustration and set it beside her dessert plate. "And I'm sorry I called you a caveman. You've actually been very kind—in your way. And in my way, I deeply appreciate it. I just don't appreciate it enough to go to bed with you. I'm sorry."

He frowned in disbelief. "I didn't *ask* you to go to bed with me. I just *told* you I don't want to take you to bed."

"That's good," Ginnie said. "Because you're right. I don't believe in sex without a meaningful relationship. You and I are too different. Good grief, if this were twenty years ago, you'd be rushing off to Vietnam to get yourself shot. And somehow, you'd manage to be proud of it."

"Damned straight." His mouth quirked humorlessly. "And if this were twenty years ago, you'd be running around in love beads, putting daisies in gun barrels and babbling about flower power. If you were a guy, you'd be burning your draft card. And you'd manage to feel proud about *that*."

Ginnie raised her chin a fraction of an inch higher. "For your information, my father *did* burn his draft card. As a symbol that he believed in peace. He went to jail for that belief. And for refusing to go to Vietnam. And you know what? I *am* proud of him."

Wayne stared at her for a long moment. "Well. We seem to have a problem."

Ginnie looked at him uneasily. There was more emotion in his voice than she had heard before, but it was harsh and tightly reined in. The candlelight seemed to flash in the dark depths of his eyes.

"My father went to Vietnam," he said. "He had beliefs, too, and he died for them. And you know what? I'm proud of him. And nobody's going to talk me out of it, no matter how high their damned ideals are."

Ginnie drew in her breath so sharply it hurt. Her sympathies, always quickly touched, rose swiftly, crowding out all thoughts of ideology. "I'm sorry," she said, her throat tight. "I really am."

He dropped his napkin on the tablecloth. There was infinite bitterness in the action. "Sorry? Then you're one of the few. It's the war everybody wants to forget. Nobody called him a hero. Nobody wanted to believe he could be one. Well, here's a news flash for you, Flower Power—it may have been a bad war, but some damned good men died in it."

"I said I was sorry. I meant it."

He eyed her with scientific assessment. He nodded. "That's the hell of it. You probably do mean it. And at the same time, you still think he was a war monger. And me, too. Well, kid, somebody has to mind the store. It was the job we chose. I'm sorry you don't like it."

Ginnie stared at him in dismay. So that's why he'd gone into the military, she told herself. He'd followed in his father's footsteps. He believed his father was a hero and he'd emulated him. But the accident ended that dream. And she was just starting to realize how much that dream's death had cost him.

She took another deep breath. "I was just brought up differently, that's all. To believe in resolving things without force. To defend things by reason and by law—whenever possible."

He sighed in disgust. "Fine. Whenever possible. But reality isn't that tidy. Reason doesn't work with unreasonable people. Law can't stop the unlawful ones. Sometimes the only answer is force. You know it as well as I do. When somebody's shooting at you, you don't reason with him. You get a gun yourself—and you use it."

Ginnie shrugged with hopelessness. She could never make him understand the depth of her feelings. "Force. War. Guns." She shook her head.

"Ginnie, these things are not my *fault*. They're just part of the way the world works."

"I grew up being taught that the way the world works can be changed."

"Well, kid," he said cynically, "believe whatever you want. But it doesn't make much difference. Things haven't changed yet."

She had been staring at the way her silver knife shone in the candlelight. Now she raised her eyes and looked at him again. "What did force and violence and guns ever do for you? Except kill your father and almost kill you? I'd think you'd hate them."

He started to answer, but instead said nothing. His lips thinned and it was his turn to shake his head. When he finally spoke, his voice was edged with resignation. "Come on. I'll take you home. It's late."

She knew the conversation was over. His expression had gone completely emotionless. It was as if he had closed a door in her face, shutting her out. She remembered what he had said in the car, right before he kissed her. *I try not to have feelings.*

What was it? she thought. What made him so inward and solitary?

She sensed far more had happened to him than just the accident, terrible as it was. But what had it been?

As they walked back out into the chilling night, she cast him a questioning glance. His profile was as unpliant as that of a statue. He stared straight out at the darkness, a man complete in himself, who didn't need anything or anybody.

"Wayne?" she said softly, wondering if she should apologize to him yet again. It had been a long twenty-four hours, terrifying, exhausting and frustrating. She was so tired and confused, it was as if her mind had been ravaged by fire. She had said many things in the course of the day that she should not have. "Wayne?" she repeated.

Perhaps the wind carried her voice away and he did not hear her. Perhaps he heard her and simply chose not to answer. He said nothing. He did not even look at her.

But as they started across the icy parking lot, he put his arm around her to keep her from slipping. The arm was strong and solid, and felt absolutely dependable.

She stole another glimpse at him. He seemed lost in his own thoughts. Although his arm wrapped securely around her, it was as if he had forgotten she was there. He protected her completely and automatically because that's the kind of thing he did. It was the kind of man he was.

And that was the moment, as foolish as it was, she fell a little bit in love with him.

"WILL YOU BE ALL RIGHT?" he asked her at her door. "You want me to come in and check your place?"

She shook her head. The new locks were strong, sophisticated, and they showed no sign of having been disturbed. She knew if he came in, she wouldn't want him to leave. She didn't even trust herself to shake his hand good-night. "Thanks for everything. I mean it."

"Get some sleep. You're dead on your feet." He gave her his grave half smile.

Don't smile like that, Ginnie thought wearily. *It'll kill me. I don't have that much strength left.* She tried to divert herself from her knotted emotions by the complex action of undoing all her new locks.

His smile faded as he watched her. "If you need me, I'm right here. You can count on it."

Ginnie nodded. She knew she could.

"And lock all those back up once you get inside. Don't take any chances."

"I won't." She managed a weak smile. She hoped he would say something about seeing her again, but he did not. *Oh, God,* Ginnie thought, her head hurting again, *he's like the Lone Ranger. He'll only be here if there's trouble. Otherwise he'll just be on his way, riding into the sunset.* If she were going to be attracted to somebody after Del, why couldn't it be a nice gregarious accountant with an urge to settle down?

She slipped inside the apartment, turning on the light. She closed the door and carefully relocked all the locks. She turned and looked around, examining the room.

The bathroom door was open. If she tilted her head, she could see inside. She peeked at the bathtub. It was empty.

She exhaled in relief. Until that moment, she hadn't even realized she was holding her breath.

The apartment was slightly larger than her own, its layout a bit more eccentric. But what was most different was how crowded it was. Everything was overstuffed and over-decorated. There were too many books spilling out of the bookshelves, too many knickknacks and souvenirs crowding the other shelves, too many letters and notes and clippings spilling across the dining room table.

The table had evidently served as a desktop, for it held stacks of mail, bundles of cancelled checks, untidy piles of receipts. Earlier in the day, when Ginnie had first seen the place, she had been taken aback by the clutter. It spoke to her all too clearly of life suddenly interrupted, of the unexpectedness of death.

She took off her coat, shivering slightly at the chill in the apartment. This morning, as she had moved her things in, she had paused to look at the papers arrayed on the table.

The man who had lived there until such a short time ago had been named Francis Parker "Pat" Sutherland. She remembered seeing him once or twice, a big, bluff man between forty and fifty. He'd had a ruddy face and a full head of curly gray hair.

Wayne had said Sutherland had been a social worker working on some special project that involved the homeless, and that he had lived in the apartment for perhaps six months. That was all Ginnie knew of him, except that no heirs had come forward to claim his possessions.

Sutherland's furniture was costly, the prints that jammed his walls expensively framed. His closet was crowded with good clothes. If he did not have a great many people in his life, he had filled it with a great many things.

Ginnie kicked off her boots and turned up the thermostat. She walked through the apartment, hugging herself for warmth.

She moved through the crowded little kitchen, glad that she was so tired. Fatigue numbed her against the too many reminders of Sutherland's sudden departure from life.

In the sink sat a cereal bowl with the encrusted remains of Sutherland's last breakfast. His coffee cup sat beside it, green spots of mold growing in its bottom. The morning newspaper from two weeks ago was flung carelessly on the kitchen table. A story had been clipped from its front page.

She forced herself to go into the bathroom. She glanced nervously at the tub again. It was still empty. She swallowed hard.

On the edge of the sink sat a shaving mug and a crumpled tube of toothpaste. On a shelf next to the medicine cabinet lay a set of black hair brushes that needed cleaning. They were full of Sutherland's gray hairs.

Ginnie swallowed hard again and went back into the living room. The bathroom made her feel like an invader of Sutherland's privacy, a voyeur.

She glanced at his bills and receipts lying on the table. They seemed as boring as anyone's, but they also struck her as private, something she had no right to disturb.

She walked into the bedroom and flinched slightly at the sight of the bed. The spread was rumpled, the pillows slightly askew, and the edge of the sheet hung out crookedly, barely touching the floor.

She had not thought to bring fresh bedding with her, but knew she could not sleep on the sheets where Sutherland had spent his last night. Opening the bedroom's big linen closet, she took out fresh sheets and pillowcases. Sutherland's heirs—or his spirit—would just have to forgive her for taking the liberty.

She yawned and pulled off the spread, then the sheets. One pillow fell to the floor with an odd *thunk*. Ginnie bent to pick it up, then froze as if hypnotized.

A book lay under the pillow, tucked into the pillowcase. It was a well-worn book with a dull green cover. In dim letters the cover announced the title and author, *Passing Through* by Louisa Anne Newsome.

How strange, she thought, a tingle running through her. She picked the book up. Sutherland must have been reading in bed, grown tired and shoved it under the spare pillow.

She straightened, then sat on the bed, the fresh sheets forgotten. Several pieces of paper, folded over, had been thrust between the pages. She opened the book and uncreased them, smoothing them out.

One was a story of Junior Hopkins that had been clipped from the front page of the paper. It showed the familiar black-and-white photograph of a young man with long pale hair and stupefied eyes. It told the equally familiar story of a boy, troubled by drugs and personal demons, who had drifted to New Hampshire, then vanished into thin air. Now his family had mounted an ambitious search for him.

Why? Ginnie thought. *Why did he have this in the book?* Did he know Junior Hopkins? His work, after all, had been with the homeless. The second sheet of paper was even more puzzling. It was a list of the tenants of Hawthorne Towers. It looked as if Sutherland had copied it from the mailboxes in the lobby. Most of the names were crossed off. Nine were not.

Carl and Nancy Burbage
Emile Swengler
Paul N. Donner
George Fairfax
Mary K. Treat
E. L. Prouty
Virginia Prince
Wayne Priborski

Ginnie studied the list with rising consternation. What had made Sutherland cross the other names off the list? What had made him keep these, including her own and Wayne's, on it?

She looked at the third and last piece of paper. It was a sort of crude map of the building, floor by floor, showing the placement of each apartment. Nine were marked in red and labeled.

Burbages?? (don't fit pattern—But.)
Swengler!

Donner...
Fairfax...
Treat?!
Prouty...
Prince X
Priborski? (Students gone too much.)
Sutherland?

In addition, three areas in the basement were outlined in red and marked. All three were marked, simply, LOCKED.

What is this? Ginnie asked herself, frowning. Why were these apartments singled out, and what were the strange notations beside each name? Why was her name the only one marked with an *X* and what did the mark mean?

She was suddenly frightened again.

She lifted the papers and looked down at the open book, at the pages they had marked. The left-hand page was blank. On the right a new chapter began. Its title stood forth in bold-face type. "To the Dark Tower."

Ginnie read the opening paragraphs.

Nowadays the building is called Hawthorne Towers. In my day it was called the Merrimack Academy. When it was first built, it was called either "The Noble Experiment" or "Hawthorne's Folly," depending upon one's view.

But it has always, from the beginning, been called "haunted."

Chapter Nine

Ginnie forgot how late it was, how exhausted she was. She still read on.

The story that Louisa Anne Newsome recounted of Hawthorne Towers was disturbing. Some of the girls of Merrimack Academy reported that their rooms had been disturbed, small items taken. A few insisted they could not shake the unpleasant feeling that they were "being watched," or that they had sensed "a presence" in their rooms.

Louisa Anne Newsome herself experienced the ghostly sense of being spied on, especially at night. She awoke more than once with the certainty someone had been standing in her room, watching her sleep. Both the headmaster, William Pilsner, and his wife insisted such a thing was impossible: the blinds and curtains of Louisa's room had been shut tight, the door securely bolted.

Louisa's sister, Mary, two years older, also attended the academy. After Mary was attacked in her sleep, both she and Louisa begged their parents to withdraw them from the school. They did so, but both girls were affected by the experience and became, in Louisa's words, "obsessed" with the occult.

As for what happened at the Towers, the nighttime attack on Mary was the second such at the academy. No more occurred after Mary and Louisa left. William Pilsner, the headmaster, was suspected by some. Others suspected his stepson, although the boy was small for his age and did not seem outwardly interested in girls. Still others believed it was a woman, one of the students, or possibly Pilsner's wife or one of his daughters. Pilsner died six months after Louisa Anne and Mary Newsome left. None of the incidents was ever solved, but no more occurred.

Ginnie frowned over the story and read it a second time. Although it was dramatically told in parts, the verifiable facts were few. A cynic might have called the whole tale the concoction of overimaginative schoolgirls so ripe for excitement they were willing to scare themselves.

Louisa Newsome truly believed the building had been haunted. But while she was skilled at recreating the atmosphere of events, she marshalled woefully few hard facts.

Those who lived on neighboring farms told us that the building had a reputation for evil ever since it was erected in 1867. The wife of the farmer who brought the school its milk, a French Canadian woman, would not come near the Towers, even by the light of day. *"C'est une demeure diabolique,"* she would say. It is the devil's dwelling.

From its first days, she said, the young women who worked in the mills and lived in the Towers told tales of "eerie sounds echoing through the night, of rustlings and incoherent whisperings and the tortured noise of gasping breaths. More than one morning, a troubled girl would recount being awakened by the ghostly touch of a cold hand upon her sleep-warmed cheek, a chill kiss pressed against her throat.

Then, maddeningly, Louisa Newsome veered away from the ghost tales themselves and into her own theories of ghosts. "For this, after all," she wrote, "is to be primarily an account of my own thoughts about the supernatural."

She gave long, intricate reports of experiments she and her sister made with a Ouija board, of seances and automatic writing. She wrote of mediums and card readers, crystal gazers and clairvoyants.

Although Ginnie found it interesting, it also struck her as unfocused and rambling, wandering randomly from one subject to another.

She rubbed her eyes. She realized she was so tired that she had just read almost two whole pages without having any idea of what she had read.

She yawned and turned back the pages to reread them. Pat Sutherland's bedside light was on, throwing a muted circle of light around her on the unmade bed. His alarm clock said the time was five minutes after one o'clock.

She was so weary, she forgot she was lying on a bare mattress with an untidy welter of blankets at her feet. She even forgot that this bed was where the unfortunate Pat Sutherland had spent his last night alive.

She narrowed her eyes and tried to concentrate on Louisa Anne Newsome's theory of mediumship and ectoplasm. Her eyelids grew heavier and heavier. The book slipped from her hands and fell softly on the striped mattress ticking.

Ginnie dreamed of Del. It was a long, involved dream that took place on a dark and misty plain in Indiana. Del was with her, then he disappeared, leaving her alone. On the horizon, a tornado cloud appeared, black and churning toward her. It seemed as high as the sky itself, it was coming straight toward her and there was no shelter.

Then, through the twilight darkness, she saw a little house, a cozy little house with curtains at the window. Somehow she knew Del was inside, but when she beat on the door, he wouldn't open it, even though the cloud roared nearer.

"You'll have to find your own way," Del taunted.

"You'll have to find your own way," A woman's voice echoed. It was the woman he had left Ginnie for.

As the wind rose and the sky grew darker, she heard them laughing in the safety of their house. She turned, but there was nowhere to run except into the dark and lashing storm.

"Go away," a voice said. It wasn't Del's voice and she couldn't tell where it came from. The roar of the wind was so loud she wasn't sure she had heard it at all.

"You have to go away," the voice repeated as she fought against the gale. Dust was blinding her and she heard things breaking, limbs and tree trunks. She still couldn't recognize the voice. She realized she wanted Wayne but didn't know how to find him.

She reached out her hand for him but found nothing but the empty cold of the wind. "Wayne! Where are you?" she cried in the soundless voice of dreams.

"You have to leave this place," the voice said. "It's very dangerous for you."

Someone kissed her cheek, extremely softly.

Ginnie stirred, troubled, because she knew she hadn't dreamed the kiss. Something dangerous was happening to her, something real, and she had to fight it, if she could only struggle up through the depths of sleep.

A hand, she sensed, was touching her neck. Was it a real hand or a dream hand? It seemed preternaturally strong, and it gripped her throat.

Wake up, some deep part of her mind screamed in alarm, and Ginnie fought to obey.

With great effort, she opened her eyes, but the hand on her throat tightened. Her lids fluttered, she gasped and caught the briefest glimmer of light. Then the light swam away and all she saw was darkness.

The remaining wisps of dream vanished. The real world vanished, as well. She sank into the blackness of unconsciousness as if she would drown in it.

SHE DIDN'T KNOW where she was.

Her eyes were closed and she was plunged in blackness. The blackness throbbed, a dull, menacing ache.

Painfully she opened her eyes. All she saw was blackness. Her heart pounded as if it were a drum played by an insane musician.

She put a hand to her throat because it hurt. Above the sound of her own driving blood, she heard another sound rushing softly across the darkness.

Water, she thought, muddled by the darkness. *I hear water.*

Then she went rigid against the mattress, her hand still at her throat. She knew what the noise was.

Water was running in the bathtub. *She was in the darkness and the corpse had come back.*

She lay listening to the ripple and gurgle from the bathroom. In a cold torrent, memories poured back, murky and confused.

She had been reading. She was in Sutherland's apartment. She had been reading a book about ghosts in Hawthorne Towers.

But she had fallen asleep with the light on. Now the room was black and someone or something was in the bathroom.

The corpse is back, she thought again in panic. She felt a surge of terror so sharp it was like a physical blow.

No, she told herself, her heart beating harder still. *No, it was no ghost.*

Someone had been in the room with her. Someone had turned off the light and put a hand to her neck as she struggled to wake. That hand had pushed her into unconsciousness. She could still feel its warm print on her throat.

The sound of water splashed and gurgled through the darkness. *He's going to drown me,* Ginnie thought in panic, *just like the man in the bathtub.*

Carefully, barely breathing, she raised up on an elbow. The motion made her dizzy, and for a moment the blackness was shot through with tiny, dancing sparks.

She narrowed her eyes, trying to focus on the luminous face of the clock. She could barely make it out: 2:38.

In the bathroom, the water ran and quietly splashed. On and on it surged. There was no other noise except the beating of her heart.

She wanted to scream, but her throat hurt and she was too breathless. She wanted to run, but knew she couldn't find her way through the unfamiliar darkness.

She reached for the lamp switch. A fresh throb of pain shot through her head. Her hand trembling, she turned the lamp on. Its friendly circle of light glowed familiarly on the mattress and fell into shadows at the edge of the room.

Everything was undisturbed, she thought, the blood banging in her temples. Then she looked down at the mattress and at the floor beside the bed. No, everything was not the same. Her scalp prickled as if a jolt of electricity had been pumped through her body.

The book was gone. Louisa Anne Newsome's worn green book was nowhere to be seen. Nor were the sheets of paper that had been thrust between its pages. They had been taken.

And now, beside her bed was a round fluffy pink rug. Once more she felt a wave of sickness. She recognized the rug. It was the one that had been stolen from her bathroom.

Two nights, ago, it had been spotted with something like blood. Now it was stainless, so clean and soft it had obviously been freshly laundered.

From the darkened bathroom came the steady sound of running water.

I dreamed it all, Ginnie thought drunkenly. *I'm dreaming this now. It isn't really happening.*

Carefully, experimentally, she put her stocking feet on the floor. The pink rug felt soft and yielding beneath them.

She tried to stand, and the ache in her head hammered away, all too real. Breathing shallowly, she looked around the room. In a corner leaned a golf bag, full of clubs.

She took three unsteady steps toward the bag, then stopped, listening. Only the gurgle of the water echoed through the apartment.

She drew out a golf club, not knowing what sort it was, only that it had a heavy metal head. She tried to make herself breathe deeply, for she still felt dizzy and her head throbbed worse than before.

It's a nightmare, she told herself again. *I'm in a nightmare and I'll wake up soon.*

But nothing changed. The bathroom door still stood half-open, darkness within. She crept toward it, holding the golf club. Her knees were unsteady, but she made herself go.

She flicked on the hall light. Shadows fled away or changed places, but nothing else happened. Ginnie took another deep breath, then kicked the bathroom door farther open. "I've got a club," she cried.

She had meant her voice to sound threatening. It sounded only desperate and the crash of the door overwhelmed it. There was silence again, except for the sound of water.

She stepped to the doorway. She reached inside and switched on the light with a motion so swift she could not believe she made it.

As the light blazed on, she took an automatic step backward, but she could not keep her eyes from traveling to the tub. She grimaced and her knees threatened to give way.

But the tub was white and completely empty.

The water sparkled as it coursed from the faucet and swirled down the drain in clear, innocent ripples.

Ginnie stared at the stream of water. For a moment she almost thought she could see the dead man sitting there again, his bloodshot eyes staring from under his hat, dirty water dripping from his mouth.

She gritted her teeth and forced the image back. She stumbled to the tub and turned off the water, her motion almost savage. The drain burbled, then was silent.

She turned, then, and ran toward the front door. The light from the hall illuminated it only partly and she had trouble unlocking the new locks. They rattled and her fingers shook as she tried to subdue them. She dropped the golf club as she jerked the last chain free.

She swung the door open and suddenly Wayne was there.

He was shirtless, barefoot, and his dark hair hung in his eyes. "Ginnie?" he said. "What's wrong? I heard a crash—"

She threw herself into his arms. Only half-coherent, she tried to choke out the story. But she still couldn't get her breath. For a long moment, she could only lean her forehead against his warm, bare shoulder, panting like a runner who had gone past her limit. She closed her eyes, as if to shut out the memories.

He held her tightly, he ran comforting fingers over her hair to smooth it, he pressed his mouth against her ear to speak softly. "It's all right. You're all right. Talk to me. Get your breath. Shh. Now—slowly."

Raggedly, in bits and snatches, she recounted the story, not in the right order and not clearly, but she got it out.

Wayne brushed her hair back from her fevered face. "Let me get it straight. You found a book."

She nodded, biting her lip. "Yes. Newsome's book."

"And papers."

She nodded again. "With our names on them. And Mrs. Treat's. And the Burbages'. And Paul Donner's. And Mr. Prouty's. I forget them all."

"Shh. Take it easy." He brushed a tear away, and it was the first time Ginnie realized there were tears. She was ashamed to have shown weakness and looked away from him, staring down at the worn carpeting of the hall.

Wayne lifted her chin so that she had to look into his eyes again. She was surprised by the intensity of the concern on his face. "Tell me again," he said. "You fell asleep. But you heard somebody."

She bit her lip again. "A hand was on my throat."

He touched her throat. There were no bruises, only faint pink marks. He frowned. "Somebody choked you?"

"Not exactly choked," Ginnie said. "It was like my mind went dark. Like a candle blown out."

"You're sure it wasn't a dream?"

"I'm sure. Wayne, the rug's back. The one from my bathroom. Only it's clean. Somebody was *there*."

Gently, he disengaged her arms from around his neck. He draped one arm around her shoulders and drew her toward his place. "Come on," he said. "You'd better stay with me."

He led her, unprotesting, inside his apartment and then into his bedroom. He turned on the bedside lamp. The upper sheet and blankets were flung back from the bed.

"Take the bed," he said, making her sit on its edge. She nodded, too numb to argue. She looked up at him, glad that he was such a powerful man.

"Look," he said, his hands on his hips. "I'm going to check out your place."

She paled. She didn't want to go back there. She'd felt too vulnerable there, too threatened.

He gave a curt shake of his dark head. "No. You don't have to go back. Just me. Are you afraid to stay here alone?"

"No," she answered. *Liar,* she told herself.

"Okay," he said patiently. "I'll be right back."

He left. Ginnie collapsed against his pillow, hugging it to her. The bed was still warm from his body, still comforting with the clean, tangy scent of him. She inhaled that scent, felt that warmth gratefully, almost greedily.

She lay there, in the tumble of his bedclothes for a long moment, her heartbeat finally slowing to an almost normal pace.

A profound uneasiness still surged through her. She tried to remember what the voice had said. *You have to go away. This place is dangerous. Was that it?* Suddenly that was all she wanted to do—go away, leave this place. She hugged Wayne's pillow to her more tightly and buried her face against its clean crispness.

She heard Wayne come back in, heard him lock the door. Soundlessly, he moved into the bedroom, but she sensed his presence there. "Are you all right?"

She nodded, her face still against the pillow.

He sat on the bed beside her. He put one hand on her shoulder. "It's all right, Ginnie. There's nobody there."

She said nothing, only hugged the pillow tighter.

He was silent. He rubbed her shoulder, massaging the taut muscles. "I don't see how anybody could have got in," he said at last. "Gin, I think you had a bad dream."

She turned over onto her back, staring up at him. His face was serious, almost solemn. "I didn't dream it," she said. "That rug—it wasn't there. And the book's gone."

He shook his head. His hand moved to her cheek and rested against it. "Ginnie, the place was locked tight as a drum. From the inside. Nobody could have gotten in. Nobody."

Hurt and resentment shone in her eyes. "What about the book, the rug?"

He brushed the hair back from her forehead. "Maybe you dreamed the book. Maybe the rug was there the whole time. Sutherland's place is full of stuff. One rug is like another. How can you tell it's yours?"

She pushed his hand away and turned her face from him. She stared off into the shadows at the edge of the room. "And the water? And the hand on my throat?"

"Ginnie—I'm sorry. Nobody could have gotten in."

She put her hand to her throat. He drew it away and stared down at her. "You've hardly got a mark on you. Nothing you couldn't have done in your sleep."

This time she flung his hand away. She glared at him. "So I strangled myself, got up and turned on the water—"

"You *said* nobody choked you—"

"Well, he knocked me out. I should know. I was there. But you think I'm hysterical. I suppose you think I imagined the dead man in the bathtub, too."

She sat up and started to rise, but he grabbed her by the wrist and pulled her back to the bed. "Where do you think you're going?"

"I don't know. Anywhere. I can't stay here any longer. I won't. It doesn't matter if you believe me or not, because I know what happened."

She started to rise again, but he gripped her by both shoulders and held her in place. "Settle down. You don't have any place to go. At least you know you're safe here."

In frustration, Ginnie tried to shake his hands off, then stopped struggling. She was suddenly weary to the bone. She realized she didn't have shoes or a coat or even her car keys. Everything was back in Sutherland's apartment, and she didn't want to go back there alone, not tonight.

She sighed in exasperation. Wayne's hands seemed to burn into her and she wished he would release her. "If you don't believe me, the police certainly won't," she said bitterly.

"I'd like to believe you. But the door to the fire escape is locked from the inside. So was the front door—you know, you had to unlock it. Nobody could get in those windows. There's no way a human being could have gotten in that apartment."

His words shook her. She blinked hard. She remembered Mrs. Treat's pronouncement that a ghost had appeared to her once and would again.

"Then maybe whatever it was wasn't human," she said.

Chapter Ten

"No. You can't think that way. Ghosts don't exist. There's no such thing," Wayne said.

Ginnie shook her head. The lamplight made red fires glint in her hair, and Wayne resisted the impulse to brush it back from her forehead again. He touched this woman too much. He always found himself touching her, as if it were beyond his power not to. Even now, he couldn't quite force himself to take his hands away. They felt as if they belonged there.

"Mrs. Treat said somebody was trying to get to me. That he wouldn't stop until I helped him—"

"Mrs. Treat's crazy."

Ginnie shook her head again. "But he didn't ask for help. He told me to leave. He—he's trying to scare me."

She looked so worn that Wayne squeezed her shoulders harder, trying to infuse his own energy into her.

She smiled and straightened her back. "Well—" she shrugged "—he scared me. Which is what he wanted to do. I guess I shouldn't give him any more satisfaction."

Damn, Wayne thought. He wanted to believe nothing worse had happened to her than a bad dream. Reason demanded that he believe it. "Don't do this to yourself," he said.

"He *likes* to scare, apparently," Ginnie said, determined to marshal her courage. "That's what Newsome's book said. He likes scaring women. I'm not the first. He attacked Louisa Newsome's sister. He got into locked rooms in her day, too.''

Wayne studied her, frowning with perplexity. He didn't like her talking like this. It wasn't rational. He told himself again that she was overtired, caught up in nightmares.

''Ginnie.'' The set of his mouth was grim.

He didn't understand and he didn't believe her. She wished he would grip her arms with less ferocity, that his expression would not, for once, be so stony. She wished that he would simply take her in his arms and hold her. He was solid and real and dependable and she longed to lay her head against his shoulder, not to quarrel with him. He was, she knew, trying to be kind. Perhaps she could not expect him to believe her; perhaps it was asking too much.

She shrugged again. ''I know. I shouldn't talk about such things.'' Her voice was quiet. ''I'm sorry. I didn't mean to panic. I'll be fine.''

The smile she gave him was without cheer. He didn't smile himself. He looked into her eyes, but she looked away.

Ginnie, he thought, *look at me. Turn to me.*

She kept her gaze on the shadows. It was as if she were mentally building a wall against him, brick by brick.

It was just as well, he thought. Let her build it and put broken glass on the top. It was safer, saner for them both.

He knew that if she would lean against him now the way she had done in the hall, he would not leave this bed.

He wanted to feel her hair tickling his shoulder again, feel her breath warm against his bare chest. If she needed to come into his arms, he would hold her all night long. He would make love to her until she had no room in her mind for fear or cold or death.

No, he thought. She wasn't the kind to lean. And he wasn't the kind to give. He didn't want to care. He didn't intend to care about another woman as long as he lived.

Still, he thought, her lips were beautiful, her hair was like silk to the touch and dark fire to the eye, and her skin was as white as porcelain. Her body pleased him infinitely, and when he touched her, as he did now, it filled him with hunger to touch her more.

No, he thought again. He let his hands drop from her shoulders. He stood. "Get some sleep," he said gruffly. "I'll be in the next room if you need me." He turned his back on her and walked out.

Ginnie wanted to say, Stay with me, but she did not. She watched him go. His bare brown back formed a triangle, broad at the shoulders, narrow at the waist. But it was marred.

With a shock, she saw his scars for the first time. Both from the gunshot and operations, they covered the area across both shoulder blades, a welter of ragged edges and the mark of two long incisions, edged by stitches.

My God, Ginnie thought, *it looks as if he had wings removed.*

And she realized, with a sense of dismay, that was, in a way, exactly what had happened to him. The accident had ripped his wings away. He could no longer fly.

GINNIE SLEPT UNEASILY and could not have slept at all if Wayne had not been near. But that he was near was disturbing in its own right and in a different way. She awoke too early in the morning and knew she would not sleep again. Restless thoughts played in her brain like a gathering of unruly imps.

She had slept in only her bra and panties. Now she arose and, to ward off the chill, put on Wayne's robe, which had been hanging on the back of the bedroom door. It was too broad in the shoulders, but the length was nearly right. She belted it tightly and padded barefoot toward the kitchen.

The apartment was colder than usual. She wondered if the heat had gone off during the night.

First, she told herself, she would make a cup of tea. Then she would gather up her courage and go back to Sutherland's apartment to look for the book. Then, whether she found it or not, she would decide what to do next. Last night her ghostly visitor had told her to leave. She had to decide whether it would be wisdom or cowardice to do so.

She entered the living room and paused. Wayne lay on the couch, his back to her. The blue blanket with which he had covered himself had slipped to the floor.

She hesitated a moment, then went to the couch and picked up the blanket. She held it a moment, wondering if she would awaken him if she covered him again.

It was odd to see him so still when she was used to him being full of intensity and coiled energy. His arms and shoulders were so bunched with muscles that, even in sleep, his body did not seem truly in repose.

Once more she stared at the scars on his back. She winced thinking of the wound; that damned fool Clooney must have blasted half of Wayne's back away. White scar tissue marked the ragged areas where the bullet had ripped the flesh apart.

Like they tore away your wings. Before she realized what she was doing, she reached out and touched his left shoulder blade where it was ridged with a scar.

Swiftly he turned, one brown hand whipping out to seize her wrist. She found herself imprisoned and staring down into his black eyes.

"What are you doing?"

"The blanket. It fell. I was putting it back."

He had rolled to his back and was now in a sitting position, his legs still stretched out on the couch. "Oh, God," he groaned. "Sit." He edged over slightly to make room and pulled her down next to him. He released her wrist, then raked his hand through his hair.

"I didn't mean to startle you," she said.

He stretched, which made his muscles do any number of interesting things. "I thought your ghost had me." He regarded her with bemusement. "So how do things look by light of day? Still think Sutherland's place has phantoms?"

So, Ginnie thought, he believed her no more than he had last night. She looked away from him. "Somebody was there." She kept her voice even but she couldn't keep the resentment out of it.

He sighed. He reached over and adjusted the collar of the robe. "I didn't mean to make fun of you."

She still didn't look at him, although the warmth of his hand made her flesh tingle.

"Hey," he said, surprise in his voice.

He took her chin between his thumb and forefinger and forced her to face him. His expression had gone somber. "You're bruised," he said, lifting her chin slightly.

"What?" She blinked in surprise.

"You're bruised. Right here. Over the carotid artery." He touched her throat by the edge of her jaw.

She raised her hand and her fingers brushed his. "But last night you said—?"

He kept his hand on her throat. "It didn't show last night. It's come out since then."

"He left a mark?"

"He left a mark." Wayne looked into her eyes. She had been right. Somebody had attacked her, had had his hands on her. And like a fool, Wayne had done nothing. Nothing. He hadn't even believed her. "My God, Ginnie," he said softly. "I'm sorry."

She rose, feeling shaky again, and walked to the framed mirror that hung beside the entrance. She pushed back her hair, raised her chin and turned her head slightly. There, like a shadow under the curve of her jaw, was a dim gray spot, like the ghostly impression of fingertips.

An ironic smile formed on her lips, but her eyes smarted with tears. For the first time, she understood what it meant to want to laugh and cry at the same time. She straightened her back, determined to do neither.

"Ginnie?" Wayne said in her ear. He had moved behind her. In the mirror she could see his face, more controlled and solemn than before. The dim light gleamed on his shoulders.

Slowly, almost reluctantly, he raised his hands and clasped her upper arms, more gently than he had done the night before. He turned her to face him. She wore no makeup and the freckles stood out against her cheekbones. Her mouth, he thought, looked more beautiful than ever.

"Are you all right?" His voice was harsh but low. His hands moved lightly up and down her upper arms, as if he could not decide whether to let them settle.

"I'm relieved." She didn't want to look into his eyes and found herself staring at the strong column of his throat, the smooth sweep of his naked chest. She squared her shoulders. "It seems stupid to be grateful for a bruise. But maybe it proves I'm not crazy."

"I never thought you were crazy. I'm sorry I doubted you."

"But how did the person get in? You said nobody could have got in."

"I was wrong. Locks can be picked."

"But Wayne, why would anybody do such a thing? What's happening here?"

"We'll find out. Come on. Get dressed. Let's go look for your book."

She raised her eyes to meet his.

He didn't move and neither did she. His hands went still on her. They tightened. He drew her closer.

Ginnie's lips parted slightly and she found her hands rising, as if bewitched, to settle on his wide shoulders. His skin was warm, hard and smooth beneath her fingers.

His gaze was fastened on her mouth. Ginnie found it hard to get her breath.

"Maybe we didn't get this right the first time we tried it," he murmured. He bent his face toward hers. His lips bore down on hers.

His mouth was warm, mobile and questing. When it took Ginnie's, it conveyed all sorts of messages, some of them contradictory. It ravaged, yet was gentle. It teased, but it was perfectly serious. It was hungry, even rapacious, but it wanted to give as much as it took.

She could feel his hands moving over her back now, and the way he touched her filled her with emotions that dizzied her even more. His body beneath her fingers felt alive with sureness and passion. He touched her so that she felt both warm and cold at once; he was taking her to a place of light, he was taking her to a place of darkness. He was taking her home, he was sweeping her far away.

Without lifting his lips from hers, he opened the robe and pushed it from her shoulders. He pushed the strap of her bra down. His mouth moved to the pulse in her throat, then to her naked shoulder. His hands slipped down to span her bare waist and pull her more tightly against him.

When he bent and began to kiss the swell of her breasts, Ginnie felt faint with desire. She ran her fingers over the rough silk of his dark hair, then the scars that marred his shoulder blades.

He straightened abruptly, pulling her so close she almost gasped for air. Still she kept her hands against his bare back. "Don't touch me there," he said, his lips next to hers.

She pressed her fingers more firmly against the ruinous scars.

"Don't," he repeated and kissed her. "You shouldn't even have to look at it. It's a mess."

"I don't care," she said, kissing him back. "It's you."

"Don't say things like that." He kissed her ear, then her jaw. "You know we're going to make love, don't you?"

She nodded, her cheek against his. His was stubbled and burned slightly, but it was a burning that felt wonderful to her. "I know."

He kissed her again. "It's going to be good. Very good."

"I know that, too," she said. She mumbled the words against his lips.

"Take off the robe," he said.

She let it fall to the floor.

AFTERWARD, SHE LAY, happy and exhausted, in his arms, her face hidden against the warmth of his chest.

She felt as if her body glowed all over, but she was more than slightly dazed. Had she really, she thought, done such things as had just happened in that bed? Had she actually experienced such emotions, such physical sensations? She ran her hand along the hard sweep of his shoulder, as if to assure herself that he was really there.

He raised himself on one elbow and stared down at her, her tousled hair, her dazzled eyes.

For a long time, he said nothing at all.

Ginnie tried to turn her face away, but he put his hand to her jaw and made her look into his eyes again. Still he said nothing.

He bent his head and kissed her.

I could kiss you forever, Ginnie thought. *I could kiss you until I die.*

He drew back, but his thumb and fingers still framed her jaw.

If he would say he cared for her, Ginnie thought, everything broken in her life would seem mended; everything incomplete would seem whole again.

But all he said was "Get dressed. We'll go look for your book."

He started to give her his crooked half smile, but it seemed to die on his lips.

He stood up, pulling on his jeans. He handed her his robe. He went to the window and pushed aside the drapes, staring out at nothing except the frost.

"Look," he said. "We probably both needed that."

Ginnie, knotting the robe around her waist, could only stare at him in dismay. *We needed that?* she thought numbly. *The way people need a flu shot or a stiff drink?*

He kept gazing out the window at its curtain of ice. "I've got to tell you this, I've always been kind of a loner. You've got to understand this."

Ginnie nodded, a sinister lump rising in her throat. His hair was slightly tousled and he needed a shave, which made his face look harder than usual. The scars seemed unnaturally white against his dark skin.

He took a deep breath. "I'm at a time when I don't particularly want anybody around me. The navy was the most important thing in my life, but that's over. I've got all my money tied up in the company. I'm still recovering from the accident. It's like I'm in transition. I've got to reinvent my life. So I don't have time for anybody else. Not really.''

She nodded again. The numbness that had started with the knot in her throat had spread through her body. She felt as if she were experiencing some form of small death. "I know that," she said, her voice tight.

He glanced at her. "Did you know I'd been married?"

She felt a jolt of surprise. "No."

He looked away again. "She left me two years ago. Right before the accident. She said I was really in love with the navy. I guess I was. But I loved her. I'm getting over that, too."

So we're both on the rebound, Ginnie thought unhappily. *And we blundered into each other's paths and then into bed.*

He shrugged, his eyes still on the frost. "Everything fell apart, you know? It takes time to put it back together. So I'm not looking for anybody. You understand I don't make commitments."

Ginnie stood a little straighter, squared her shoulders. "I understand." Her voice was toneless.

So was his. He turned from her and took a clean shirt from his closet. "Good. Let's go find your book."

"Fine," Ginnie said.

But nothing at all seemed fine. It seemed dangerous and empty and tainted by some kind of betrayal.

Wayne shrugged into the shirt, glad to cover the scars. He refused to think about how good it had felt making love to her. He had let her get too close, in every sense of the word. It wouldn't happen again.

He would help her out of this mess as best he could, but then it was over. Over, dammit. Until then, he would just make sure he kept her at a distance.

GINNIE SHOOK HER HEAD. "It was here," she insisted, kneeling on the floor beside Sutherland's bed. She rose and sat dejectedly on the side of the bed. She looked up at Wayne.

He had been so closemouthed since their conversation in his bedroom that it was driving her mad. He had said nothing else about their making love. He acted as if it had never occurred.

He glanced around the room, scowling slightly. "Both doors were chained. He'd have to come through one of the windows. But I don't see how." He put his hand on the sill of the bedroom window. "This is the only one that doesn't lock. And it's up four floors. The person would have to fly." He scratched an opening in the frost and looked out, his face grim.

Ginnie studied his profile. It was regular, handsome and totally impassive. It showed no emotion at all.

"Maybe it was a vampire," she said, trying a feeble joke.

He didn't look at her and he didn't smile. "You should write down what you remember from those papers."

She nodded and stood. "I want to change these clothes. And then, I guess I should go."

He turned to face her. "Go?"

She made a helpless gesture. "I can't stay here. I can't stay in my own place. Somebody wants me to go, and I suppose the safest thing is to do just that—go."

Tell me not to, she thought. *Tell me to stay with you.*

He shrugged and looked out the window again. "I suppose you're right."

Ginnie could only stare at him.

"It's the safest thing," he said.

She took a deep breath. "What happened between us…" She couldn't finish the sentence. She didn't know how. She didn't even know what she was trying to say.

He turned to face her again, his thumbs hooked into the front pockets of his jeans. "It was just something that had to happen. That's all."

That's all. The words seemed as cool and disinterested as the stroke of a surgeon's knife. The look in his eyes was totally dispassionate.

"I suppose," she managed to say.

He shrugged one shoulder. "Change your clothes. I'll take you out for breakfast." He looked out the window again, frowning slightly.

Damn you, Ginnie thought. She gathered up her jeans, her fisherman's sweater and white fur mukluks and stalked into the bathroom.

She looked at her face in the mirror. She was pale except for a hectic flush across her cheekbones. She still had no makeup on and she looked as guileless and inexperienced as the most vulnerable schoolgirl. Her lips were still slightly swollen from his kisses.

"Fool," she said to her image. "You stupid fool."

THEY WENT BACK to Wayne's apartment. Ginnie tried to act as casual and uncaring as he did.

As he drew on the leather jacket, his phone rang. He picked up the receiver. "Priborski," he said shortly.

Ginnie watched his face as he listened. It went from emotionless to frowning. "I'll be there," he said and hung up. He went to the desk and got his automatic. He thrust it into the pocket of the jacket.

"What is it?" Ginnie asked, alarmed.

"It was Prouty. He wanted to know if you'd moved back in over there. He hears something in your apartment. He's going over to check it out."

He opened his front door and Ginnie was right behind him. "You stay here," he told her.

"No," she said flatly. He seemed determined to make all the decisions this morning and she'd had enough of it. She'd show him she was as independent as he.

"And why do you have to take that stupid gun?" she demanded.

"In case somebody else has a 'stupid gun' and wants to shoot, that's why," he said, starting down the stairs.

"It isn't necessary. It's dangerous." She stayed close behind him.

"Somebody's in your apartment."

"That doesn't mean you have to arm yourself to the teeth."

"I'm not armed to the teeth. Why are you so combative all of a sudden?"

"Me, combative? You're the one carrying the gun."

"You don't like it? Go back to my place and wait."

"No."

He swore. She remained at his side anyway.

They went through the lobby and started up the stairs to the east tower. Ginnie didn't see how he moved so quickly with his injured leg. She was having trouble catching her breath. "Slow down, can't you?"

"You wanted to come. You speed up."

"You know," she said righteously, "you're pushing yourself. You could hurt yourself."

"That'd be my problem, wouldn't it?"

What, she thought uncharitably, *did I ever think I liked about this man?* She tried not to think that an hour ago she had been in his arms and in his bed. An hour ago, his merest smile had made her heart go somersaulting off. His touch had flamed through her, making her feel things she'd never imagined feeling.

It was just something that had to happen, she thought, echoing his words. He had been ready for it and so had she. She would try to be as unconcerned about it as he was.

They approached the fourth floor. Ginnie looked up the stairs and flinched in spite of herself. "Oh, God, the light's out."

Wayne swore. He paused long enough to draw the automatic from his pocket and slide the safety off. He put an arm out to block her way. "You stay here."

"No. It's my apartment."

He didn't bother to look at her. He swore softly and started up the stairs again.

They climbed into the darkness. Ginnie's heart beat hard. She began to wish she had stayed behind. There was one small window in the hallway, but it was high in the wall and paned with ancient squares of colored glass.

"Come here." As they reached the last step, Wayne drew her to his side. Her pulses drummed so swiftly that she could hear them thudding in her ears.

They stood on the landing, looking through the gloom. Ginnie heard a groan and stiffened. Wayne's arm tightened around her.

Huddled before her door was a dark shape. She could see nothing else in the hall. Another groan sounded weakly.

"It's Prouty," Wayne said. "He's hurt."

"Oh, no," Ginnie breathed.

She broke away from Wayne and dropped to her knees beside Mr. Prouty. Light from the small window threw dim squares of green and purple and amber on the floor. It barely illuminated Mr. Prouty's body, making it a thing of shadows and dim highlights.

"Mr. Prouty," Ginnie said, putting her hands on either side of his face. Then she drew them back in horror.

They dripped with blood. She realized she was kneeling in blood, as well. It was everywhere.

Chapter Eleven

"Oh, Wayne," Ginnie breathed, looking up at his dark shape, "Somebody's killed him."

Mr. Prouty groaned and stirred.

"He's not dead, he's making noise," Wayne muttered. He squatted beside her and swore at the amount of blood. He felt the pulse in Prouty's throat. "It's strong. I don't think he's hurt badly. He's coming around."

Ginnie rose, still horrified, and pushed open Mr. Prouty's front door. Light from his front-room windows spilled into the hall.

Ginnie saw that her hands and the knees of her jeans were stained with a bright, sticky red. She fought back a wave of sickness and knelt by Mr. Prouty again.

He moaned. His eyelids fluttered. He tried to raise himself, fell back, then tried again.

Ginnie tensed, fearing he would hurt himself. She helped him sit and lean against the wall. "Are you all right?"

"What happened, Prouty?" Wayne asked. He reached out to examine the man's head wound, but Mr. Prouty shrank back in a reflex of pain.

"I—I—" he began, then groaned and sank back into silence.

"I'll get some towels," Ginnie said. She rose and went into Mr. Prouty's apartment. She kicked off her boots at the doorway because she had stepped in blood.

Alfy, Mr. Prouty's dachshund, was shut in the bedroom, whining and clawing to get out. He barked when he heard Ginnie. In the hall closet, she found a stack of clean white towels and took them. In the kitchen, she filled a stainless-steel basin with water and ice. On top of the refrigerator was a large flashlight. She took it, as well.

She flinched again at the sight of all the blood in the hallway. She made her way to Wayne and Mr. Prouty and set down the basin. She knelt beside the two men, holding the towels and switching on the flashlight.

Wayne examined the cut on the back of Mr. Prouty's head and shone the light in his eyes.

"You feel drowsy? Nauseated?"

"No—no," muttered Prouty. "Just achy. I want to go back to my place."

Ginnie wrapped ice in a towel and pressed it against the back of Mr. Prouty's head, which made the older man cringe and sharply draw in his breath.

Wayne soaked another towel and wiped the blood from Mr. Prouty's face. "What happened?" Wayne repeated.

Mr. Prouty's eyes were still dazed. "I—thought I heard something in Miss Prince's apartment. I shut Alfy up so he wouldn't bolt, then came to check. The hall lights were out. I think I hit myself on the sconce. Oouf!"

Ginnie had been trying to wipe up the welter of blood. At his words, she blinked in surprise. She raised her eyes, staring up at the wall. The light sconce, an ornate triangle of torturously shaped wrought iron, jutted five feet above the floor, its tip pointed.

She stood to examine it more closely. The lightbulb was in place, but when she tried tightening it, the socket swiveled crazily in her hand. The cord was broken.

She raised her eyes higher. The old ceiling light fixture hung unlit in the gloom. The bulbs were still in place. Standing on tiptoe, she reached and gave one bulb a slight twist. It sprang into brilliance.

She squinted at the sudden blaze and tightened the other two bulbs. Nothing more happened. They were burned out.

Mr. Prouty, pale and trembling, held the wrapped ice against the back of his head. The stained towels lay around him. His shirt was ruined and his trousers were spattered with blood. The old man suddenly seemed very fragile to her.

She looked at the sconce again, then the fixture. The old building was full of ancient wiring and worn cords; lightbulbs loosened or burned out constantly. Burbage had been changing a faulty bulb the night he was struck. Yet she was sure someone had done this on purpose.

"Wayne," she said, touching the sconce. "The lights. They must have been cut deliberately."

"We'll talk about it later," Wayne said shortly. He was trying to strip the bloody shirt off Prouty.

"Please—" Mr. Prouty muttered, pulling the shirt together again over his white chest. He seemed embarrassed that Ginnie might see his naked flesh. "I'd just like to go back to my apartment. Lie down for a while."

"Mr. Prouty," Ginnie said, "I think I should call an ambulance. And the police."

"No, no, no," he said, more emphatically than was good for him. "I'm fine. I won't go back to that hospital. I don't want the police. Nothing happened. I just bumped myself in the same place again."

He struggled to get up, so determined to rise that Ginnie relented and helped him. She put her arm around him and let him lean on her. Wayne supported him from the other side.

Wayne led him to the bathroom, sat him down on the edge of the tub and finished cleaning the wound. It was on the back of the old man's head in almost the same place as he had injured himself before. Ginnie rummaged through the medicine cabinet and found bandages.

Mr. Prouty's apartment, too, was cold as ice. He had draped a towel over the parakeets' cage to keep them warm.

Ginnie bandaged the wound. "Thank you," Prouty said, his voice quavering. "I'm fine now. I'm sorry for all the fuss. It's quite—embarrassing, really." He tried to straighten his back and sit with dignity. He could not quite succeed. Ginnie thought he looked terrible.

She held Mr. Prouty's hand and knelt before him. "We should call a doctor. You've had two serious blows to the head in a week."

He stared at her, deep weariness in his eyes. His glasses sat unevenly on his nose. Their crookedness gave him a vulnerable, uncared-for look that made Ginnie want to comfort him.

"She's right," Wayne said. He stood in the doorway, his arms crossed. Blood was drying on the shoulder of his leather jacket. "You should see a doctor. And we should call the police. You were hit."

Mr. Prouty waved the words away as if they were troublesome insects. "I don't *want* any more doctors—I wouldn't have fallen if I hadn't been a bit weak from the first accident, that's all. I was never even unconscious, just disoriented—and I wasn't hit. I just must have run into the sconce, that's all."

"Mr. Prouty, you *must* have been hit," Ginnie insisted, squeezing his hand. "It's not safe for you here."

"It is safe. I've got Alfy. I'm not leaving him or the birds. Not again. No more hospitals. No more fuss. Nobody hit me. I stumbled in the dark, that's all. I won't have people think I can't take care of myself. I'm perfectly able to take care of myself. *And* my animals. We can get along by ourselves just fine."

Alfy howled from the bedroom and his nails rattled against the door as he tried to claw his way out.

"Please," Mr. Prouty said weakly. He squeezed Ginnie's hand, then let it go. "I just want to take care of myself. And my pets." He tried to stand.

Ginnie moved to help him but he refused. He leaned his hand against the wall a moment, then stood without aid. He swayed slightly. "You've both been very helpful. But nothing happened except I made a foolish blunder. I—I'm sorry for the bother. You've both taken too much trouble. Send me your cleaning bills. It's the least I can do. I'm—perfectly able to take care of myself. Perfectly."

He started, haltingly, toward his bedroom. Ginnie moved out of his way, but Wayne did not. He stayed in the doorway, blocking it. "Prouty, what about the noise you heard in Ginnie's apartment?"

Mr. Prouty started to shake his head, but the movement obviously cost him too much pain. He grimaced. "I don't know. I'm all alone up here. Between Mrs. Treat's stories and Miss Prince's, who knows? I was concerned about her place. Perhaps it was all my imagination."

A surge of guilt welled through Ginnie and she bit her lip. It was her fault Mr. Prouty had tried to play hero, her fault he had been hurt. If he stayed, somehow that seemed her fault, too. "I know you don't believe me, but you shouldn't stay here alone," she said.

"You've both been extremely kind," he said, his shoulders sagging. "But I don't need rescuing. I just want to change my clothes and rest."

"Mr. Prouty—" Ginnie almost begged, but she could tell he wasn't listening. A look of grim resignation settled over Wayne's face.

He let the older man through the door but put his hand on Prouty's shoulder as he passed. "Get some rest. We'll talk about it when you're better. I'll check on you later."

"Yes, of course," Mr. Prouty said vaguely, and kept hobbling toward his room. Alfy whined. "I'm coming," the old man said. "Everything's fine, dear. I'm not going away again."

Ginnie looked after him with alarm and concern. "He shouldn't be alone," she said under her breath.

"He wants to be alone. I'll check on him later. I'll make sure he's all right."

"But—"

"Ginnie, he's got no signs of serious injury. Head wounds bleed a lot, but it's actually a small cut. It doesn't look like he'll have any complications."

"But—"

"He doesn't want help. We can't make him take it."

Ginnie started to protest, then did not. Perhaps Mr. Prouty didn't even remember what, precisely, had happened to him. Didn't that often happen when people had head injuries? Besides, he didn't want to admit anything untoward had happened; he didn't want his cozy and independent existence disturbed.

"Let's check out your place," Wayne muttered. "It's what we came for."

She nodded and slipped back into her boots. If she and Wayne found her apartment disturbed, then perhaps Mr. Prouty would listen and move out until things were safe again.

Wayne ushered her out of Prouty's apartment, his hand on the back of her waist. He snapped the lock on the door and, as they stepped into the hall, pulled the door shut.

Ginnie, uneasy in the half light, nodded at the sconce. "It's broken. It wasn't yesterday." She looked up at the light fixture with its one dimly burning bulb. "And that bulb was loose. Somebody could have unscrewed it."

"Somebody probably did. The problem is proving it. You have your key?"

Ginnie nodded and dug into her purse. She tried to ignore the bloody towels that littered the hall, the thin streaks of drying blood that still marked the floor. She would call Mr. Burbage and ask him to send up Robbie to clean the floor and fix the lights.

She withdrew the key and Wayne took it. He thrust it into the lock and turned it. He opened the door slowly.

As he did, a silent flood of chill air seemed to engulf them. Ginnie cringed as the coldness eddied around her, settling into her bones like fear. It was as if when Wayne opened the door, a ghost had embraced her.

A rattle and a rustle echoed from inside.

She took a step backward. "What is it?"

Wayne put his hand into his pocket, locking his fingers around the automatic. He pushed the door open wider and the cold surged around them more deeply and forcibly.

"Wayne," Ginnie said. She was no longer sure that he should go inside. She reached out to touch the sleeve of his jacket, to halt him.

But he stepped inside.

There was a sound like a spectral wind from within her apartment. She heard the rattle again, a muted, scuffling sound. She heard a fluttering noise. She heard the click as Wayne slid the off the safety of the gun.

Gray light fell into the hall from the apartment, and something like thin smoke seemed to roll, phantomlike, through the doorway. It was as if an icy mist was drifting from her rooms to spread downward through the darkness and through the rest of the building.

Ginnie shut her eyes. The cold had grown so deep, she shuddered. There was the sound of its soft rush moving around her, there was the rattle and the flutter. If Wayne moved, she couldn't hear him.

"It's all right," she heard him say after what seemed an interminable moment.

She opened her eyes. He appeared in the doorway. He reached out his hand to her.

She took it, drew a deep breath and stepped inside. Then she stopped, looking around her living room, stunned.

A film of snow had drifted across half her carpet. A veil of it lay sparkling on her couch. It dusted the little Christmas tree that stood in the corner, and wisps of white danced along the hallway floor.

Across the room, the drapes were open, the blinds up and the windows wide open. The drapes billowed out, flapping and rippling with the cold stream of air that poured in from outside. The blinds clattered and creaked with each gust.

Small flakes of snow danced into the room, twinkling and spinning in the dull morning light.

"Somebody opened the windows," Ginnie said.

Wayne nodded toward the fluttering drapes. He stepped toward them, keeping hold of her hand.

Ginnie saw something lying on the floor in the shifting scarves of snow.

She drew in her breath. She felt suddenly hollow inside, as if someone had robbed her of all life, all movement.

A book lay open, its pages riffling in the cold wind. Flakes of snow were caught, shining dimly, between its waving pages. The book's cover was dull green. She knew what it was. It was the book that had disappeared from Sutherland's rooms last night.

"Oh, no," she said.

Wayne looked at her, his eyes grave. "Newsome's book?"

She knelt and took up the book, closing it and staring numbly at its cover. She nodded.

The cover of the book was cold in her hands and slightly grainy with snow. The papers it had held before were gone.

"Damn," Wayne said angrily, and shoved the automatic back into his pocket. He went to the window, leaned his hands on the sill and stared out. Across the rooftop, dead opposite, was the other tower, with his apartment and Sutherland's. Between the two, down a full story, stretched an expanse of roof so sharply angled, so thick with ice, that he could not imagine anyone navigating it.

Beyond the other tower was only gray sky and, far beneath, the snowy ground.

Ginnie rose and leaned beside him, following his gaze. There was no way up from the roof to the window. The wall was a sheer face of brick without handhold or foothold. "Nobody could get in this way," she said, shaking her head. "Nobody."

"I know."

"But somebody did. The same way they got into Sutherland's last night." She tried not to think of the unseen hand on her throat, the bruise beneath her jaw. "But where did they go after hitting Mr. Prouty? We didn't pass anybody on the stairs."

Wayne shook his head. Somebody might have hidden on the deserted third floor, but he would probably be long gone by now. At any rate, Wayne didn't intend to chance taking Ginnie down there, and he knew she wouldn't stay behind.

Whoever was doing this was starting to play too damned rough.

He straightened, examining the two window frames. "No locks?"

She shook her head. "There weren't any when I moved in. I didn't think I'd need any. Who could get in here? *What* could get in?"

Ginnie, too, straightened. She looked at the book in her hand. "It's the same one," she said softly. "It's got the same spot on the cover. Shaped almost like a butterfly."

She realized that she was shaking. Her hands, she saw, were still slightly smeared with Mr. Prouty's blood. The knees of her jeans were wet with it, and in the cold breeze they felt icy, so her knees shook, too.

Wayne gave her a long look, then turned and closed the window almost savagely. It crashed shut with a bang. He slammed the second one with almost as much force.

He put an arm around her. "Come on. Let's go back. You need to get out of those clothes. Get something to eat."

She shook harder. The cold wind was cut off, but its chill lingered so deep within her she wondered if she'd ever feel warm again.

"I'm not hungry," she muttered, still staring down at the book. "And I can't leave Mr. Prouty over there. He was attacked—worse than I was. I was only knocked out—he could have bled to death."

"But he didn't. Worry about yourself."

"He won't even call the police," Ginnie said in frustration.

"Come on," Wayne ordered, steering her toward the door. "What are you going to do? Call them yourself? The man says nobody hit him, that it was an accident. Are the police going to believe you—or him?"

Ginnie stopped, trying to draw away from him. She gestured back at the room, ghostly with its partial film of snow. "And what about this? About what happened to me last night?"

He gave first the room, then her, an impatient glance. "Ginnie, you've got no hard evidence to take to the police. You never did. You say you felt a hand in the dark. You say somebody knocked you out. A book disappears. It appears again. A couple of windows open. The police are going to tell you that you don't need detectives, you need either a psychiatrist or an exorcist."

She stared into his eyes. "And which do you think I need?"

He looked away, exhaling harshly. "I don't think you need either. I think you need to get out of here. As soon as possible. For your own good."

His arm was still around her, so she was achingly close. Her eyes looked bluer than eyes had any right to look.

Woman, get out now, he thought. *For your own good. And for mine.*

GINNIE KNEW SHE LOOKED alarming, the knees of her jeans soaked with blood and her boots spattered with it, but she insisted on stopping at Burbage's anyway. Perhaps her appearance would convince him that things were indeed critical in the towers.

She banged on his door until her knuckles were sore, but nobody answered. Wayne took over and his knocks were far louder than hers had been. Still nobody answered.

Paul Donner emerged from his doorway across the hall, carrying his poodle. He wore fur-trimmed boots, a fur-trimmed jacket and a fur-trimmed hat. The poodle wore a crocheted sweater of crimson.

"Hello," he said airily, "you can knock until your fist falls off, nobody's answering. They're not home. Everything's in an uproar. The heat's off, and what do the Burbages do? Pack up and leave. It's a scandal, and I, for one, don't intend to stand for it."

His gaze fell to Ginnie's knees and boots and his eyes widened. A look of repulsion spread across his face. "My God, Ginnie Prince, what happened to *you*? You look like you fell into an abattoir."

"A what?" said Ginnie.

"An *abattoir*, a slaughterhouse. Are you all right? What's happened now? Did you have some sort of accident? Can I help?"

"I'm fine. Mr. Prouty had another accident."

"Prouty? My God, is he dead? You're *drenched* with gore."

"He's not dead," Wayne said evenly. "He took another hit to the head. It bled a lot. He says he'll be fine."

"What happened? Did he trip over that nasty old dachshund?" Donner sniffed, setting Gigi down delicately in the hall. She had on her Christmas collar and leash, white leather ornamented with green.

Wayne and Ginnie exchanged looks. "We're not sure what happened," Ginnie answered. "The lights are defective in the hall up there. And the floor's—the floor's stained. I wanted Robbie or Mr. Burbage to come fix it. And maybe Robbie could walk the dog. Mr. Prouty should rest."

Donner drew on one leather glove and examined its fit. "Good luck. Robbie's gone, too, you know. Disappeared."

Ginnie stared at him. Without thinking she put her arm on Wayne's sleeve and edged a step nearer to him. "Disappeared? What do you mean?"

Donner looked up from his glove. His face was cynical. "Gone, vanished, departed, fled, split, vamoosed, left. I told you everything's topsy-turvy here. I hear his father's pitching a fit."

"Robbie's gone?" Ginnie repeated in disbelief.

"When did this happen?" Wayne didn't like Donner because he didn't trust him. The man often spoke as much for effect as to convey the truth.

"Oh, yesterday sometime," Donner said, drawing on his other glove. "He never showed up to help me move the microwave. He never went home for supper. He never went home at all. Not all night long. As you can see, the floors haven't been mopped. And the walks haven't been shoveled, and the parking lot is a sheet of ice. Someone will surely slip and die on it.'' He sighed. ''That, of course, will be the management's crowning achievement. Not discomfort. Not inconvenience. Not petty crime. But out and out actual *death*.''

''Where are the Burbages?'' Ginnie asked, concerned. Donner was frightening her. Too many things were going wrong, too fast.

Donner shrugged. ''Well, *that's* a sixty-four-thousand-dollar question. Maybe he took her out and threw her into a snow bank. She was shrieking like a banshee this morning. The whole floor could hear it.''

The hollow, sick feeling filled Ginnie again. ''She was screaming? What about?''

''Oh, I don't know,'' Donner said impatiently. ''Something about somebody taking her daughter's things. Christmas is a bad time for her supposedly. Perhaps she just shrieks to mark the occasion. Later I shrieked myself. Someone has *been* in my apartment. Well, I'm not standing for that. I'm going to go stay with my sister until everything calms down.''

Ginnie's hand tightened on Wayne's sleeve. He put his hand over hers. ''Prowlers?'' he asked carefully.

''Prowlers,'' Donner repeated emphatically. ''For almost two days and two nights, Gigi's been barking at something. Dogs *know* when something's wrong, I tell you. I went out to walk her this morning and when we came back—well, things had been trifled with.''

''Stolen?'' Ginnie asked, apprehensive.

Donner chose not to answer the question. ''I put extra locks and bolts on both doors, but I must have forgotten to fasten up when we went out. Don't tell me that somebody connected with this building didn't take those keys. It's somebody who knows our every coming and going. Of course, every time I step outside, there's that ghoul, Mrs. Treat, telling me some story about her spirit guide. Well, I suspect her sanity, but I don't suspect spirits. I suspect that lout, Robbie. I always thought he had the look of a thug in his eyes. Now Burbage isn't even here so I can lodge a complaint."

Robbie, Ginnie thought with a pang of fear and a sense of betrayal. *Robbie's always had access to the keys. He knows the building inside out. He knew that I was going to be gone to Maine. And he acted so strangely yesterday.*

"Donner," Wayne said dubiously, "how do you know somebody was in your place? Why didn't you call the police?"

Donner looked suddenly haughty. "I *did* call the police. They said they'd send a man by, but that was over three hours ago. Nobody's come. Nobody's taking this seriously. Well, *I* am."

"Was anything taken? Vandalized?" Wayne demanded.

"Yes," Donner said, more haughty than before. His expression became suddenly shuttered. "Certain items were missing. I just don't choose to discuss it any further. It's enough to tell you that something's taken. I don't intend to get hysterical about it. But consider yourselves forewarned. This place has become neither safe nor pleasant."

Ginnie tried to look confident, but suspected that she failed. "You're really leaving?" she asked Donner.

"My car is packed. I've called my sister that I'm coming—God help her and me. I've left a note for Burbage that either all this brouhaha is cleared up for once and for all—or I'm moving out. I frankly suggest everyone else do likewise. I've loved this apartment, but I will *not* tolerate these conditions. I have spoken."

He threw one end of his muffler over his shoulder dramatically and strode toward the front doors. Gigi trotted before him, as proud as a princess.

Ginnie looked at Wayne, consternation in her face. "What do you think happened to him?"

He shook his head. "He doesn't want to talk about it."

"He acted almost as if he were ashamed to talk about it."

"He's ashamed because he's afraid to admit what he's seen and heard," said a voice from the stairs, and Ginnie tensed. "The ignorant often are ashamed at first. Or angry.

Have you ever read *The Book of the Damned*? It seems we're writing a new chapter.''

Both Wayne and Ginnie turned to see Mrs. Treat descending the stairs. She moved slowly, as if tired or in pain. She wore her gray felt slippers and her shapeless gray cardigan, and her hair was untidy. Her hands were in the pockets of her commodious black skirt. Under her eyes were circles, dark and swollen. She stopped and stared at Wayne and Ginnie.

"You're bloody," she said. She sounded neither frightened nor surprised.

"You were listening," Wayne accused, his voice as flat as hers. "Didn't you hear? Prouty's been hurt again."

Mrs. Treat sighed. She put her hand over her heart. "I sensed he might be. I had such a strong impression of it. I must go see him."

Ginnie looked at the woman with dislike and impatience. Mrs. Treat always said she sensed something was going to happen, but only after it already had. And it was becoming obvious she had designs on the hapless Mr. Prouty. "I'll look out for Mr. Prouty," Ginnie said. "He's my neighbor, after all."

"No," Mrs. Treat said, "you'll be gone. You should both be gone. I was wrong."

She had reached the lobby now and stood, one hand on the dark newel post. She looked incredibly weary.

"Wrong?" Ginnie asked.

Mrs. Treat nodded. She moved toward them with a slow, halting step. When she reached them, she stood uncomfortably close, studying their faces. "Fairfax has gone," she said. "Robbie's gone. So are the Burbages. Donner. You should go, too. So should the others. I was wrong. The spirits here aren't friendly. I heard a voice last night. As clearly as I can hear you."

The set of Wayne's mouth was scornful. "Oh. All of a sudden they're *not* friendly."

"No. They were, but a new spirit has descended. A very evil one. You must go. Immediately. It's started."

Wayne's upper lip curled at the edge. "What's started?"

"The end, young man. The end has begun. Be careful or it will include you, as well. The both of you."

She put her hand on Ginnie's arm. "It wants *this* one," she said, squeezing Ginnie's wrist. "It wants her badly. But if you get in its way—" she met Wayne's eyes "—it will take you, too. You'll be as a twig in a great flame to it. You'll be helpless. You can't save her. You can't even save yourself."

Chapter Twelve

Ginnie and Wayne argued. Ginnie refused to leave the building while Mr. Prouty was there and hurt.

She sat at Wayne's table, desultorily stirring her coffee and staring out the window at the tower opposite. It was inevitable, she supposed, that she and Wayne had fought again. They always disagreed. Besides, she told herself with a slight twist in her logic, quarreling with him proved that she cared no more for him than he did for her.

She had showered and changed into clean jeans and a pink sweater, but she still felt strangely twitchy at the thought of so much blood. While she was in the shower, Wayne had compromised his principles and gone out and bought her coffee, bacon and cinnamon rolls, but she wasn't hungry. Neither was she grateful to him. She didn't want to look at him. She kept her gaze on the tower opposite.

"Eat. Stop staring at that tower. What do you think you're going to see? Bela Lugosi flying in Prouty's window?"

"I don't know." She took the smallest possible bite of her cinnamon roll, but even that seemed to stick in her throat.

Wayne opened the paper to the classified ads and frowned over them. He, too, had changed clothes. He wore faded jeans ironed to a razor-sharp crease and a white shirt, the sleeves rolled up to expose his forearms. White made his skin seem more bronzed, his hair blacker. Ginnie refused to think how handsome he must have looked in his white officer's uniform. Military types, she told herself for the thousandth time, were not her style.

She kept staring moodily out the window.

"Here's a place," Wayne muttered. "'One bedroom, appliances furnished, carport, fireplace, no pets.'"

He read off the amount for which it rented. Ginnie gave him a look that clearly said he was mad. "I can't afford that. And you might as well put the paper down. I'm not leaving."

He didn't so much as glance up. "You're leaving. Here, 'Raintree Apartments. One or two bedrooms. Energy efficient. Private patio. Clubhouse and pool privileges.'"

"I can't afford a place with a pool and a clubhouse, for God's sake. I told you, I'm not moving."

"You're moving. If I have to throw you over my shoulder and carry you out."

She glared at him. "Excuse me," she said, setting down her spoon, "but you don't tell me what to do."

He turned the page of the paper. "Wrong. That's exactly what I'm doing."

"No. This isn't the navy, I'm not your—your boatswain—and I don't take orders."

He glanced at her. It was a short look, but eloquent with masculine intolerance. "You're not safe here."

"Nobody's safe here," Ginnie protested. "But I won't leave. Not while Mr. Prouty's here. He's practically helpless now."

"He's acting like a damned fool, and if anything happens to him, it's his own damned fault," Wayne almost snarled, not bothering to look up again.

"Wayne! Don't talk like that!"

"Excuse me," he said, still staring at the paper. "I forgot your fabulous morality. Forgive me for swearing."

She made a sound of exasperation and turned away from him. Her "fabulous morality," which he so justly mocked, hadn't kept her out of bed with him.

Maybe he was right and she would be wise to go away. He certainly wasn't anxious to keep her near. Well, she thought, she didn't care. There were such things as right and wrong. There was such a thing as responsibility to one's fellow man.

She leaned her chin on her fist angrily. "I said I won't go while he's here, and that's that. He's old and weak and sick and he's got nobody to help look after Alfy."

Wayne let the paper sink. He glowered in her direction but she refused to look at him. "*I'll* help," he said.

Ginnie tossed her head. "You? Oh, right. Mr. Bedside Manner."

"I don't need any bedside manner to take some dog out for a—"

"Wayne!"

"Look, don't worry. I used to fly a jet, remember? I think I can walk a dog."

"It's not the dog. It's Mr. Prouty himself."

"You want Prouty to move out? Is that what it takes? I'll get him to move out. I'll talk to him again."

"Wayne—he's too proud. And he's not going to be separated from those animals, you know that."

He picked up the paper again, turning the page with a rattle. "I'll find him a place where the animals can stay. I'll get him out. First, let me get you out. One weak sister at a time, okay?"

Ginnie faced him again and shot him a fierce gaze. "I'm not a weak sister, you male chauvinist—" She could not quite bring herself to say *pig*.

Wayne could. "You forgot *pig*. What's the matter? Too *nice* to say it?"

She stood. "All right. I'm no weak sister, you male chauvinist tattooed yankee pig."

He still didn't look at her, but he laughed. "'Tattooed yankee pig'? I like that. You know, for a pacifist, you've got a hell of a smart mouth. Deep down, you *like* to fight."

"I don't like to fight," Ginnie said furiously. Then she was mad at herself for allowing him to make her furious. "I just said I'm no weak sister. I can take perfectly good care of myself."

"Yeah. Right." He favored her with a brief, dark glance. "That's good, because you know, I can't go on taking care of you. I haven't got time. I've got other things to do, believe it or not."

She turned from him again and crossed her arms. She went to the window and stared off toward the tower, unseeing. He could make her angrier than anyone she'd ever known, and his words hurt.

She supposed he had taken care of her. But she had done her best to be strong. She hadn't meant to faint over the dead man; she hadn't meant to panic when someone choked her, but it had been truly terrifying. She didn't mean to be silly over Mr. Prouty, but seeing him lying in the hall covered with blood was enough to scare anybody.

She had tried, as hard as she could, to keep on going the last few days, no matter what happened.

Now Wayne spoke as if she were nothing more than a nuisance, a weakling and a millstone around his neck. He had made love to her out of curiosity and simple animal hunger. Now he wanted her out of his way, gone.

But oddly, what bothered Ginnie worst was that he was going to stay on alone in this horrible place. Above all else, she was frightened for him. It didn't matter if what threatened was natural or supernatural. Everyone else might run, but he wouldn't. He'd take on a whole legion of devils, even if it meant death.

She bent her head slightly and raised her hand to her eyes. This was not, she told herself, the time for tears, especially over a stubborn, arrogant, uncaring man.

"Oh, God." Something akin to despair edged Wayne's voice. "Are you crying?"

"No," Ginnie practically snapped. "Only weak sisters cry. I have a headache. You gave it to me."

He stared at her back, slim but wide-shouldered for a woman. He shouldn't be sharp with her. She'd been through hell in the last few days.

She wasn't tough, but she was strong, as strong as they came. She was lovely, and sexy, too, so sexy she put a lump in his throat, but she drove him crazy in ways he couldn't begin to number.

He didn't want to care about her, he didn't want to care about anybody; he didn't want to get involved. Still, he found himself putting down the paper and rising from his chair.

"Look," he said, stepping toward her, "we give each other a headache. Truce for a while, okay?"

And he found, to his dismay, that he was touching her again. He stood behind her, his hands on her upper arms. "Hey," he said. She was silent "Ginnie. Look at me."

She turned to face him. He put his hands on her arms again and looked into her eyes, then at her lips.

"The thing is," she said, blinking up at him, "I don't want to leave you here, either. I'd worry about you."

Her voice broke slightly. There was nothing erotic in the way she reached over and adjusted the collar of his shirt, but it made Wayne's heart contract so hard, it hurt him. Her gesture was shyly affectionate. It was almost—he hesitated to use the word—loving.

He had a sudden impulse to take her in his arms, press her against him, simply hold her. He wanted to feel her body slim and warm against his, to bury his face in the silk of her hair, to get drunk on the touch and scent of her.

He resisted because he was a man who was good at resisting things. He wondered if how he felt showed in his face. He hoped it didn't. He took his hands away from her. "If I get Prouty to go, will you go, too?" he asked gruffly.

"I want you to leave, too."

"No. Don't care about me, Ginnie. Because I don't care about anybody. I can't. I told you that. Understand?"

He didn't care. He wouldn't care. It was as simple as that. She understood all too well.

She nodded stiffly, and her hand dropped away from his shoulder. Once more they looked into each other's eyes. And then they looked away.

"I just don't get involved with people," he said, moving back to the table. He shrugged one shoulder. "It's nothing personal."

Ginnie stared out the window again. "Nothing personal."

He sat down and picked up the paper again. "Sit and eat," he said.

Ginnie sat down, but she knew she couldn't eat. She stared at the paper that hid his face. She looked at his hands, sure and brown against the paper's whiteness.

She disliked being contentious with him, but she almost feared tenderness from him worse. "Why'd you get the tattoo?" she said, just to say something.

"I was drunk. It seemed like a good idea at the time."

"Why don't you drink anymore?"

"I changed my ways, that's all."

"Because of the accident?"

"Yeah," he said. "Because of the accident."

She sank back into silence. She put her chin on her hand again and stared unhappily at the paper.

"Here's one," Wayne muttered. "'Parkside Apartments. Furnished or unfurnished. Lake view. Tennis courts. Clubhouse. Indoor pool.' What about if you roomed with another woman? Then you could split the rent."

Ginnie scanned the headlines mechanically, barely hearing him. There was trouble in the Middle East and a fight over taxes at the state capital. There was no new lead in the disappearance of Junior Hopkins, and two more policemen had resigned because of the bribery scandals. A lumber truck had crashed on highway 101, and an unidentified man had been found drowned in the Merrimack River.

Ginnie reread the last headline. She felt suddenly dazed, almost giddy. "Did you hear me?" Wayne said.

"Wayne," she said softly, "they found a body in the river."

"So?"

"A drowned man. They don't know who he is. What if he's my drowned man?"

The paper lowered. He studied her, his face unreadable.

She pointed at the story, a tiny one in the bottom corner. "They found an unidentified man in the Merrimack. Late last night. Drowned. They think he's a vagrant. What if he was the man in my tub?"

He closed the paper and scanned the front page. Shortly before midnight, the man had been pulled from the icy Merrimack. He had no identification, but authorities theorized he was homeless, a street person.

Wayne looked at her again. "Ginnie," he said, "you don't want to go to the morgue."

She bit her lip. She had never seen a morgue, except in television shows. Until she'd seen the dead man in her tub, she'd never seen a corpse except powdered and surrounded by flowers in a funeral home. Wayne was right. She bit her lip harder. "Maybe I don't have a choice," she said. "It's what I have to do."

He folded the paper and laid it beside his coffee cup. He looked at her for a long moment. "I'll go with you," he said at last.

She shook her head. She stared out the window again. "No. I'll go alone. You're right. You've got other things to do besides baby-sit for me."

He sighed harshly. "I didn't mean that. It was just talk, all right? You should have somebody with you."

"No. You should stay. Mr. Prouty might need you."

"Mr. Prouty," Wayne said in disgust. "You want me to devote the rest of my life to him?"

"No, but—"

"I'll call him, make sure he's all right, then go with you." He paused, his jaw set as if he were searching for words. "I didn't mean it when I called you a weak sister. I was hot under the collar, all right? There are some places a person shouldn't go alone. A morgue is one of them."

Ginnie, still stared out the window. At last she gave a reluctant nod.

He was right. A morgue was no place to go alone.

MR. PROUTY HAD an unlisted number, so Wayne went to his apartment, leaving Ginnie alone. The rooms seemed preternaturally empty without him, and his absence filled her with a strange restlessness.

She stood by the window, looking at the east tower. It rose, an enigma of brick, against the gray air. Snow had started to fall thickly again.

Suddenly she saw someone moving toward the woods. It was a man, a large man in a dark coat and dark hat. He moved steadily, and he had a sack of some sort across his shoulder.

Ginnie tensed and strained her eyes. It was Mr. Swengler, she was sure. But why was he going to the woods and what was he carrying?

Her first impulse was to go to the phone to call Wayne. She turned, then stopped, remembering she couldn't; she didn't have Prouty's number. She moved back to the window.

Swengler was hobbling determinedly toward the wall of trees that lined the river. In a moment, he would disappear from her sight. The way the snow was falling and the wind blowing, his tracks would soon be erased.

Ginnie held her breath and watched a few seconds longer. She made a swift decision. She snatched up her jacket and hat and gloves, pulling them on as she opened the door and made her way downstairs.

Halfway down the stairs, it occurred to her that she should have left a note for Wayne. She paused, then went on. There wasn't time to go back.

When she opened the outside door, the wind cut cruelly. She made her way around to the back of the apartments, in the direction Swengler had gone. Snow stung her eyes and the cold air bit her face. She wished she'd brought her muffler.

She floundered toward the woods as quickly as she could, traveling a wavering path, hoping to find Swengler's tracks. The snow was deeper than she'd thought, and she marveled that the old man had moved so swiftly through it.

At last, almost at the edge of the woods, she discovered his footprints, already drifting over. Although she was long-legged, his tracks were too far apart for her to step in. He was, Ginnie remembered with a sinking heart, an extremely large man, perhaps six feet four.

She paused beneath the first row of cedars, squinting into the forest. The trees were black against the snow, and they creaked and moaned in the wind. Ginnie realized that she didn't want to meet Mr. Swengler in the coldness and dark of the woods. She turned up her collar and shivered slightly.

If she were careful, she thought, if she stayed observant, he at least could not surprise her. He had been moving with his head down, intent only on the ground before him. She moved off about fifteen feet to the side of his tracks. If he came back the same way he had gone, he might not even see her footprints. She jammed her cold hands deeply into her pockets and trudged on, her eyes narrowed against the snow.

Except for the sound of the wind and the trees, the woods were silent with the eerie silence of new snow. Inside the woods, the world seemed reduced to black-and-white: the dark trunks of trees, the green-black of cedar and pine needles, the shifting, blowing blankness of the snow.

Swengler's tracks moved in a surprisingly straight line, as if he knew exactly where he was going and how to get there.

Near the river's edge, by a grove of birches ghostly in the snow, his footprints took a sharp turn to the north, to run parallel with the river itself. The river was dark, steely gray and partly frozen. In a few places, it foamed as it surged past the great stones in its bed. Ginnie thought of the man found dead in the river and shivered again. No grave, outside of the arctic, could be colder.

This was no time to think of dead men or graves, Ginnie chided herself. Swengler's tracks angled off again, back in the direction of the towers. She pushed her hands more deeply into her pockets and kept following. Surely he wasn't simply doubling back, was he? Surely he wasn't doing something as simple and ordinary as taking a walk.

She rounded a particularly large pine and stopped, holding her breath. There, perhaps fifty feet ahead, Mr. Swengler knelt in the snow. The intervening scrub cedars and bare blackberry canes almost screened him from her sight.

He was on his knees, his back to her, by a tumbled heap of granite boulders overgrown with dead vines. He was putting a heavy stone into place, as if covering something.

Ginnie stood watching, barely daring to breathe. Swengler dusted snow back over the stone he had moved, then crept backward, sweeping the snow with his empty sack to hide any sign that he had knelt there. At last he rose and stared at the sky a long time.

Then he turned and looked about him. He turned his face slowly, then stopped just when his eyes seemed to meet Ginnie's full on. She felt as if her heart tripped and fell down hard. *Oh, God. He sees me.*

But then he kept turning, his eyes sweeping the woods around him. He hadn't seen her, after all. She started breathing again.

Swengler turned the collar of his black coat higher. He folded the empty sack and thrust it into his coat pocket. He raised his hawklike profile to the sky once more. Then he set his face toward the towers and started home.

Ginnie waited until he was out of sight. After he left, she forced herself to count to five hundred, even though her feet were growing numb and her hands and face tingled painfully with the stab of the cold.

Then she made her way to the formation of rocks. Most of them were massive. Some great natural force, glacier or quake, must have heaped them there. They were large enough, Ginnie thought uneasily, to hide a body beneath their craggy mass.

That's ridiculous, she told herself sternly and knelt where Swengler had been moments before. Nothing short of a bulldozer could move the largest rocks. She worked to pry away the far smaller one he had set in place. Its weight reminded her again that although Swengler was aged, he was a powerful man.

At last, gasping at the effort, she rolled the rock away. Beneath it, a hole as wide as a dinner plate yawned blackly.

Ginnie grimaced with apprehension. The thing looked as if it plunged down through the other side of the earth. It had been dug beneath an old root as thick as a strong man's arm. It must have once been the burrow of an animal.

She thought of things hiding down in the darkness, things with sharp teeth. She didn't want to put her hand inside. She gritted her teeth and remembered Wayne's words: *weak sister.*

She plunged her hand inside. At first she could feel nothing except the sides of the hole.

Her hand brushed something. She inhaled sharply. Her fingers closed around a cylindrical shape and she drew it out.

She sat back on her heels and stared at the object with stupification. It was a can of chicken-noodle soup with a red-and-white label.

Soup? thought Ginnie, blinking in surprise. *A man comes out to the woods in a snow storm to hide a can of soup?*

She set down the can and reached inside again. She touched something that felt like another can. She withdrew it and stared down at it. A green-and-white labeled can of tuna.

''Tuna,'' Ginnie said under her breath. Gold or gems or money or a murder weapon would have surprised her less. The one thing she had not been expecting hidden in the heart of the woods was tuna fish.

She reached inside again. And again. And again.

Another can of chicken-noodle soup. Sixteen ounces of stewed tomatoes. Thirty-two ounces of fruit cocktail. She found, in total, twenty-eight cans of food, most of them soup.

Our friendly woodland grocery store, Ginnie thought, shaking her head. She stretched her arm inside again. This time she felt something that seemed to rustle slightly. She closed her fingers around its edge and drew it out.

It was a small, clear plastic bag. Within the bag was a second bag, and within it was a box wrapped heavily in aluminum foil.

She opened the first bag and then the second. The box was small, but heavy. She unwrapped the layers of foil. The box was red cardboard. In black-and-white letters its label said, SURESHOT CARTRIDGES, .22 caliber.

Oh, no, Ginnie thought. This was closer to what she had been expecting. She opened the box's lid. The bullets nestled snugly inside, little coppery cylinders.

She closed the box again and thrust it into her pocket. She didn't know why Swengler was hiding bullets, but she would feel safer if he couldn't find them again. She took a deep breath and plunged her hand into the hole once more.

She reached as far as she could. Her fingertips brushed something. She stretched a bit farther and managed, at last, to get a purchase on it and drag it out.

It was a rolled up bundle of old newspapers tied with strips of black plastic. In its center was a lady's umbrella, protruding from both ends. The umbrella was navy blue with little bright green whales printed on the fabric. The curved handle was the same cheerful green. There was also a woman's gold necklace and two gold earrings.

Ginnie looked at the bundle in perplexity. Soup, bullets and an umbrella with whales on it. And a woman's jewelry.

She could deduce only one thing from the collection: Emile Swengler was mad as a hatter.

Hurriedly she put the umbrella, jewelry and canned goods back into the hole. Using all her strength, she rolled the stone back into place. Then, as Swengler had done, she backed away, dusting the area with snow to erase her tracks.

She stood, shrugging more deeply into her coat, and started off in the same direction Swengler had taken, back toward the towers.

The box of bullets seemed to weigh heavily in her pocket. The bullets were suspicious, she thought, troubled. But they proved nothing. Nobody, to her knowledge, had been shot.

The dead man had been drowned, of that she was almost sure.

She took care, once more, to keep well to the side of Swengler's tracks. Snow fell harder now, but the wind had stilled. She glanced at the sky. It must be about noon, but the sun was hidden. The sky hung low, a leaden gray.

She kept expecting Swengler to loom up in front of her, a black shape against the falling snow. His eyes would be ferocious beneath his white eyebrows, and he would seize her, demanding to know why she was following him. What would she say?

But he didn't appear. The wind stirred in the limbs. Her boots crunched softly in the snow. It was so quiet, she could hear herself breathe.

She felt almost safe when she reached the edge of the woods. She looked about. Hawthorne Towers, huge and silent, rose against the sky. Snow blanketed the expanse of ground between her and the building.

Tucking her head down against the cold, she covered the distance as quickly as she could. Her shoulders sagged with relief when she reached the front doors. She stepped inside quickly, grateful for the embrace of the warmth.

After the unending glare of whiteness outside, it took her eyes a moment to adjust to the dim light of the lobby. With a start, she saw Mr. Swengler standing by the foot of the stairs.

He still wore his heavy black coat. His hands were in the pockets and the collar was turned up high. Under the black brim of his hat, his eyebrows seemed almost supernaturally white. He stared straight at her.

For the first time she noticed his eyes, which were the same leaden gray as the winter sky. Unblinking, they seemed as dead as the eyes of the drowned man. But they were accusing, too.

He knows, Ginnie thought, her muscles tightening. *He knows.*

Chapter Thirteen

Ginnie tensed for flight.

Swengler stopped her. He seemed enormous in his black clothes. His face was stiff with indignation, and the gray eyes still hadn't blinked.

"Young voman." His lower lip trembled with rage. "Young voman, vhy vere you in the voods?"

He took another step toward her. He glowered down. The eyes beneath the shaggy white eyebrows no longer looked dead to Ginnie. They looked insane.

"I was taking a walk," she lied, stepping swiftly to the side and heading for the stairs.

He snatched at her arm, but she was too quick. She dodged and started up the stairs as quickly as she could.

"Young voman! Vhy vere you in the voods?" His voice boomed behind her. He had moved to the bottom of the stairs and glared up after her. "Young voman! Vhy vere you in the voods?"

Ginnie reached the second-floor landing. She half expected Swengler to lunge up the stairs after her and seize her by the ankle. She couldn't move swiftly enough. Her legs felt slow from the cold and heavy from moving through the snow.

But he didn't seem to be following her.

She started to take the stairs two at a time. She wanted to get past the deserted third floor as quickly as possible. As she approached the third-floor landing, she glanced backward, just to make sure Swengler wasn't in pursuit, murder in his pale eyes.

She ran into something as hard as a wall and felt her arms suddenly pinned to her sides.

Someone had her.

Oh, God, Swengler cut me off, she thought in panic, and struggled to escape. She couldn't—so she screamed.

"What's wrong with you?" Wayne demanded, holding her so she couldn't bolt. "Where were you?"

He had scared her so badly, she couldn't speak.

He gripped her more tightly, shaking her slightly to bring her back to herself. "Where were you going?"

"Upstairs," she managed to say. "Where were you going?"

"Downstairs."

"Why?" She couldn't get her breath.

"To look for you. I thought the goblins had you."

She wished her heart would stop hammering so insanely. She could feel its beat shaking all through her body. "Why'd you grab me?"

"I didn't. You ran into me. Where've you been?"

"The woods."

"Why?"

She shook her head, took a deep breath. "I followed Mr. Swengler and he caught me. He's got some sort of cache in the woods. With bullets in it."

"What?" Wayne frowned. "Start at the beginning."

"Let's go to your place first. And lock the door."

ONCE INSIDE, she made herself a cup of strong coffee and told him the whole story, showing him the box of bullets. When she finished, she rose and made a second cup.

"You shouldn't drink that stuff," he said, "as wound up as you are."

"Spare me," Ginnie said, standing by the counter and stirring the coffee. She nodded at the box of bullets on the table. "What do you think?"

Wayne picked up the box. "He sounds like some kind of survivalist or world-ender. Stashing stores against the coming famine or something."

She leaned against the counter and took a sip of coffee. "But why bullets?"

Wayne raised an eyebrow in speculation. "If the world ever does go crash, bullets will be more valuable than money. Think about it."

She shook her head. "I don't want to. I don't want to think about him. Do you suppose we should call the police?"

He sighed. "Ginnie, it's not illegal to hide soup in the woods. Bullets, either. The old guy's kind of crazy. But he hasn't actually done anything."

She sat down at the table again. She put her head in her hands. He caught me. "I feel like a fool."

"It's not illegal to feel like a fool, either. Everybody does, sooner or later."

She closed her eyes. Her head throbbed. "Give me some good news. Tell me you talked Mr. Prouty into moving out."

There was a beat of silence.

"I talked Prouty into moving out."

She squeezed her eyes shut more tightly. "No, really. Tell me what happened."

"I did. I talked Prouty into moving out. I'm helping him go tonight."

Her eyes snapped open. She looked at him suspiciously. "Really?"

"Really."

"But how?" she demanded.

He shrugged. "We reasoned together. It's a thing men do. You should try it some time. Reason, I mean."

She put her head in her hands again. "Have I called you a male chauvinist pig lately?"

"Yes."

"So how did you 'reason' with him?"

"I told him the building was practically empty, Robbie and the Burbages were gone, the heat's off, somebody just burgled Donner, and the next time he had an accident, nobody might find him. He could lie there while the animals starved. I told him, too, that you should go and you wouldn't leave if he didn't. Besides that, he's had time to think things over. He realizes he can't take that dog up and down the stairs in the shape he's in."

She uncovered her eyes and looked at him again. He sat with his arms folded across his chest. His face told her he was serious; he had actually talked sense into Prouty.

He turned toward the living room, frowning. "Did you hear something?"

"No. You mean it? Mr. Prouty will really go somewhere else?" she asked.

"He has a stepsister who rents cabins by the lake. They'll let him bring the animals and they'll look in on him. He'll stay till he's recovered."

Ginnie sighed with relief. "Congratulations. I didn't think you could do it. He's leaving tonight?"

"Tonight. Which means you go, too. You should start packing."

She bit her lip. "I have to go to the morgue first."

He frowned. "Haven't you had enough excitement for one day? Wait."

"No," she said. "I can't wait. I'd rather get it over with. It'd be all I'd think about."

"Do it tomorrow. First get out of here and get a good night's rest."

She crossed her arms and shook her head. "No. It might help to identify him. He probably has a family somewhere, wondering what's happened to him."

"Oh, God," he said with a sigh, "morality. It's become a question of morality."

She looked at him unhappily. "I suppose."

There was a knock at the door. Ginnie started. She had visions of Mr. Swengler towering there, all in black, like a vigilante from hell. She and Wayne looked at each other.

He rose, went to the door and swung it open. A bearlike man with a ruddy face and black beard stood there. He wore a knit cap and a plaid jacket that made him look like a lumberjack. He had a sheepish smile on his face and a book in his hands. It was half-wrapped in torn brown paper.

"I knocked at your neighbor's door, but nobody answered," he said. "My name's Bill LePage. I live down the road. I should have tried to make it here sooner, but I own a service station and this weather's had me runnin', man. This book—" he held it out toward Wayne "—came for your neighbor yesterday afternoon. The courier company left it at my house by mistake. The kids tore it open—thought it was a Christmas present. Sorry about that. Will you give it to your neighbor and explain? I'd appreciate it."

Wayne answered with a curt nod. He took the book. The man gave him another sheepish smile. "You got a spooky place here, you know? Like, where *is* everybody?"

"Christmas," Wayne said by way of explanation.

The man cast a glance around the hall. "Yeah. Well, to each his own. This place is got a little too much atmosphere for my taste, know what I mean?" He smiled again and gave Wayne a mock salute. "Well, Merry Christmas. Sorry again about the wrapping. You know kids."

He left, and Ginnie heard him whistling as he started to descend the staircase. Wayne closed the door and turned to her. She crossed the room and looked at the book in his hands. It was old, the black cover battered. Its title had long ago worn away.

"What is it?" she asked.

"Something for Sutherland," he said, smoothing out the torn wrapper. "From someplace called The Antiquarian Book Service."

"You didn't tell him Sutherland was dead."

He raised one shoulder dismissively. "What good will it do? We'll put it in Sutherland's place with the rest of his stuff."

"What's it about? It looks ancient."

He opened it. The title page was yellowed and foxed. In ornate letters it said, *"Haunted New Hampshire, A Compendium of Places Populated by Specters, Wraithes and Shades."* It was dated 1929.

"Good grief," Ginnie said, taking the book from him. "Why do you suppose he ordered this?"

She turned the page to the table of contents and ran her finger down the chapters. "I don't see this place mentioned. Do you suppose it's in here?"

"Maybe. He had some reason for wanting it."

She stared at it a moment. "Do you think it'd be all right if I looked through it?"

He lifted his shoulder again, his mouth expressionless. "Sutherland won't care."

"This book. This one and the Newsome Book," she mused. "I'd like to look them both over."

"Yeah," he said. "Later. We've got to get going. I have to be back here at six to help Prouty. Right now, you'd better call the police. We've got a dead man to see."

THE DETECTIVE WHO MET Wayne and Ginnie at the medical examiner's was named Sergeant Harkis. He did not bother to be polite. He was a small, squarely built man of about forty, with a bulldog jaw and a balding head. He led them into a cramped, sterile-looking room with humming fluorescent lights and a small television monitor on a counter. The screen showed an empty room.

The look Harkis gave Ginnie fell just short of contemptuous. "Let me get this straight. You saw a dead guy in your bathtub. But he went away."

Ginnie kept her chin defiantly high. "That's right."

"Yeah," Harkis said. "I heard about you."

"I know it sounds crazy," she said defensively. "And I know that nobody believes me. But I saw a man. I want to know if this is the same man."

"Some people got an odd idea of how to amuse themselves. Me, I prefer football on TV, not looking at some floater."

"Floater?" Ginnie said warily.

"Drowning victim," he said without emotion. "Not that this guy was floating. He got hung up in some snags." He glanced down at the information he had taken down from her over the phone. "Hawthorne Towers, eh? Maybe we should build a special road between there and here. We had somebody from there last month. Only he was on the other side of the wall."

Wayne shot him a questioning look. "Sutherland? Why was he here?"

Harkis shrugged. "Medical examiner looks at all unattended deaths. Unless the victim has a history of some condition. It's routine."

"I thought Sutherland had a heart attack," Wayne said. "I thought he had a history of heart trouble."

"Naw," Harkis said. "Had a fall in a motel. Been drinking and hit his head, then bled to death."

"Wait a minute," Wayne said. "I thought—"

Harkis, ready to move on to more current things, ignored him. He pushed a button and spoke into intercom. "Harold? You in there? Or are you dead, too? Come on. We got a customer out here. Roll out the meat tray."

Ginnie glanced uncomfortably at Wayne. "I didn't know they did this with television." Wayne, in his leather jacket, stood with his thumbs hooked in his belt. He shook his head and shrugged. He was still frowning.

Harkis looked at the TV screen, unimpressed. "All the modern conveniences. Come on, Harold. Wheel him out for our viewing pleasure."

A thin young man with horn-rimmed glasses appeared on the screen. He glanced at the camera as if he might smile and wave, then seemed to think better of it.

He reached and somehow adjusted the camera so it moved in closer to what looked like a large metal file drawer. Using both hands, he pulled the drawer out. A sheeted figure lay on it. The top quarter of the figure filled the screen.

"Oh, God," Ginnie said, and forced herself not to turn away. Wayne's arm went around her waist.

The attendant pulled the sheet back. Ginnie tensed and drew in her breath. The man's chest was bare and livid. The face that lay, eyes closed, on the coldly shining metal seemed both familiar and unfamiliar.

It was not, by any means, a pleasant face. The flesh was discolored, the features swollen. Compared to the tormented face of the man in the bathtub, this one, for all the trauma it had suffered, seemed almost restful.

Wayne gripped Ginnie more tightly.

"Okay, Harold," Harkis said, sounding bored. "Play Hollywood. Give us some camera angles."

The camera began to move. It closed in on the face and panned it, showing first the left profile, then the full face, then the right. Ginnie forced herself to watch.

The man was unshaven, which matched her memory. He looked somewhere between forty and fifty, which also matched. She thought in life he must have had a craggy face, heavy at the jowls, weathered, and that, too, seemed familiar.

But she was confused. When she had seen the man, his mouth and eyes were open. He'd worn a hat, so she had not seen his hair. This man had thinning brown hair shot through with gray. It needed a trim. He had a scar on his forehead that she didn't remember, but perhaps it had been hidden by the hat.

The camera rested on a full-face shot. *So this is what death looks like,* Ginnie thought. *It looks terrible.*

Harkis watched dispassionately. "Well, lady, what do you think? Is this your friend in the bathtub or not?"

Ginnie forced herself to keep her gaze on the man's battered countenance. He must have been pummeled by the river currents and probably frozen as well. She was starting to feel more than a little ill.

"Well?" said Harkis.

"I don't know," she finally said.

"Ah," Harkis breathed. "You don't know. I drive clear over here, and you don't know. Well, take your time. I can stay here as long as you can."

Ginnie took another deep breath. "What color are his eyes."

Harkis sighed and spoke into the intercom. "Harold, what color are his eyes?"

From somewhere off camera there was a rattle of papers, then Harold's voice. "Blue."

She nodded. "That's right."

"Oh," Harkis said. "That's right. Very good. You want any more information?"

Ginnie squared her shoulders. "What do you have?"

Harkis spoke into the intercom again. "Harold, you got the unvital statistics?"

The papers rattled once more. Harold spoke in a thin voice. "White male Caucasian, five foot ten, approximately one hundred ninety pounds, age approximately forty-seven years. Distinguishing marks: scar on center of forehead, appendix scar, scar on right foot. Mole on back of neck. Unhealed puncture on right forearm—may have sold blood just before death. No autopsy report yet. No dental, either, it's the weekend. But I'd say he drowned. He had a lot of river water in him."

"Ring any bells?" Harkis asked. He lit a cigarette without asking if anyone minded.

Ginnie shook her head. "He looks the same—sort of. But different, too. The man I saw was dressed. His eyes were open."

Harkis exhaled smoke through his nose. He looked like a squat, bored dragon. "The same, but different. Okay. How was he dressed? Harold, the lady wants to say something about how Wet Willy was dressed."

"Clothes make the man," said Harold brightly.

"You're on," Harkis told her.

Ginnie cleared her throat self-consciously. She spoke into the intercom. "Some of his clothes were wet and some were dry." *How stupid,* she thought. *They found him in the river. By then everything was wet. Start over.*

"He had a brown hat. I think the kind they call a fedora."

"Negative," said Harold. "No hat."

So, of course, his hat fell off, thought Ginnie. She pushed her hair back irritably and started again.

"He had a brown overcoat, kind of worn. A whitish shirt. Gray pants. No tie. Brown shoes. He had wool gloves, either tan or gray. One—" she closed her eyes, remembering "—the left one—had a hole in the finger. The little finger. His fingernail was dirty."

There was silence. The camera stayed trained on the dead man's face.

"Bingo," Harold said quietly. "You got it, lady. She's right, Harkis."

The expression on Harkis's face changed perceptibly. He looked at Ginnie, all traces of boredom gone. She looked at Wayne. Slowly, he smiled at her. For the first time in what seemed a long time, she smiled, too.

She had finally hit. Somebody was finally listening. *Bingo,* she thought. *You got it, lady.*

"I'm going to have to ask you some questions," Harkis said.

"Ask away," Ginnie said. She was ready.

"Somebody finally believes me," Ginnie said as they drove back. She snuggled down more deeply into the car seat. "They finally believe I saw *something*."

"Yeah?" Wayne said, frowning out at the snow that drifted through the beams of the headlights. "Don't get too happy. Next thing, because you knew what he had on, they'll think you pushed him in the river."

She straightened, no longer relaxed. "They wouldn't."

He didn't look at her. His face in the failing light was grim. "You're the only lead they've got. You really think they'll believe your apartment is where you saw him?"

A wave of bewilderment washed over her. It was mixed with indignation. "They couldn't possibly suspect *I* had something to do with this—"

"Why not? You suspected them, remember? You've got a bunch of cops that are shorthanded. Everybody's on their backs. You're probably going to be questioned again. More than once. And at some point, they're going to try to prove you're lying.''

"Oh, great," Ginnie muttered. "I try to do my civic duty and I end up being a suspect. Great. Is this what they mean in the military when they say, 'Never volunteer'?''

"This is what they mean."

She slumped back against the seat again. "Let them question me," she said fatalistically. "I did what I had to do.''

He gave her a brief, sidelong glance. "Yeah. You did what you had to do." He turned his gaze back to the road.

"That man was dead before he ever got in the river," she said. "And that means somebody moved his body. Somebody's trying to cover up something about his death. I have a duty to report a fact like that."

"You've got a duty to take care of yourself. Look, Ginnie, there's a lot of suspicious stuff going on. Too much. I'm going to take you back, help you load your car, then follow you downtown to the Hilton. It's a big hotel, there are a lot of people there. You should be safe."

Ginnie said nothing. She did not even nod. He had insisted she pack her suitcases before they left for Concord. She'd been trying not to think about the moment she would actually load them up.

"I can't afford the Hilton," she said at last. "There's a little motel out on the turnpike, the Lucky Clover. I'll go there."

"*I* can afford it," he said. "I want you at the Hilton. The security's better. You'll be safer."

"I won't let you pay for me," she said between her teeth. "I don't accept things like that from men." What did he think? Buying her time in an expensive hotel would be a way of settling accounts over going to bed with her?

He swore softly. "Could you shake off your Midwestern morality for once? Money? That's what's bothering you? It's not moral to let me help you? All right—you can pay me back. Geez. This is your safety we're talking about."

Suddenly Ginnie was weary again. He was right, of course. She was being ridiculous. It was only her safety he was concerned about. She sank more tiredly against the seat. "I'm sorry."

He wasn't mollified. "And stop being sorry, will you? You're always sorry. You drive me nuts. First you get mad. Then you get guilty because you got mad." Under his breath he swore again.

"I'm sorry," Ginnie said automatically, then almost bit her tongue. "I mean, I'm not sorry. Forget I said anything."

"Lord," he said, sounding wearier than she did, and angry, as well. He took a deep breath. "Let's start over. Look. There's a lot of things that don't make sense about what's been happening. When you get away from all this, I want you to try to think, okay? Look over Newsome's book again. See if you missed anything. Think about the papers that were in it. The ones that were taken. Write down everything you can remember about them."

She shook her head hopelessly. "I told you. One was just a newspaper article on Junior Hopkins. Another one was a list. Our names were on it with some kid of strange system of symbols or something."

"You can't remember them?"

"Not exactly. They were mostly punctuation marks. Except my name had an *X* by it. Yours had a question mark, I think. And some had two, like a question mark and an exclamation point. Mrs. Treat's did, I think. But I couldn't make out any meaning. It made no sense."

"And the last paper?"

"I told you. A rough map of the building. It showed where all the people on the list live. And it had some storage areas or something in the basement marked."

"The basement," he said thoughtfully. "What about the third floor? Anything marked on the third floor?"

She thought, biting her lower lip in frustration. "I can't remember. It was late. I was tired."

"Okay," he said. "Just keep trying. Me, I'd like to find out more about Sutherland's death. I was sure somebody said it was a heart attack. But Harkis called it an accident."

"Who said it was a heart attack?"

"Burbage, I think," Wayne said.

He had asked Harkis about it again at the morgue. But by then, Harkis had become the man who asked questions. He hadn't been interested in answering them, and Wayne knew why. Ginnie's strange story had raised Harkis's suspicions. He would give them no more information. He would watch them. He would listen to them. He would probe them and weigh what they said. But he would tell them nothing.

THE HILTON WAS LUXURIOUS enough for the hordes of presidential candidates who descended on New Hampshire every four years hoping to win points in its early primary. It was even luxurious enough for the superstars of network news who came to cover the vote. Ginnie walked through the same lobby that George Bush had once walked through, but she didn't feel a sense of awe or one of history. All she felt was loss. She would be here. Wayne would not.

Wayne registered her under another name, Linda Irvine. He said that was just to be on the safe side.

He insisted on taking her suitcases to the room itself and checking it out. He looked around the place, seemed satisfied that it was safe, then handed her the keys. "The only other person who needs to know how to find you right now is Harkis," he said. "Call him. Then get yourself a decent meal. You never eat right. It might be safer to use room service for a while. Then get some rest."

The key was still warm from his touch. She fingered it and looked into his eyes. "You have to go back?"

He nodded. "I have to load up Prouty's car. I should drive him. I can take a cab back to my place."

Ginnie spoke up with unaccustomed boldness. "I could come pick you up and take you back."

He glanced away, shaking his head. "The weather's too bad. You stay put. I'll see you."

She cranked her boldness up another notch. "Will you? When?"

"I'll call you," he said. "Maybe tomorrow."

He started out the door. Ginnie put her hand on his sleeve. He stopped. "Wayne," she said, worry in her eyes. "Be careful, will you? You'll be alone over there with Mrs. Treat and Swengler, and I don't trust either of them."

He gave her his half smile, the one that made her heart seem to tumble through limitless space. "I'm not afraid of them."

She kept her hand on the leather of his sleeve. "Even if he buries things in the woods and she talks to ghosts?"

He looked down at her fingers, pale against the darkness of his sleeve. He knew better than to kiss her goodbye, because it would end up the same way as this morning, her in his arms and the two of them in bed. He couldn't afford to get used to that. He didn't want to need her. It was important for him to be able to walk off and leave her when the time came.

Still, the worry on her face gnawed at him. *No,* he thought, *don't worry about her. Don't care that she cares. Just make sure she's safe, then go.* He smiled a bit more widely.

"Hey," he said. "Don't worry about me. I'm immortal."

He put his hands in his pockets so that he wouldn't touch her again. He walked out the door.

Chapter Fourteen

He just walked out, Ginnie kept thinking. *He didn't even say goodbye. He didn't kiss me or so much as shake my hand. It might as well have been Mr. Prouty he was dropping off, not a woman that he'd made love to this morning.*

All right, she told herself. *He's making it clear—he doesn't want a relationship. He's a lone wolf. He's got his gallant streak, but it's almost against his will. He doesn't make commitments. He goes his own way. He probably regrets what happened this morning as much as I do.*

She tried, for the hundredth time since he'd left, to put him out of her mind.

She sat at the desk in the hotel room, running a hand through her hair. She bent over a sheet of hotel stationery, trying to reconstruct the list that she'd found in Louisa Newsome's book.

Wayne Priborski ?
Ginnie Prince X
Paul Donner ?
Emile Swengler ?!
Mrs. Treat ?!
George Fairfax ?
Sutherland ? (Something about students being gone too
                    often)
Mr. Prouty ?

And something else, she thought. Hadn't there been something about "Here" and the initials T.G. And some other puzzling list—"Check—"Dead—"Sp."—something like that?

Mr. and Mrs Burbage, she wondered, what about them? Their names, too, had been marked and set to the side, with some note about their not fitting the pattern.

She shook her head. She thought she had the names right, but she had no confidence that she correctly recalled the strange notations behind them. She was almost sure Sutherland had made a question mark by his own name, but that puzzled her. What could it possibly be that he didn't know about himself?

She took a sip of the coffee she had ordered from room service. It was already cold. She'd ordered a sandwich as well, but could not eat it.

A random thought of Wayne crossed her mind. *Don't think about him,* she told herself. *Try to remember the map. The map.*

She took another sheet of stationery. She sketched a crude outline of Hawthorne Towers as seen from the front. On the fourth floor of the east tower, she and Mr. Prouty lived. *Has Wayne taken Mr. Prouty to his new temporary home yet?*

On the fourth floor of the west tower lived Wayne and, formerly, Sutherland—*Why was Wayne so disturbed to find out Sutherland hadn't died of a heart attack,* Ginnie wondered. *Does he suspect something sinister that he wasn't telling me? Should I call and ask him? No,* she told herself sternly, *I shouldn't.*

Nobody lived on the third floor of either side. She kept that section of the building blank. The only people on the list who lived on the second floor were George Fairfax and Mrs. Treat. *Why did Mrs. Treat first want me to stay, then warn me to go,* Ginnie wondered. *Why has she taken such an obvious dislike to Wayne? And where has George Fairfax gone?*

She wrote down a cluster of names in the section marking the east side of the first floor. Mr. and Mrs. Burbage had the large center apartment. *Where have* they, *gone so suddenly,* Ginnie wondered. *And why has Mrs. Burbage been screaming? Had someone really taken her daughter's things, or had she imagined it? Or was it over something else altogether? Was it Burbage who had told Wayne, wrongly, that Sutherland died of a heart attack? If so, had it been a simple mistake? Or a deliberate lie?*

Paul Donner. Ginnie chewed her pencil so hard she left marks in its yellow paint. Donner claimed something had been stolen from his apartment, but he wouldn't say what. Why?

And lastly, Mr. Swengler. Swengler was the one tenant in the building who truly frightened Ginnie. He was a solitary man, a powerful man, and because she had seen madness flashing deep in his eyes, she believed him to be a dangerous one, as well. A man who hid things in the woods. Things like bullets.

She studied the crude map she'd drawn. Its constellation of names told her nothing. She sighed and took another drink of cold coffee. It tasted like muddy water and made her think of the dirty river where the dead man had been found. She put the cup aside.

Beneath the sketch of the building, she made a rough outline of the basement. On Sutherland's map, several areas had been outlined in red. But which ones? And where, exactly were they located?

She gritted her teeth. She was not good at remembering floor plans or mapping spatial relationships. Although laundry facilities were in the basement, she avoided using them because the basement was vast, dark, damp and all too reminiscent of an enormous grave. She had never bothered to rent a storage cubicle down there. She could imagine rats in the darkness.

She tried to remember what parts of the basement had been outlined, but couldn't. She circled the east end and the west end. But she wasn't sure. The basement held a number of storage areas, both for tenants and management, but she had never wanted to explore them. It was too dank, too full of corners and shadows.

She tried to remember who went frequently to the basement. Burbage, of course. And Robbie. *And where was Robbie? He'd been acting oddly, and he often talked of leaving. But would he pick Christmastime to leave? Had he tried to frighten me? Or was he frightened himself?*

Who else had she seen going into or coming from the basement? She remembered Mrs. Treat carrying her laundry basket down. Ginnie remembered once being startled by Mr. Swengler coming up the stairs. Paul Donner once claimed the old man would slip down there at nights, doing God knew what.

Mr. Prouty had at least one storage cubicle down there, but so did other tenants, including some of the students. Paul Donner had been in the basement recently, too, looking for Gigi. Ginnie remembered him going down there the morning she'd found the mutilated picture in her apartment. She massaged her temples tiredly.

Glancing at the bedside clock, she saw it was almost nine o'clock. Surely Wayne would be back from helping Mr. Prouty by now, she thought. Perhaps she really should call him and make sure everything was all right. She could tell him that she'd tried to reconstruct the map, but it conveyed no message to her. She could ask him, too, if he knew more about the basement than she did.

No, she told herself firmly. If he wanted to talk to her, he knew where to find her. She did not want to pursue him.

She took Sutherland's two books, plumped up the pillows on the bed and lay down with a sigh. *Homework,* she thought grimly, opening Louisa Newsome's book again. She turned once more to the chapter "To the Dark Tower."

She reread it carefully, including every tedious word of Newsome's theories on the spirit world. The story was as intriguing, yet as vague as she remembered.

Ginnie sighed when she finished the account. Perhaps she was still missing something of significance. She turned the pages back, summoned all her willpower and started to read the chapter yet again. Louisa Newsome's speculations seemed even more tiresome than before, even more tortuously reasoned.

"Ectoplasm can most easily materialize on this plane when it finds psychic energy receptive to its essence. This energy does not, of course, have to be conscious..."

Ginnie frowned with irritation. Sometimes it seemed as if the book had been written by two different people, one a powerful if elusive storyteller, the other, a rambling bore obsessed with spiritualism.

She even forced herself to read the next four chapters to see if Newsome returned to the events at Hawthorne Towers to explain them more fully. She did not. She hinted only that her play about a woman in love with a ghost was based on the psychic experiences of her sister, Mary.

At eleven o'clock, Ginnie could stand no more. She took a break to watch the news. The news, she found, was depressing, but not nearly so depressing as the prospect of finishing Newsome's book. After the broadcast, she indulged herself by taking a shower and washing her hair.

She turned down the covers and climbed into bed. Squaring her shoulders, she reached for Newsome's book again, but decided she could face no more of it. She picked up *Haunted New Hampshire* instead. Its chapter titles told her nothing; it had no index. There was no way to tell if Hawthorne Towers, under any of its numerous names, was even mentioned, except to read the whole thing. She opened the book and started at the beginning.

Slightly before two o'clock, she found what she had been looking for. She had almost dozed off, for the writer, Lambert Strethers II, had an ornate style and a love of irrelevant detail.

But in the ninth chapter, irrelevant detail slowly assumed a jolting significance to Ginnie.

It was the express wish of Samuel Watson to build a resort not only of surpassing beauty, but of the latest modernity and to this end, he planned the great edifice that came to be known in our day as Kinnard Hospital and situated it by the banks of the scenic Merrimack, in the midst of a pleasant wood of birch, maple and evergreens.

At this point, Ginnie had only yawned and thought of turning out the light. It was not until the next sentence that she realized the writer was describing Hawthorne Towers.

His dream, alas, was not to be realized, for the Angel of Death took him to his reward, leaving his nephew, General Malachi Hawthorne, to finish the task, a consummation not to take place for some four years, for General Hawthorne was fighting to preserve the union of his country in the War between the States.

Ginnie sat up straighter and rubbed her eyes. This was the first she knew that General Hawthorne hadn't originally planned the building or meant it as a dormitory for mill workers. She read on.

We may see the extent of Samuel Watson's dream of a palatial resort from this account taken from a local newspaper.

"The building will be four stories, with great fireplaces of marble or granite in every room, a richly appointed restaurant on the first floor with light fixtures and windows, wall paper and fabrics by the designer William Morris of the English firm of Morris, Marshall, Faulkner & Company.

"Those wishing to dine in their rooms may have food brought, fresh, by a personal waiter from the fully equipped basement kitchens, via one of two large dumbwaiters. These innovative elevators are powered by steam, like those recently developed in New York,

and may rise, in perfect silence, four stories in the span
of a minute.

"To ensure the freshness of food and drink, sup-
plies and ice will be kept at hand in another innovative
arrangement. An interior springhouse and ice house,
located in the cellar, will neighbor the kitchen itself.
Chefs will use the latest Rumford iron stoves imported
from Munich..."

Ginnie got out of bed and turned on the overhead light.
She sat down at the desk and unmindful that the book didn't
belong to her, began to underline certain words and
phrases—"...dumbwaiters...four stories in the span of a
minute...interior springhouse..."

My God, thought Ginnie, *the place had two dumbwaiters going clear from the basement to the towers. And an
interior springhouse.*

A springhouse, she knew, was a structure built over a cool
spring or brook. It had been a common means of refriger-
ation in the nineteenth century. It had either no floor or a
partial floor, just a walkway to get to the shelves that held
the cooled foodstuffs. And if a spring had bubbled up in the
cellar of Hawthorne Towers a century ago, it might still be
there, behind one of the locked doors in the basement.

A man could be drowned in spring water without ever
leaving the building, she thought in horror. And then he
could be moved to her room. Or any room serviced by the
old dumbwaiters.

My God, she thought again, reading on, *nobody was
getting in through the doors or windows. They must have
been able to get in somehow from the inside.*

She felt almost feverish with the discovery, shaky and a
bit weak. Hastily, she read the rest of the story.

Samuel Watson died, leaving the building unfinished, its
interior still unadorned. Malachi Hawthorne returned from
the war and disdained such luxury and frippery. He put his
family fortune into the milling industry, which was beginning to thrive in New England, and he made the building

into a dormitory for the young women who flocked to work there.

Hawthorne, tempered by battles and a year in the hellish prison camp of Andersonville, was fanatical about the welfare of these young women. He was not unscarred by his experiences. For the rest of his life, he would suffer bouts of claustrophobia, a fear of being confined.

In spite of his own problems, however, he made the building a model of practicality and clean communal living. He lived on the premises himself with his mother and spinster sister. He tore out all of his uncle's expensive and newfangled innovations.

But had he? Ginnie wondered. Or had he kept the dumbwaiters for his personal use? Perhaps he only meant to keep a paternal eye on the young women at first, to ensure that their ways and morals were as pure as he wished. Or, perhaps his year in prison camp had given him a horror of being confined to a dwelling without hiding places or escape routes. Perhaps something, some primitive fear, either for himself or his charges, made him keep secret passages in the building, known only to himself.

For, as Ginnie's eyes rushed over the print, she became more positive that such passages must have existed. By 1898, the dormitory had been in service over thirty years and the general was an old man of almost seventy.

It was in 1898 that women in the dormitory began to complain of mysterious happenings, great and small. There was the sensation of "being watched." There was the unexplained disappearance of "personal items" from locked rooms. Finally, in 1903, there was the first instance of a young woman claiming to have been awakened by someone touching her in her sleep. The occurrences continued, with rising seriousness, until 1909, when the general died.

His nephew inherited the building and converted it to a boys' school. A few mysterious incidents were reported, and a local legend began that the place was haunted by the General's restless ghost.

In 1918, the nephew again converted the building, this time to a resort, which it remained until 1926, when his son inherited the property and converted it to a sanatorium.

The story ended. But Ginnie knew what happened next. The building had been converted to a girls' academy. It was to this school that Louisa Anne Newsome had gone. Once more, a ghost seemed to walk.

Seemed, Ginnie thought, grinding her teeth in concentration. But if the old building had secrets, others, in the course of time, could have learned them.

She looked at her crude map of Hawthorne Towers again, the list of names. Now she saw the pattern Sutherland had written of. She put aside the Burbages' names, for they did not, indeed, fit in. She put aside Wayne's name and Sutherland's. That was part of a different pattern.

George Fairfax and Mary Treat lived over Paul Donner and Emile Swengler, respectively. The third floor was empty, but Ginnie and Mr. Prouty lived in the corresponding rooms on the fourth floor. *And all six of them lived over the storage area in the east end of the basement.*

If the old dumbwaiter or elevator passage still existed, its shaft could be located between each of the pairs of rooms. It could run from the basement to any of the six apartments. And the two on the third floor.

Suddenly Ginnie understood why the picture that had hung in her hallway never stayed in place. It must cover some sort of entrance. And she understood what she thought had been one of the lists Sutherland had made: "Check—Dead—Sp." It was not a list. It was a statement. Check the dead space. The old building had been remodeled so many times, it was full of dead spaces. And some hid only God knew what.

A sick feeling stirred in the pit of her stomach. Somebody among her neighbors had known about the passages and used them. Somebody could use them now.

And Wayne, unsuspecting, was there alone on the fourth floor of the west tower.

His apartment and Sutherland's were located dead opposite from hers. It was logical that the second dumbwaiter be located opposite, as well. Somehow, Sutherland must have known something was going on. Had he eliminated the students as part of it because they were a shifting population, "too often gone?" Did he suspect it was one of the permanent residents, someone always there?

Somebody had got into her place. Somebody had got into Sutherland's. And somebody could get into Wayne's.

She sat for a moment, staring down at the book and her map, as if paralyzed.

Then she arose so fast that she upset the desk chair. She rummaged through her purse and drew out the slip of paper Wayne had given her with his number on it. Going to the bedside table, she picked up the phone and with shaking hands, punched out his number.

He'll think I'm crazy, she told herself giddily. *I'll get all tangled up and won't be able to explain it clearly. I'll have to be very organized. I'll have to say, "Get out of there immediately." And he'll get that chip-on-the-shoulder tone in his voice and say, "Why?"*

She listened to his phone ring the first time. She thought, *I'll say very calmly, "I think there are two secret passages in the building. One runs from the basement to my room and probably Prouty's. One runs to Sutherland's and probably to yours. You need to get out of there right away."*

His phone rang again.

Ginnie's mind spun on. *I'll say, "There's a good chance there's an old-fashioned springhouse in the basement. That's where the dead man could have drowned." I'll say "I've got proof. It's all in Sutherland's book. Come see. But whatever you do, get out of there now. It's dangerous."*

His phone rang a third time.

Ginnie stood, running her hand nervously through her bangs. Sutherland's book, she thought, biting her lip. The key was in the book Sutherland had and the one he ordered. He suspected—and probably was on the trail of something.

The phone rang a fourth time. It seemed to echo hollowly in her ear.

Sutherland was on the trail. But he died. Suddenly.

Oh, my God, Ginnie said again to herself and felt sicker than before. Had Sutherland been *murdered*? Had somebody known he was close to learning the secret and killed him?

Mr. Prouty had almost been killed, why not Sutherland?

"Wayne," she said between her teeth *"answer. Answer, damn you."*

But the phone rang on and on.

And no one answered.

Chapter Fifteen

The snow had stopped, but snowplows had not reached most streets. They stretched white and featureless under the cloudy sky. Beneath their treacherously placid surface was a crumpled blanket of ice, slush frozen to the hardness of stone.

When Ginnie left the hotel, downtown looked like a ghost city. The Christmas lights, wreathed with crystalline mist, shone down on empty streets and deserted sidewalks. Above them, the sky seemed almost supernaturally black.

She wanted to speed, to stamp the accelerator to the floor, but she didn't dare. The road slid and slithered beneath her wheels like a great glistening snake. The tension of being forced to go so slowly and with such painstaking care made every muscle in her body ache.

She had snatched clothes out of her suitcase without even looking at them. She wore jeans, a yellow silk blouse and tennis shoes without stockings. She had thrown on everything over her camisole pajamas.

She had on her coat, which she'd forgotten to button, and her muffler, but had run out without her hat and gloves. Her hair was still slightly damp from the shower. Her car's heater, which had been working only erratically, stopped working altogether. She had to roll down a window to keep the windshield from fogging over. By the time she got to the outskirts of the city, she realized that her hands, locked on the wheel, were numb with cold.

It had hardly occurred to her to call the police. She knew they wouldn't believe her, either that the building could be honeycombed with passages or that Wayne might be in danger. They would listen to her with their forced politeness, then laugh when she hung up.

But the farther Ginnie drove into the black and icy night, the more she was convinced her hunch was true. For eighty years, off and on, residents of the towers had been plagued by strange visitations. Locked rooms had been entered. Something had seemed to walk through walls with the ease of one of Mrs. Treat's beloved phantoms.

Except, she told herself, Mrs. Treat was wrong and Wayne was right. No phantoms existed. What did—what had to—was a series of people who had known a secret. And the secret, simply, was that there was another way, besides doors or windows, to enter certain rooms in Hawthorne Towers.

She pulled onto the New Cumbria Turnpike. It twisted, a dull white ribbon, between walls of black pine. Its surface was even slicker than the city's streets, and Ginnie slowed the car's pace to almost a crawl.

She tried to clinch the wheel more tightly with her stiff fingers. She had to believe she wasn't on a fool's errand. Someone could get into rooms at will, and they had to be using the dumbwaiters, she told herself. Wayne could be in danger. Why hadn't he answered his phone?

By the time she reached the front doors of Hawthorne Towers, she felt only willpower and nervous energy propelled her onward. Her feet, in the flimsy tennis shoes, were as numb as a set of wooden stumps, and she could no longer bend her fingers.

She opened the front door and the lights of the lobby, dim as they were, made her squint painfully. The warm air felt almost smothering in her nostrils, oppressive in her lungs, yet it didn't warm her chilled body.

She looked around the lobby nervously. Childishly, she had hoped to see Wayne standing there. He was not. Nothing stirred. Silence hung in the air like a weight.

Keeping her hands in her pockets, she ran up the stairs. Wayne had to be in his apartment. He had to.

The silent building seemed so immense and the stairwell to stretch so far upward, that the sound of her steps was lost. They made only an infinitely small *pat, pat, pat* in the quiet.

Holding her breath, she hurried past the landing of the third floor. Its shadows looked longer and darker to her than usual, its quiet hung more ominously. *Where was Wayne?* she fretted. *Why hadn't he answered?* Her heart knocked against her breastbone in a drunken drumbeat.

She ran. When she reached the fourth floor, she threw herself against Wayne's door and hammered it with both fists. She tried to call out his name, but couldn't find her voice. Only a rasping gasp came out: "Wayne—please!"

Then the door swung open. Wayne stood there, wearing his black leather jacket.

He looked beautiful to her, truly gorgeous—strong and healthy and whole. Ginnie almost fell into his arms. She clung to him, relieved that he was all right, burying her face against the warm leather.

"What the—" he said.

"Got to get out—" she panted against his chest.

"Where were you?" he demanded. "I called. I was just going to the hotel to look for you."

"Secret passages," Ginnie said, drawing back and staring into his eyes. "Dumbwaiters. And water in the basement."

He touched her face. "What? You're frozen. Your hair's wet. What have you done to yourself? Ginnie?"

She nodded, groping for words. "I came to warn you. Somebody can get in here, too. To your place. I'm almost sure."

He gripped her by the arms. He spoke slowly and calmly, as if to a child or a person on the edge of hysteria. "Shh. Quiet. I tried to call you because it's over, Ginnie. It's finished. There's no more danger."

She nodded, contradicting him. "Yes. Yes, there is."

He shook his head. "No. Nobody's creeping into anybody's place uninvited again. The ghosts are laid to rest."

"No." She tried to slow down, to sound controlled and rational. "There weren't any ghosts. I don't know who it was, but—"

"I do."

She blinked in surprise. She stared at him. "What?"

"I know who it was. Who's been causing all the trouble. Swengler. But he won't cause any more."

She was too full of the need to tell him her own complicated story to comprehend what he said. "Swengler?"

He dug into his pocket. He pulled out a jingling ring of keys. "Burbage's keys," he said, pressing them into her cold hand. "Swengler had them the whole time. He doesn't any more."

"Swengler?" she repeated, still not understanding. She clenched the keys tightly, as if assuring herself of their reality.

Wayne drew her inside and closed the door. He made her sit on the couch. He knelt on one knee in front of her and began massaging her cold hand. He said, "As soon as I got back tonight—"

"Mr. Prouty—is he all right?" Ginnie asked. "He and Alfy and the birds? They're all gone?"

Wayne took the keys from her and thrust them back into his pocket. He rubbed her hands so hard they tingled. "Prouty's fine. The birds and Alfy are fine. They're out of here and safe. When I got back, I started watching. From down in the lobby, in the shadows. Waiting for Swengler to go out again."

"Swengler?" Ginnie said.

Wayne began to work on her wrists. "You'd found his cache in the woods. He knew it. I figured he'd be driven to move it, and this time he'd probably wait until night. If I was lucky, I'd see him go. I was lucky. He went out at about midnight. I followed him." He gave her a half smile. "I made sure I did a better job of it than you did."

She still felt cut off from the import of what he was saying. Only the warmth and sureness of his touch seemed real, that and the familiar darkness of his eyes. "He has another cache?"

Wayne nodded. "Probably more than one. He moved his things to one farther north and nearer the river. I watched him and after I was sure he'd left, I checked it out. The keys were hidden in it. I took them. He must have hit Burbage and stolen them. I found a gun, too. And more bullets, food. The old guy's set for Armageddon. He must have been the one who stole things from Donner. And the Burbages."

She shook her head. "But why would he do all those things? Hit Mr. Prouty? Choke me? Steal the book and give it back?"

He rose, keeping her hand in his, then sat beside her. "Ginnie, he's not sane. Who knows why? He probably couldn't explain himself. Maybe he thought people were after his hidden treasures."

"No," she insisted, licking her lower lip. It stung. She must have bitten it on the way over. "No. It's not that simple. What about the man in the bathtub? Where did he drown? And why was he in my place?"

"I don't know," Wayne said, squeezing her hand. "Maybe the guy was a vagrant. Maybe he happened onto one of Swengler's stores and the old man found him. Maybe it was the cache beside the river. But Swengler caught him. They struggled. Swengler held him under—he's a powerful guy. The man died. Swengler panicked and hid the body."

Ginnie frowned, still dazed by cold and confused by Wayne's explanation. "But why my place? It makes no sense."

"I know it makes no sense. But it's the only answer. Swengler had the keys. He was the only one who could have done it. What have you done to yourself, Ginnie? You still look frozen. What in God's name brought you back here?"

You did, she almost replied. She looked down at her hand in his. He was being kind because she'd been frightened, that was all. That was the way it had always been. "I found something in Sutherland's book. It scared me. I tried to call you. You didn't answer."

"I was out hiding behind snowdrifts. You look like you hid *in* one."

He smoothed her hair back from her forehead. She wished he wouldn't do things like that. She turned her face away so he would stop.

"My heater stopped working. I had to drive with the window down so I could see."

"You drove all the way over here with the window down? It's ten below out there. My God, Ginnie—" For the first time, he looked at her feet. The tennis shoes were soaked from wading through the snow in the parking lot. Her ankles and feet had turned an angry red.

With one fluid movement, Wayne moved farther down the seat, took Ginnie by the ankles and swung her feet onto the couch so that she sat with her legs stretched out, her feet in his lap. He unfastened her shoes and dropped them to the floor. He massaged her feet, rubbing first one, then the other.

"What in God's name made you even come out? Nothing's that important."

You are, she wanted to say. He was making her feet burn and prickle. His hands chafed, stroked and kneaded them, forcing warmth into them again. It hurt and felt wonderful at the same time.

"You said something in Sutherland's book scared you," Wayne muttered. "What?"

Haltingly, Ginnie began to tell him about the dumbwaiter and the indoor springhouse, about old Malachi Hawthorne and the mill girls.

The further she tumbled into the story, the more strained and preposterous it sounded, even to her own ears.

"And this whole time there could have been secret entrances," she finished lamely. "And Sutherland could have started to suspect it."

Wayne sat with her feet in his lap, his hands around her ankles. He simply stared at her, the line of his mouth unreadable. "Secret entrances," he said tonelessly.

"I know it sounds farfetched," she mumbled, wiggling her toes self-consciously. "But it would explain everything."

He patted the pocket of his jacket. She heard the faint, muffled jingle of the keys. "These explain everything."

Ginnie sucked at her lower lip. She shook her head. "They don't explain how anybody could get into Sutherland's place after I had the locks changed."

He frowned. He clasped her around the ankle again. "Secret passages? It sounds like something out of the late, late movie."

"I know," she admitted. She crossed her arms and hugged herself. She was getting warm at last, and it filled her with tingling and restlessness. "But how else could somebody get into Sutherland's?"

"I've lived in this place eight months. I'd notice something like that. I'd know by now if it had secret panels." He said the words *secret panels* with a maximum of sarcasm.

"Not if they were good ones," Ginnie insisted. "Did you ever go to the House of Seven Gables down in Salem? It has a passage that it'd be impossible to spot if you didn't know it was there. They think it was used for smuggling."

"Maybe Swengler got lucky," Wayne argued. "Maybe one of his keys worked in Sutherland's door, by accident. Maybe you left something unlocked."

"You know I didn't leave anything unlocked," she argued back. "You checked everything out yourself."

"You," he said, taking her by the feet and turning her so they set on the floor again, "need to get your feet on the ground."

He sat with his elbows propped on his knees, his hands lightly clasped. She could feel that he was deliberately putting distance between them again. His mouth took on an almost mocking twist. "But you came all this way to save me from the monsters in the walls. I'm touched."

"Wayne," she said, an edge in her voice, "don't patronize me. The story sounds wild, but there *are* facts in it. Two dumbwaiters *were* supposed to be built into this building. So was some kind of interior springhouse. And this place has a history of mysterious goings-on."

Impatiently she rose and went into the hallway, to the spot like the one in her own apartment where the painting would never stay hung. "It has to be here," she said. "It has to be."

She ran her hands along the wall but could feel nothing. She pushed at it, but nothing moved. She knocked at it, but it didn't sound hollow. Wayne had followed her, and he watched her, his face dubious. Ginnie pounded on the wall one final time in frustration, then leaned it against it, almost ready to weep. "It must open from the other side," she said. "That must be it."

He reached into his pocket, took out the keys, dangling the key ring from its chain so that it spun slowly. "If it bothers you this much, we can go look."

Ginnie stood up straight and turned to him. "What?"

He looked at the keys, then her. "We can go look in the basement."

"Now?" she asked. She stared at him in horror. It was well after two o'clock in the morning.

He let the keys spin slowly. "You won't rest until you know, will you?"

She swallowed once, hard. "No. I won't."

He tossed the key ring in the air and caught it neatly. "I believe you enough to go look. And to take a gun when I go."

"No," she said firmly. "Don't take the gun."

"It's part of the deal," he answered with equal firmness. "I go into the basement, I go with a gun. Swengler should be in dreamland, but who knows? And the way he hoards stuff, he's probably got a hundred guns."

"You were born in the wrong century," Ginnie said with disgust. "You should have been a cowboy."

"Whoopy-ti-yi-yay," he said. "Put on your shoes."

"I HATE THIS PLACE," Ginnie said with a shudder. "Even with the lights on, it looks like the lights are off."

The basement was a gloomy, cavernous space, floored and walled with flagstones. The laundry room alone, directly at the foot of the stairs, was modern and well lit. The rest of it, divided confusedly by various enclosed spaces, stretched out, losing itself in shadows and illogical corners.

"I can't believe this was my idea," Wayne said. His face was grim. "Now, what do we look for first?"

She glanced uneasily into the shadows. "I don't quite know. I guess to see if the springhouse is really here. It could be. This place is always damp enough. In the summer, you can feel it on the walls."

Even now, in the dead of winter, she could smell the sickly scent of mildew and oozing moisture. The air was frigid, and she was glad she'd kept her coat on. Her feet, in the wet shoes, were chilled to the point of pain by the cold stone.

"Reconnaissance for one room with spring," he muttered. He switched on the flashlight he'd brought. The back of the basement was not lit at all. It was never used.

Ginnie nodded at a long, unpainted wall toward the rear. "Strethers's book said the hotel's kitchen was supposed to be in the basement. That big space closed off back there, do you suppose that was meant to be it?"

"You're the detective," Wayne said. "Let's check. Stay close to me."

Ginnie resisted putting her hand on his arm just to have the reassurance of touching him. They moved deeper into the darkness, following the cone of light from the flashlight.

"The space here is cut up so eccentrically," she murmured. She kept her voice low, almost a whisper, out of instinct.

"It is all over the building. The place must have been remodeled a dozen times. Down here, they must have staked out a room whenever they wanted one. There's no pattern to it."

The door in the long wall was old. Its wood had never been painted, but age and damp had turned it dark, almost black. Its lock plate was thick with rust.

"Hold this." Wayne handed her the light. "This may take some doing."

He studied the keys and picked one that looked old-fashioned. It would not fit into the lock. He tried a second key. It did not fit, either. He took a third. It slid into the lock roughly, but wouldn't turn. He set his teeth and gave the key another twist. It turned. He touched the doorknob. He pushed the door inward. It creaked.

Wordlessly, he took the light from her. He put his other hand in his pocket with the gun. He stepped inside.

Ginnie stayed close behind him. She watched over his shoulder as the light swept the room. It seemed empty. Cobwebs clung like a fog to the crude ceiling, draped every corner.

A scuttling sound made Ginnie flinch. The light flashed on the dull hide of an animal. The thing froze, glaring into the brightness. The blaze of light turned its pupils red. It bared sharp teeth, then skulked away through a hole in the wooden wall.

"It's only a rat," Wayne said.

"Only," Ginnie returned. She put a hand to her chest and felt the fast thudding of her heart, even through her coat.

Wayne shone the light around the barren room. "Nothing but rat droppings and spiders," Wayne said.

"And no way to tell if it was meant to be a kitchen." Ginnie shook her head. "It looks as if it was walled in but never finished."

He pulled the door shut and locked it with almost as much difficulty as he'd opened it. "What next? You choose. You read the book."

She chewed nervously at her sore lower lip. "The book said the springhouse—was supposed to be close to the kitchen. If this was meant to be the kitchen, then it should be nearby."

He shone the beam of light on one neighboring door, then another. "Choose," he said.

Ginnie thought. She pointed at the room nearest the large one. It was small and set farther back than the other. "That one."

"You got it."

He handed her the light again. She held it steady as he tried the same three keys in the same order. The third, the one that had opened the other door, slid in, fitting smoothly. He twisted it easily. "I hate to tell you this," he said between his teeth, "but this works a little too well. Somebody's been using this one." He pushed the door open.

Ginnie heard the gurgle of water. The sound gave her a surge of elation and a prickle of fear at the same time. She automatically shone the light on the floor inside. A murky little stream sparkled and leaped. Water. A spring.

Then Ginnie raised her eyes and her heart froze in midbeat. She sucked in her breath in hopeless horror.

Above the gurgling stream dangled two motionless human feet in scuffed brown boots.

Ginnie jerked the beam upward in horror, then stifled a scream.

Robbie, dead, swung by a rope around his neck.

Chapter Sixteen

Wayne grabbed her and made her hide her face against his chest. He took the flashlight from her and aimed its beam at Robbie's face.

He winced. The movies, he thought, didn't prepare you for the sight of someone who had actually hanged. Robbie's features were swollen and blackened and his staring eyes were red from burst veins. His tongue lolled grotesquely from his mouth.

Wayne drew Ginnie closer. "Don't look," he ordered.

"He didn't run away. He killed himself," she said, squeezing her eyes more tightly shut.

"Or somebody did it for him." He turned the light away from Robbie's face and to the ground.

Beneath the boy's feet, water bubbled up merrily. It ran above ground for a yard and a half, a dirty little cascade four and a half feet wide. Then it disappeared underground again, running toward the river. Bordering it on all sides was a framework about three feet wide, made of ancient boards.

The walls were lined with empty, dusty wooden shelves. The temperature was cold enough to turn Wayne's breath into a frosty cloud. It had also kept the body cold; Wayne could not tell how long the boy had been dead.

On the floor, not far from Robbie's dangling feet, was a wooden crate. The colors on its ragged label had faded long ago. Haskell's Blueberries, Dover, Delaware.

The homeliness of the detail filled Wayne with grim irony. To ascend to one's death by a blueberry box seemed without dignity, merely pathetic.

He squeezed Ginnie's shoulder. "We need the police."

Ginnie shuddered. She scrubbed her tears away with the flat of her hand, but she could not make herself turn and look at Robbie's ruined face again. "Shouldn't we cut him down—or something? We can't leave him there like—that."

Wayne shook his head. He didn't know. Perhaps the police wouldn't want anything disturbed; if he touched the boy's body, he would be destroying evidence or something.

He looked again at the hanging body, the crate with its tattered label. *Forget the police,* he thought. Ginnie was right. They couldn't leave him there like that. He was hardly more than a kid. It wouldn't be human.

"I'll do it," he said. "I've got a knife. Are you all right?" He tilted her chin up and made her look at him.

She started to nod, but was too honest. She shook her head. "I've seen too many dead people lately."

"We both have." He wished now he'd called the police as soon as he'd found Swengler's keys. Instead, he'd tried to find Ginnie first and everything got tangled up, and now she'd had to face another gruesome piece of work.

He shrugged to himself, trying to be philosophical. What difference could the police have made? They never would have believed Ginnie's story. They would have made only the most cursory search of the basement. However the hand was dealt, it would have been played like this: it would have to be Ginnie and he who ended up in the basement, opening this damned door.

"I feel terrible," Ginnie said, swept away in a wave of grief. "Why? Why was he so unhappy? Why didn't he let somebody know? Didn't any of us care enough?"

Wayne shook his head. "We don't know that he did it. Somebody may have wanted him out of the way. And tried to make it look like suicide."

"But why?"

"I don't know. Maybe it has to do with the dead man and this room. Robbie knew this building better than anybody, better even than Burbage. Maybe he knew too much."

Ginnie pushed a hand through her hair. Instinctively, she knew Wayne was right. Robbie's death had to be connected to that of the man in the bathtub, connected to everything that had happened. Maybe, she thought with weary hope, it's over now and this is the end of it. Maybe the dying will stop now.

"Look," Wayne said, his voice gruff, "Go back where it's light. Wait for me. I'll take care of this."

She took a deep breath. "No," she said. "You'll need help."

He tried to give her an encouraging smile, but it came out bitter.

Cutting down the body was worse than Ginnie had thought, worse than anything she could have imagined. The flashlight, set upon a shelf, only half lit the springhouse, casting weird shadows. She had to stand on the crate, hacking awkwardly at the rope, while Wayne held up Robbie. She tried to cut as high as possible on the rope so she wouldn't have to look at Robbie's face again, but that was impossible. She gritted her teeth and kept sawing at the tough hemp fibers.

Wayne stood under the boy, in icy water halfway to his knees. He held Robbie in a parody of an embrace, taking the weight so the body would no longer dangle from the rope and wouldn't fall into the water when it was cut down.

Ginnie chopped and carved at the rope, tears of frustration stinging her eyes. It was a thick rope, difficult to cut. She didn't see how Wayne could bear the weight of Robbie's body and keep standing in the swift tumble of the cold water. She saw him grimace and knew pain was shooting through his leg.

Finally the blade bit through the last strand of the rope. "Thank God," she breathed, but she immediately had to step down and help Wayne struggle with the body. Robbie was an awkward bundle, and Wayne had to wrestle the boy to the ledge without dropping him.

Together she and Wayne managed to stretch him out on the wooden ledge. Ginnie could not help seeing the boy's face again, but, she thought numbly, she was getting used to it. It was only poor Robbie, she thought. Poor, poor Robbie, who never got his chance to go on to bigger things. He looked shrunken in death, and younger than his twenty-two years.

"God," said Wayne. It was as much a prayer as an oath. He still stood in the water. He stripped off his jacket and laid it over Robbie's face. He turned to an empty part of the ledge and started to lift himself out. Ginnie reached a hand to help him.

Then everything happened at once.

A loud noise exploded through the air so powerfully that Ginnie felt almost deafened. The crash reminded her of the big gunpowder firecrackers of her childhood. She jerked backward in reflex.

Almost simultaneously with the noise, Wayne spun, then lunged forward, falling on his hands and knees into the water.

He wore a white shirt. Suddenly, to Ginnie's horror, the back of it was crimson with blood. It seemed to bloom there like a great strange flower.

"God!" Wayne said again. He gasped. He tried to raise himself, then fell backward, collapsing into the stream.

For a split second Ginnie saw that blood welled out of the front of his shirt, too. Then the water closed over his face.

"Wayne!" she screamed. She waded into the freezing spring and grabbed for him. She was too alarmed to even feel the cold. "Wayne!" She seized him beneath the arms and when she tried to lift him, fell herself.

Gasping at the shock and the wetness, she righted herself and managed to drag him, sputtering, to the surface. Her coat, soaked with water, was now smeared with his blood, as well. Blood danced through the water, a cloud of dirty pink.

Wayne tried to clamber up on the ledge with Ginnie straining to help him, but he couldn't stand. "I've been shot," he panted. "Get the gun—get the gun."

He snatched at the jacket covering Robbie, fumbling in its pocket. The gun fell to the boards and skittered to the corner, four feet out of his reach. When he tried to stretch for it, the pain of the exertion doubled him over. His left hand flew to his ribs to clutch his wound. His right remained stretched toward the gun.

"Oh, Mr. Priborski," said a displeased voice. "Always so combative. Can't you at least die in peace? No more struggling, young man. No more."

Wayne's lip curled in a snarl. He held his hand against the wound, as if keeping his life inside him. He was still doubled over, half lying, half sitting against the corner of the ledge, trying to reach the gun. The water came halfway to his chest. "Swengler," he said, turning his gaze up to the sound of the voice, hate in his eyes.

Ginnie had scrambled onto the ledge to help Wayne. Now she crouched with her back to the automatic, staring at the door.

A man appeared, his face shadowy, gun in hand.

Her heart hammering in her throat, Ginnie stared at him in terror. *It must be Swengler,* she thought. He had found them and now he would kill them both.

But the voice had not been like Swengler's. It had been one far more familiar. She watched, paralyzed, as the man took a step nearer the dim light of the room. The faint glow played on his face. Ginnie went numb.

It was not Emile Swengler in the doorway.

It was Edward Lawson Prouty. He wore his familiar bulky parka, the funny hat with the earflaps. His big glasses made him look like a stern owl.

"Mr. Prouty," Ginnie said in confusion and wonder. What was he doing in the basement? He was supposed to be safe at a cabin by the lake. Why did he have a gun?

Had he come to save them?

"Prouty, you son of a bitch, you shot me," Wayne snarled.

"Yes," Prouty answered. "And you'll die of it. I could put you out of your misery. But I won't. You've been a most annoying young man. Well, curiosity killed the cat."

"Mr. Prouty, what are you doing?" Ginnie asked. She felt as if she had stumbled into an incomprehensible nightmare. She was still crouched, motionless, on the ledge. Wayne needed her, but Mr. Prouty held a gun trained on them both. "Help me get him out."

"Stay where you are, my dear," Prouty said. "I regret that I'm going to have to kill you, as well. I did everything in my power to avoid it, but now it has to be done. Don't worry. I'll make sure it's quick. Unlike him, you won't suffer."

Ginnie shook her head dazedly. "Mr. Prouty, put down the gun. Let me help Wayne. He's hurt."

Prouty gave her a stern look. "Of course, he's hurt, my dear. That's the *point*. I can't have the two of you running about, calling in the police. Not tonight. I have work to do. I'm forced to burn this place down. The two of you have persisted and persisted in getting in my way, forcing my hand." He shook his head solemnly. "I knew you should avoid this young man, Miss Prince. Look at the pretty pass he's brought you to."

Wayne leaned back against the ledge, still grasping his ribs. His face was pale and his teeth had started to chatter. "Let Ginnie go," he said. "You don't want to kill her."

Prouty nodded as if he felt a slight remorse. "True. I don't." He turned his attention back to Ginnie. "And I want you to understand, Miss Prince, that when I kill you, it's with true sadness. I like you. I always have. I tried very hard to get you to think you hadn't seen what you had. But Robbie had already ruined any hope of that. Then I tried equally hard to get you to move away and simply let me be. But your friend here—" he gave the gun a slight wag toward Wayne "—your friend meddled. And Robbie couldn't keep a secret. He started to crumble. It's they who've driven us to this point. I have no choice, I want you to know that.''

Ginnie's mind went cold at his words. A chilling calm invaded her mind and body, and all of her senses seemed heightened. If she was extremely careful, she and Wayne might have the most slender of chances. The instinctive and icy calm had descended on her to help her find what that chance might be.

She spoke cautiously. ''Mr. Prouty, you can't just stand there and watch a man die.''

''But I can, my dear, I've done it often. It's rather an interesting process. Death *is* actually beautiful, you know. Such a lovely stillness steals over the body. All pain ends. It can be so very peaceful if done right. Some people, however—'' he gestured first at Wayne, then at Robbie's body ''—seem born to die badly.''

His words made her mind go colder than before. ''You— killed Robbie?'' she asked.

She could feel Wayne's eyes on her and knew exactly what he wanted. He wanted her to distract Prouty so he could go for the gun. But he'd never reach it, she thought, it was too far and he was hurt too badly. The water around him was a fainter pink, but he was still bleeding, even if more slowly.

''Robbie bungled things badly,'' Mr. Prouty said, obviously displeased at the memory. ''Then he grew rattled and kept bungling more. It was a vicious circle. He was responsible for his own sad end. I merely held him at gunpoint and made him put the noose over his head.'' He gave a little chuckle. ''But he wouldn't step off the box. I had to kick it out from under him.''

The gun, she could see Wayne telling her. *Get the gun in my hands.* She glanced at him. He leaned, panting, against the ledge, the water lapping just beneath his chest. His left hand, pale beneath the water, still gripped his wound.

Slowly, without asking permission, Ginnie stood. Prouty let her. She tried to keep her eyes from the gun. It was only a yard away from her feet. If she could kick it just right—it would be within Wayne's reach. But as soon as he moved for it, Prouty would shoot him again, and this time he would surely kill him. But if she did nothing, Wayne would bleed to death. She needed to make a decision quickly.

"Why are you doing this, Mr. Prouty?" Ginnie asked carefully. "You're not a bad man."

"No. I'm not a bad man. I'm a very good one. I've never done anything except for a good cause. But I fell, and that drunken fool had gone and died, and Robbie panicked and moved the body. Then everything got into a terrible muddle." He paused and alertness sparkled in his eyes. "You and Mr. Priborski keep stealing glances at that gun, Miss Prince. Please don't do anything foolish."

Ginnie gauged the distance between the gun and Wayne. Her knees felt shaky, her whole soaked body trembled and her feet were numb with cold. She wasn't sure she could even connect with the gun if she tried to kick it. She forced herself not to look at it again.

"You said—you said somebody died and Robbie moved him. Was that the man I saw?"

A look of profound irritation settled over Prouty's round face. "Yes. Robbie got him drunk and locked him in down here with a bottle. But he didn't drug the wine well enough to make sure he stayed quiet. During the night, the fool rolled into the spring and I suppose he was too drunk to get out. Who knows how many lives he cost the world with his perfectly senseless death? And the next morning, before Robbie even knew he was dead, I fell and that harpy Mrs. Treat got my key. Robbie couldn't put the body in my apartment. She might turn up at anytime. He didn't know what to do with it. He was afraid to leave it here. Someone had stolen the keys. So, like a fool, he put it in your place. Couldn't the idiot realize it was no safer there?"

If I kick this gun, Wayne will die trying to get it, Ginnie thought. *If I don't, he'll die anyway. What should I do?*

Distract Prouty, she thought. *Keep him talking.*

"May I take off this coat?" she asked, raising her arms slightly to emphasize how wet it was. "It's really uncomfortable." She wondered, rather wildly, if she could throw the coat at his face, cut off his sight for a crucial second.

"No, my dear, no tricks. You might try to fling it at me."

Ginnie worried her lower lip. It had started bleeding inside and she could taste the warm saltiness of her blood. Prouty had easily anticipated her move with the coat. What could she do that he wouldn't anticipate? Another idea flickered into life. She drew off her muffler. It was long and hand-knitted and heavy with water. "Let me tie up his wound, Mr. Prouty. Please. Don't let him bleed to death."

"Don't worry, Miss Prince. He won't suffer at the end. At the end, they just rather—drift away."

Mentally she measured the distance between herself and Prouty. If she whipped the muffler into his face, she might distract him for a second or two. But she was too far from him—six feet at least. And she would have to find a way to get the gun to Wayne at the same time. The look in Wayne's eyes frightened her. He was telling her to move, quickly, before it was too late.

Distract Prouty so you can do something, she thought. *Keep him talking.* She spoke in a surprisingly calm voice.

"You said that because the man died, lives would be lost. What did you mean?" She willed her hands to keep from shaking as she fingered the wet fringe of the heavy scarf.

"Because, my dear," Mr. Prouty said, "a dead man's blood is dead, too. It's good for nothing. I can't use it."

Horrified, Ginnie could only stare at him. *Blood?* she thought. *Prouty had wanted blood?*

Slowly, facts that had been unrelated to her began to fall together and assume a terrifying significance. She remembered that the drowned man had a puncture on his arm, as if he'd sold blood. She'd heard that desperate people sometimes sold their blood.

And Mr. Prouty worked at a blood bank.

"You wanted his blood?" she said, her voice almost a whisper.

"Thousands of fine people desperately need blood. My own mother died for lack of suitable blood. But these—

these creatures walk around good for nothing, sleeping in gutters and picking out of garbage cans. Their lives are a hell of useless misery. I end that misery, Miss Prince. And save worthwhile lives doing it. The homeless and wretched are painlessly put to rest. Their blood is used to heal the sick. I've eased a great deal of suffering, Miss Prince. A great deal."

She looked at him with a sort of horrified wonder. He admitted killing, but he saw himself as a sort of angel of mercy. She merely nodded, as if she was beginning to understand.

"You work at the blood bank. That man—the one in the bathtub—the police said he'd given blood. Is that where you met him?" *Stay calm,* she thought. *Do what you have to do. Say what you have to say.*

"Plasma, my dear. I work at the plasma bank. And he didn't *give* anything. He sold it. Type AB negative. He was a dirty man, but he had clean blood. And a rare type. They all did. They served humanity far better dead than alive. All of them."

"All of them? There were others?" Her heart hammered.

"There were others." Prouty nodded as if the news should be obvious. "Seven. Do you know how many pints of blood the human body holds? Eight. That's fifty-six pints of blood, my dear, rare blood that saved precious lives. When a facility can't find what it needs elsewhere, it can always find it here. I'm famous for supplying it. And I do almost all the paperwork—nobody ever realizes that we're a few pints ahead now and then. What did those men have to live for? Nothing. I ended their pointless existences. And saved lives doing it."

Ginnie forced herself not to look at Wayne. She was afraid if he was worse, she would be too shaken to do anything.

Inhaling deeply, she kept her eyes on Prouty's round, grim face. She toyed again with the muffler, as if twisting it out of nervousness.

"You took blood," she said, as if reciting a lesson he had just taught her. "From homeless men. Somehow you got them here and did it." Her voice shook and she willed it to be steady. "But you needed Robbie's help. To get them here? Or to take them away? Did he know what was going on?"

Prouty shook his head. The dim light glinted on his glasses. "Not really, Miss Prince. He was stupid. I'd tell him the ones to look for. He'd promise them shelter, bring them here and let them drink themselves into a stupor. The wine was drugged, to make sure they stayed out. I kept them down here till morning to get the alcohol out of their systems. The drug lasted longer. Then Robbie brought them to my rooms. But he never knew what happened to them. And he knew better than to ask. Later he just disposed of— packages for me. Rather small—packages."

Ginnie tried to take a step toward him, but he used the gun to motion for her to stay in place.

"I don't understand," she said, trying to sound bewildered. "Robbie'd bring them up to your apartment—still drugged—and you just . . . killed them?"

An irritable look crossed his face. "I strapped them on a table and I took their blood. During the process, they . . . slipped away. They never knew what happened. Unlike Mr. Priborski here."

Ginnie took a deep breath. In spite of herself she glanced at Wayne. His paleness alarmed her, but the set of his face, although rigid with pain, was fierce. *Move,* he was telling her. *Move, or we're dead.*

"If you really have all that equipment, why didn't Mrs. Treat find it?" Ginnie asked. She toyed with the scarf and once more measured the distance between herself and Prouty.

"I keep it hidden." Behind his glasses his eyes crinkled in satisfaction. "There's a secret space between your apartment and mine. There used to be a great many secret spaces and passages in this building years ago. How I loved them— they were a boy's paradise. But fools have walled most of them over without even knowing. A pity. But all things must end.''

Ginnie heard a ragged edge enter Wayne's breathing and it frightened her. She look at him in alarm.

"It's okay," Wayne said between his teeth. "It's still okay."

But she heard the strain in his voice and her calm began to erode. She tried to ignore her fear and keep Prouty occupied. "Years ago?" she asked. "You loved them when you were a boy?"

"I grew up in this building," Prouty said. A bitter smile played around his lips. "My stepfather was headmaster when it was a girls' school. He was a petty tyrant and it was a lonely life here, being the only boy—and one that everyone made fun of. But the building was my friend. And it told me all its secrets. There were wonderful things hidden in this building. Wonderful things."

She heard Wayne draw in his breath too sharply, the sound filled with too much pain. She held herself steady. "Then you were the one watching those girls, weren't you?" she asked Prouty. "All those years ago. And you've watched me, too, haven't you?"

Prouty's face went suddenly cold and she knew at once she'd made a tactical error. "I don't want to talk about it," he said, almost petulantly. Ginnie saw that he didn't mind acknowledging that he murdered people. But he was ashamed that he spied on them.

He wants me to think he's a hero, she thought desperately. *He's standing here about to kill me, but he still wants me to think that he's a hero.*

She took a deep breath. "Mr. Prouty, I understand. I'm sorry you have to do what you're going to do. But don't let me die in vain. Please. Take my blood, too."

She raised her left arm toward him, as if offering him her elbow to escort her somewhere. She took half a step toward him.

"What?" Prouty asked. "Stay back. Don't move."

"My blood isn't rare," she said earnestly, "but it's type O—the universal donor. It could help a lot of people. Please. Dying wouldn't be so bad if I knew part of me was living on, helping other people. Think of it—eight pints. Type O. It could help almost anyone."

"I don't—" For the first time, Prouty seemed unsettled. "I don't—type O?"

She nodded. "That's all I ask. Take it. So I don't die for nothing. Like him—" she gestured at Wayne "—or him." She pointed at Robbie's body. "He died for nothing, Mr. Prouty. Please don't do that to me—use me for somebody's good."

For a split second, Prouty's gaze rested on Robbie and he looked almost guilty.

Ginnie lunged forward, slapping Prouty across the face with the soaked scarf as if it were a whip. He flinched backward, his glasses knocked askew. Ginnie flung the scarf at his face as she dropped to her knees, reached for the gun and slid it across the boards to Wayne.

He lurched for it, his face contorted with pain and determination. His hand closed around it.

Ginnie sprang back into the corner, crouching again, trying to keep out of the way. Instinctively, she hugged herself.

Wayne knocked the safety off the automatic and aimed at Prouty.

Prouty, recovered, his face red and trembling with intensity, aimed at Wayne.

A spurt of fire leaped from each barrel. Ginnie closed her eyes.

The noise of two guns firing filled the little room with such a staggering thunder that Ginnie felt thrown against the wall by it. Her ears rang so loudly that once more she thought she had been deafened.

Something hard smashed against her shin. *I've been shot,* she thought. She heard metal clatter on the floor.

Almost against her will, she opened her eyes. There, on the floor before her, at the very edge of the ledge, lay Wayne's automatic. It had struck her leg.

Oh, God, Wayne's dead, she thought, and turned her eyes to him.

His back was to the corner of the opposite ledge. He was struggling to rise, but he could not. His left hand was still pressed to his side. His right he held awkwardly out from his body. It dripped with blood. He had been hit again.

Ginnie was terrified for him.

It was the expression on his face that frightened her most. A kind of disbelieving despair shone in his eyes. He looked at Ginnie. It was only for a second, but it seemed a lifetime.

They both looked at the doorway. Prouty still stood there, gun in hand. Anger warred with bitterness in his round face. His thick lips crooked downward at one corner.

He raised the gun and aimed it directly at Wayne's head. His hand trembled slightly. From the look on his face, it trembled from rage.

Wayne, his hand dripping blood into the water, lifted his chin defiantly. "Let the woman go."

"Never," Prouty said between his teeth. His voice, too, shook with emotion.

Wayne fought back a grimace of pain. His upper lip curled in almost animal threat. "Let her go. If you don't, I swear I'll come back from the dead and get you. I swear I will. You'll wish it was you who died and not me."

A fine sweat glistened on Prouty's upper lip. His opened parka made him look shorter and plumper than usual, but the eyes behind the glasses were as cold as a snake's.

"Nobody comes back from the dead," he said.

His hand began to shake harder. It shook so badly that he grasped his wrist with his other hand, police style. But still he could not hold the gun steady. Its aim began to stagger drunkenly.

Ginnie pressed against the wall harder. She saw a drop of blood fall from beneath Prouty's parka to land on the toe of his boot. It glistened like a dark jewel against the black rubber. Another fell, and then another.

Prouty took an unsteady step backward. He couldn't keep his hands from quivering. He tried to keep the gun trained on Wayne's face, but could not. His own face, florid before, was going sickly pale.

"You hurt me," Prouty accused, fury and resentment vibrating in his voice. "You hurt me."

"Yeah," Wayne said. "That's the point."

Prouty blinked in anger. He was beginning to look almost stupified with pain. He put his left hand under his parka. He withdrew it slowly, then stared down at it with horror. His fingers were thickly scarlet with his own blood.

He could barely keep the gun level now. He stared at Wayne with righteous rage. "This is my *blood*." Involuntarily, he took another step backward. This time he staggered slightly. He stretched his bloody fingers toward Wayne in denunciation. "This is my *blood*."

"Right. It makes a difference when it's yours." Wayne's face was tight, his nostrils flared.

"I'm going to k-kill you." Prouty's voice broke in the middle of the threat. He sounded like a child. He tried to take a step forward. He tried to aim the gun with both hands again. It shook more wildly than before. His eyes began to roll dazedly.

"I'll kill you both!" he cried, but when he pulled the trigger, the gun was pointed at the ceiling. The recoil threw him even farther backward.

Once again the roar of the gun made Ginnie flinch. She looked at the doorway.

Prouty was gone. She heard him crash against something in the darkness. She heard him sob. She heard him fall. There was silence.

She looked at Wayne. "My God. You killed him."

He gritted his teeth in pain. "You don't know. Get the gun." Suppressed agony resonated in his voice.

Ginnie ignored his words and scurried across the ledge to his side. Still clenching his teeth, he leaned his head back, closed his eyes, and said, "Don't worry about me. It's not that bad. Get the gun."

Ginnie hooked her arms beneath his. "This may hurt," she said. She set her mouth and using all her strength, tried to lift him.

"Don't," he ordered, and she must have hurt him, because there was even more pain in his voice this time. She made herself ignore it. She had to get him out of the water, to stanch his wounds.

She took a firmer grip on him. "Help me," she said in his ear. "Try to stand when I lift. Help me."

He shook his head, his eyes still closed. "Don't. You're not strong enough."

"I'm strong enough," Ginnie said, her lips against his ear. "Believe me. I'm strong enough."

This time she refused to stop at the limits of her strength. Charged with adrenaline, she pushed beyond them. "Oh, God," Wayne panted as she wrestled his body upward. "Oh, boy."

She tugged with the last surge of her power, and he, to end the pain as much as anything, heaved himself upward and backward. He lay on his back, gasping, his eyes squeezed shut. His lips moved, but he said nothing.

Stop the bleeding, Ginnie thought. *First, stop the bleeding.*

She snatched up her muffler from where it had fallen. She bound it swiftly and tightly around his bloody right hand.

He opened his eyes. They looked feverish to her, disoriented. "Ginnie," he said, "get the gun—"

"Shh." She hesitated a moment, then ripped open his shirt. She took the knife she had used to cut the rope and slit away as much of the cloth as she could. She wadded it up and packed it against the wound.

It wasn't enough. There was an exit wound as well, and she needed enough cloth to bind both injuries. She hesitated a moment, breathing hard and licking her lower lip.

Then she did what she had to do. She pushed aside Wayne's jacket from Robbie's body and cut away the boy's sweatshirt.

She tore and folded like a crazy woman, making crude compresses. She forced Wayne to sit. She bit her lip again, hard, when he clamped his mouth tight to keep from crying out.

"I'm sorry," she pleaded. "We've got to stop the blood. Let me get the rest of this shirt off you."

She cut the last of his white shirt away, folded it into a crude pad and thrust it against the wound in his back.

"Now," she told him, struggling to keep calm, to make her every movement efficient, "now I'm going to try to tie them in place. Lift your arms. Like you're going to put them around me." She shrugged out of her coat and then slipped off her blouse to use as a bandage. Her wet camisole clung to her body, chilling her.

He draped his good arm around her. As she leaned near him to get the blouse in place, she could feel his wet hair against her cheek and bare shoulder. She looped the blouse around him, pulling it tight by the arms.

"Fine," she said. "Fine. Now I'll tie it. Bear with me. I've never done this before."

He kept his good hand on her shoulder. He leaned back against the wall again. "Ginnie," he said weakly, "get the gun."

She nodded, making a bulky knot of the sleeves. "As soon as you're through. God, what a terrible job. You look like a ragbag. A Boy Scout would be drummed out of the corps for this."

He gripped her shoulder tighter. "Listen—"

"Shh," she said. "Oh, Wayne, look. You look like something out of a bad mummy movie. It's terrible. Here." She tried to make him lie down. He wouldn't. She took his hand from her shoulder and made him hold his bandage more firmly in place. "There. That'll help. I'll put my coat over you. Then I'll get help."

She grabbed up the coat, spread it wide and settled it over him. She tried to tuck it around him, but her efforts seemed crude, even in her concern.

"Ginnie . . ." he said, almost fiercely.

"I know, I know," she nodded. She touched his cheek, which was cold. "I'll get the gun. Oh, God, Wayne, you're so cold."

He closed his eyes tightly and shook his head as if to clear it. She didn't know how much longer he could remain conscious.

She moved away from him reluctantly. She crawled wearily the few feet to where the gun rested. She knelt and picked it up with her left hand. Once more its heaviness surprised her. She felt a wave of repugnance wash over her. *Guns,* she thought. *For the second time, he's nearly been killed by a gun.*

"Put it down, Miss Prince. It's too late." Mr. Prouty's voice sounded in her ears like a death knell.

Ginnie looked up, stunned. She felt as if someone had suddenly plunged her into some sort of frozen electricity. Her stomach lurched, her skin tingled and she literally felt the hair on her arms stand up. She knelt, her wet hair in her eyes, the gun resting in her left hand.

She stared up into Prouty's cold, angry eyes. He stood in the doorway, leaning heavily against the frame. He still held the gun. He was still shaking, as well, but not as hard as before. If he was still in pain, it no longer showed. A terrifying calm seemed to have descended on him.

In disbelief, she looked from him to Wayne.

Wayne had thrown off her coat. He sat, bare-chested, the crude bandage around his middle. He was so pale, it horrified her, and the bandages were already soaking through with blood. With terror, she realized he was probably growing too weak to move.

"Ginnie," he said, his eyes fastened on hers, "shoot him."

Ginnie stared at Wayne without comprehension.

"Dog," Mr. Prouty spat at him in contempt. "Young man, you'll die like a dog. You're dying now."

Wayne took a deep breath. He glanced at Prouty, but his eyes returned to Ginnie. They had never seemed so black to her.

"Ginnie," he repeated through his teeth, *"shoot him."*

Ginnie looked at Wayne and then again at Prouty. Prouty's mouth was curled in a determined line. He had the gun aimed at her chest. She suddenly felt naked and hopelessly vulnerable. There was nothing between her and Mr. Prouty's gun except a few feet of empty air.

"Put the gun down, Miss Prince," he ordered. "Put it *down*." She stared at him. His hand had begun to shake again, but he managed to keep the gun pointed at her chest.

She looked at the gun lying in her hand. It was black, heavy, squat, ugly. She put her right hand on it. She slipped her finger through the trigger. It seemed like an obscene act to her.

"Don't," Prouty warned. "I'll shoot first. My hand's not as steady as it could be, so I probably can't kill you with the first shot from here. You'll suffer. You can make it easy for yourself. Or you can make it hard."

She knelt there, both hands on the gun. Her heart beat so hard she was sure that Mr. Prouty could see its thudding beneath her flesh. He could see it clearly enough to aim straight at it and explode it.

"Ginnie," Wayne almost snarled. "Shoot him."

I don't know how to kill anybody, Ginnie thought. *I don't even know how to shoot a gun.* Her finger inched more tightly around the trigger.

"If you put it down now," Mr. Prouty said, his tone beguiling, "I'll come over and put this gun to your temple. It will be very quick and you won't feel a thing. You won't have to watch your belligerent friend die. You'll be at peace."

Ginnie stared down at the gun in her hands. "You can't kill us. You won't get away with it."

"Ah, my dear." He almost smiled, then flinched, as if he'd had a twinge of pain. Once more he held his wrist to steady his aim. "No one need ever know how you died. I came back to burn this place. Nothing but ashes will be left. And Robbie's body in the spring—they'll think he did it all. Including killing you. I tried my best to get everyone out of the building. I did my best."

Ginnie lifted her eyes to meet his again. "You can't burn it. Mrs. Treat and Swengler are still here."

"Through no fault of mine," Prouty said. He flinched again. He leaned a little more heavily against the door frame. "They wouldn't go. That must mean they're meant to die."

Ginnie stared at him. Superficially, he still looked like her neighbor, Mr. Prouty, who was plump and fussy and slightly comic and who doted on his animals. He had Mr. Prouty's hat and coat and pudgy face and fleshy hands. But he was a monster.

"Ginnie," Wayne practically screamed, "Shoot him! Shoot!"

Ginnie raised the gun, but her hands shook worse than Prouty's.

"Don't," Prouty warned her. His face had gone as hard as stone.

Ginnie tried to point the gun at him. Tears welled in her eyes, almost blinding her.

"Don't," Prouty said, almost kindly. "You won't be able to. You'll see."

Ginnie's arms trembled as well as her hands. She tried to look down the barrel of the gun, to see if its site was on him. She couldn't tell.

"Oh, my dear," Mr. Prouty said regretfully. True sorrow seemed to tremble in his voice.

"Shoot him!" Wayne screamed.

Ginnie held the gun straight out and aimed it at Prouty's chest. She wanted to pull the trigger, but something deep within her could not let her.

Prouty leaned against the door harder still, using the firmness of its support to steady his aim. "I'm sorry," he said. "I really am."

Ginnie pulled the trigger. But it was too late. His shot rang out first.

Chapter Seventeen

Ginnie was hurled back against the wall as if lightning had ripped through her shoulder and pinned her, liked a pierced insect, to the boards.

She didn't know if she had hit Prouty. She was too stunned to know anything except pain.

"Ginnie!" She heard Wayne's cry. She had fallen on her right side, and she was vaguely aware that Prouty was stumbling toward her, a sick determination on his face. The gun was still in his hand.

Ginnie tried to raise herself. She could not. Her right arm didn't work. It didn't do anything except flame with anguish. She raised her head to look for the gun but could not see it.

Then the bulk of Prouty's body filled her field of vision, blocking out everything else. Heavily, he knelt beside her, his breath rasping. The dim light cast dark shadows on his features, coarsening them. He bent down wearily and stared into her eyes. She stared into his.

She tried to speak. She opened her lips, but nothing came out. Her stricken breathing was the only noise she made. Prouty reached out, patting her cheek distractedly. His hand was cold and unsteady.

"I'm sorry," he grunted. Tears glinted in his eyes. A string of spittle hung from his lower lip. "You shouldn't have made me do it. But it won't hurt long. I'll fix it."

He reached over to where Robbie's corpse lay stretched. Awkwardly, he pulled the black jacket to himself. The effort seemed to cost him a great deal.

Tenderly he covered Ginnie's upper body with the jacket. He tucked it in so it would stay secure. "It's better if we have some clothes on, isn't it?" he asked.

He patted her cheek again. His breath was more labored and raspier than before.

He sat back on his heels, staring down at her. He swayed slightly. The tear in his left eye spilled over and ran down his cheek. He did not wipe it away. Sweat shone once more on his upper lip. His nose was starting to run. He sniffled.

"I really do regret this, you know. You were always very good to Alfy."

He put the barrel of the gun to her temple. The coldness made her shudder.

He soothed her, his hand stroking her covered shoulder. "Shh. It won't hurt long. Goodbye, my dear."

He paused. The sound of his exhalation was long, rattling, labored. He swayed again.

The barrel of the gun scraped down her face, scratching her cheek. In perfect silence, Mr. Prouty crumpled and fell across her body.

Ginnie cried out. He was a heavy man and his inert weight felt as if it were smothering her, crushing her. His arm lay extended across her face and she couldn't turn her head.

He's dead, she thought.

He moved. Ginnie's heart seemed to stop beating.

He moved again, pressing against her hard. He moved a third time, pinning her more hopelessly against the floor.

She couldn't stop herself. She screamed.

Then Prouty seemed to fly away. She could think of no other description. One moment his body sprawled across hers, pressing against it. The next he seemed to levitate and fly with a crash into the corner.

Wayne pulled her to a sitting position. She stared, dazed, at his face. Beneath the veil of his tan, he was as pale as a man carved from ivory. "Are you all right?"

The jacket had fallen away. He touched her bare shoulder. "Can you move your arm?" he asked. "Try."

She nodded obediently. She tried to move her arm. She could not.

He touched her face. He smoothed her hair back. "Okay," he said. "Okay. Take it easy. I'll try to get upstairs to a phone." He untied her blouse from around his middle.

He dragged himself, in a sitting position, to the edge of the ledge, wet the shirt, then dragged himself back. "Okay," he said again. He pressed the shirt to her shoulder. "You okay?" He bent and kissed her lips. His own were cold. "You okay, huh? You okay?"

She put her good arm around his neck and pressed her forehead against his left shoulder. "Prouty?" she asked. Her whole body trembled. "Wayne? Hold me?"

He coiled his good arm around her, held her tight. "Prouty's dead. I think maybe you don't want to look at him."

She nodded wordlessly. She didn't want to look. "You're sure he's dead?"

"I'm sure."

"I felt him move."

"No."

"Yes. I did. I know I did."

"That was me, trying to get hold of him. He's dead. I was going for him and he just crumpled up and died."

Her arm tightened around his neck. "What?"

He pressed his face against her left shoulder. His breath was warm against her cold skin. "Ginnie, trust me. I was about to grab him from behind. But he fell over. I know a dead man when I see one. You killed him."

She could say nothing. She'd killed.

It was a terrible thought, and all she could do was cling to Wayne. He must have used almost the last of his strength trying to save her. She could not let him go.

Somewhere in the distance, they heard a siren. It grew nearer. Another siren's wail joined the first.

Ginnie ran her left hand over Wayne's wet hair. She kissed his cheek. "Somebody upstairs must have heard. They must have phoned the police. Mrs. Treat?"

Wayne nuzzled her cheek. "Mrs. Treat wouldn't have to use a phone. She'd use telepathy."

Ginnie hugged him, even though it made her shoulder hurt. She burrowed more safely against his chest. "I can't believe you. You're making jokes."

"Yeah. Well. As long as you don't expect good jokes. Two dead guys in the same room. Couple of holes in me and you, it impairs the sense of humor. Jeez, Ginnie, you sure you're okay?"

The sirens grew nearer, keening and wailing.

"Wayne, I think I can walk. Let me go upstairs. We don't know for sure those sirens are for us."

His arm tightened around her possessively. "No. Stay. I think I'm going to need you. They're for us, all right."

She drew back and looked at him with concern. There had been an uncharacteristic catch in his voice. "How do you know they're for us?" she asked, smoothing his hair again.

His breathing had become shallow. "It sounded just like that the last time I got shot."

He looked around the room a bit wildly, as if his sight were failing. She was alarmed by his appearance.

"Ginnie?" he said. "Ginnie? I think you better hold me."

He collapsed, sagging into her arms.

Ginnie held him as tightly as she could. She, who had once thought the police her enemy, prayed they would get there in time.

AFTER ONLY ONE DAY, Ginnie hated the hospital. She hated its smell, its food, its rules and the stupid short-tailed gown they gave her to wear.

Most of all, she hated that she couldn't see or talk to Wayne. The police wanted their separate stories untainted by any hint of collaboration. She knew only that he was in good condition.

She, herself, felt terrible. Prouty's bullet had nicked the bone of her upper arm, but had done no damage that would not repair itself. A worse problem was that in her weakened condition, both pneumonia and the flu threatened and she wasn't reacting well to her medication.

The doctors said she needed rest, but it was hard to rest when detectives kept perching around her bed like talkative buzzards.

"And then what happened?" they would ask. "And where was Mr. Prouty in relationship to yourself when this occurred?" It was Harkis, the detective she had met at the medical examiner's, who prodded her longest and most relentlessly.

There were too many other detectives for Ginnie to keep straight. They were coming in from other cities, even other states, trying to track down missing men who might have fallen victim to Prouty.

"What did he say about the disposal of the victim's remains?" they asked repeatedly. Ginnie could only recount Prouty's sinister remark about Robbie getting rid of "small packages." On the evening news, she heard that the bog between the apartment building and Robbie's farm was being searched. She didn't want to think about what might be found.

Above everything else, haunting her like some dark specter was the sickening realization that she had killed a man. It did not matter that he was a bad man. She had looked another human being in the face and she had shot him. Mr. Prouty had been a killer. Now she was, too.

When Harkis returned that evening, she was tired, headachey, troubled and slightly feverish. She didn't want to see another policeman, only Wayne.

Harkis came in the door looking somewhat uncomfortable and carrying a box covered with silver foil.

"Me again," he said. He set the box on the bedside tray. "I brought you some peanut brittle."

Ginnie looked at the box, then at Harkis. He seemed tired and had a five o'clock shadow. It was kind of him to bring her a present, but she was afraid he was going to grill her again.

She managed a weak and insincere smile. "Thanks. When can I see him?"

Harkis shrugged. He sat down on an institutional-looking green chair. "Couple of days."

"A couple of *days*?" Ginnie protested. She wanted to see Wayne now. She wanted to be with him now.

"He's probably gonna be out of here before you are. He was hurt worse, but he's in good shape. You, they tell me, aren't. You're anemic, underweight, run down. You should take better care of yourself."

Ginnie sighed wearily. The doctors kept telling her the same thing, and she was tired of hearing it.

"How's Mr. Swengler?" she asked. The old man had been arrested for stealing the keys.

"He needs help," said Harkis, shaking his head. "Strange story. He'd been in one of Hitler's concentration camps—weighed a hundred and ten pounds when he got out. Survived, but as he got older, he got obsessed with having enough to eat. He thought Burbage was using the keys to steal his food, so he hit him and took them. Then he started stealing himself—a dozen cans of soup from the Burbages. Stole the daughter's umbrella and some jewelry, too. Upset Mrs. Burbage a lot. Stole a gun from Fairfax's place and a rib roast and a Wiener schnitzle from that Donner character."

If Ginnie had felt better, she would have laughed. Paul Donner had been burgled of a Wiener schnitzle? No wonder he refused to say what had happened to him.

"Fairfax," she said, her voice was hoarse. "Did you find him?"

Harkis nodded. "He was at his brother's for Christmas, that was all."

Ginnie relaxed a bit. She had been afraid that George Fairfax, too, might have been one of Prouty's victims.

Harkis crossed his legs, cocking his left foot on his right knee. He cleared his throat. "I came to tell you that they found a body in the bog. Part of a body. They expect to find others."

Ginnie turned away, a wave of faintness washing over her.

Harkis cleared his throat again. "They also found the old dumbwaiter systems. Right where you figured they ran. Still in working order. Pretty amazing. The basement entrances are hidden by the storage cubicles. Prouty had rented the two with access to them."

She stared up at the ceiling. Everytime she heard Prouty's name, she felt weepy. She fought the sensation back down. "How'd he get into the apartments?"

Harkis cocked an eyebrow. "Very ingenious system. Touch a lever inside the wall and part of the paneling just slides away. But it was covered up on the other floors by remodeling. The only places he could still get into were the two towers."

She tried to take a deep breath for strength, but the air rattled weakly in her chest. "Is that why Robbie put the body in my room?"

He nodded again. "Now we know it for sure. Prouty left a journal. We found it at the cabin he'd rented. It was written in a cipher. It was as if he wanted proof of what he'd done, yet he didn't want it. The cipher was a fairly simple one. Only took the cryptologist about fifteen minutes to break it."

All of Ginnie's bones were starting to ache, but she raised herself slightly, her eyes narrowed in disbelief at Harkis's words. "You mean he kept *records* of what he'd done? That's crazy."

Harkis shrugged. "Hey. Serial killers are always arrogant. Deep down, they want somebody to know how smart they've been. His notes were sketchy at the end, but there's enough to tell the story."

Ginnie sank back against the pillow again. "I can't believe this. So why was the body in *my* bathtub?"

Harkis held his hands out in a gesture that said the answer was simple. "Prouty fell. Then Robbie found the victim dead. He didn't have anybody to tell him what to do, so he panicked. He couldn't take the body out in broad daylight. He couldn't do it that night because it stormed. But he thought he had to put it somewhere, and all he could think of was the tower rooms. Not Sutherland's, because nobody knew when one of Sutherland's heirs or a lawyer might turn up. Not Prouty's. Mrs. Treat had grabbed the key. Priborski was home. You weren't supposed to be back for two days. Yours was the safest place. But you did come back."

Ginnie pushed her good hand through her hair. Her forehead felt hot. "So Robbie was probably *in* my apartment when I came home. Or in the passage."

"Right. You left, he got the body back into the passage. But he left evidence the body'd been there. So he came back and moved that. He stashed the body someplace and the next night dumped it in the river. Then Prouty killed him."

She shook her head sadly. "And Robbie mutilated the picture? He had to. Mr. Prouty was still in the hospital."

"Right again," Harkis said. "You were the only person who'd seen the body, so he tried to scare you out. He shouldn't have. If he hadn't, you might have thought the whole thing had been some sort of crazy hallucination. Prouty didn't like the idea of driving you out at first, but when you and Priborski stayed on his trail, he had no choice but to keep it up."

Ginnie massaged her temples wearily. "But why?"

Harkis looked uncomfortable. "There were spy holes in those walls, Miss Prince. In all the tower rooms. He was watching you the night you found Sutherland's book and the papers. I'm sorry to tell you this, Miss Prince, but he liked watching you at night. It's one reason he didn't want you to move at first."

Ginnie turned her face away, feeling another wave of nausea. Tears of shame and anger stung her eyes.

"Prouty'd searched Sutherland's place before, but you found something he hadn't. He had to know exactly what it was. He knew you could get another copy of the book, so he put it in your place—to scare you. Sutherland's notes he didn't want you to have."

Ginnie had forced her tears back, but her head was starting to ache badly. She wished Harkis would go so she could buzz for an aspirin. Still, there were questions she wanted answered, so many questions.

"So he did spy," she said with distaste. The knowledge left her feeling slightly soiled.

"Whoever built that place designed it so he could watch people in their rooms. Prouty found out about that when he was hardly more than a kid, and made the most of it. And when the building became apartments, he moved back to enjoy it again."

Ginnie shook her head, then wished she hadn't. It made the pain seem to crash from one side of the skull to the other. She tried to ignore it. "But when Wayne and I found Mr. Prouty knocked out, was he only pretending? And what happened to Sutherland? Did Mr. Prouty kill him, too?"

Harkis shrugged affably. "The coroner said Prouty had a razor cut on the back of his head. Probably inflicted it himself. He wanted to scare you out, and head wounds bleed like crazy. Besides, this was Prouty you were dealing with. It may not have even all been his blood."

Ginnie lay back against the pillow, her voice bitter. "Why did he say he wouldn't leave, then change his mind?"

"He was desperate, trying anything to get you to go. He felt the trap closing. You see, his world began closing in when people started looking for Junior Hopkins. Prouty got him. It's all there in the cypher. Hopkins had sold blood to the plasma bank. Type O with a bunch of rare negatives tacked on. The plasma bank, incidentally, now has five pints of the stuff. It came from Hopkins, all right."

Ginnie felt another wave of nausea. She didn't want to think what had happened to Junior Hopkins at Prouty's hands.

"Then," Harkis continued with a shrug, "everything started going wrong for Prouty. Sutherland got on his trail. Prouty thought he was rid of him, but then the keys were stolen, which meant somebody had access to every part of the building. That scared him. Then the drifter drowned and

Robbie bungled getting rid of the body. Robbie got scared, and when he got scared, he talked too much—that's why he had to die. In the meantime, you and Priborski had picked up Sutherland's trail again.''

He exhaled sharply. "He knew it had to end then. He shut down the heat, hoping it'd drive people away. He got into the passages and was the voice Mrs. Treat heard saying everybody should leave—but she'll never admit to that.''

He shook his head. "He kept getting more desperate. Finally he decided that even with people still in the building, he'd torch it. Nobody would ever know about the passages or what he'd done.''

Ginnie sighed and settled back more snugly into the pillow. Although she thought she could bear to hear no more, there were still questions she needed answered. Once they were, she wanted only two things. Rest. And Wayne. She wanted him so badly, the need hurt worse than her arm and her head and everything else combined.

"He thought events almost ordained he burn the building,'' Harkis mused. "Oh, yeah, he felt the trap closing, all right.''

"And Robbie?'' Ginnie asked, rubbing her hot forehead. In some ways, Robbie bothered her most of all. "How did he get mixed up in it?''

Harkis shook his head. "Prouty picked his targets at the plasma bank. But he was too smart to be seen with them. He sent Robbie out to bring them back to the Towers, promising them shelter. The kid would drug them and in the morning, deliver them to Prouty's place using the dumbwaiter. But Robbie probably never knew what happened to them. Prouty wouldn't want him to know, and the kid was trained not to question anybody older or smarter.''

Poor Robbie, she thought. But she felt sick thinking about it.

"As to why, the kid apparently did it for money,'' Harkis said with a cynical twist to his mouth. "We found he had a bank account nobody knew about—almost seven hundred dollars. He wanted to get away from home. Well, he did. Just not the way he planned.''

Not the way he'd planned, Ginnie thought, gritting her teeth at the pain in her head.

''Now, as for Prouty,'' Harkis said with a sage nod, ''what he told you was true. His mother died down in Florida because of problems with a transfusion. She had a rare blood type. It happened five years ago. Blood was his business, but he couldn't help her. It must have put him over the edge.''

Ginnie forced herself to keep listening, but she had to close her eyes. Dizziness was descending on her, like a great spinning angel that wanted to bear her away to nothingness. ''Sutherland?'' she managed to say.

Harkis's raspy voice was flat and factual. ''Prouty got him. On Thanksgiving night, Sutherland thought he saw Junior Hopkins going into the back entrance of the cellar, right behind someone whose face he didn't see. He was so sure, he went down to the basement to check it out. But nobody was there.

''Sutherland worked with the city's soup-kitchen project. He knew Hopkins. When it became obvious that Hopkins had disappeared, Sutherland got suspicious. Hopkins wasn't the first homeless person to vanish suddenly from around here. He was just the first one anybody cared about. Another drifter—long gone by then—had told Sutherland once that somebody had tried to get him to come to the Towers, but the guy was suspicious and hadn't gone.

''Sutherland started putting two and two together. He became convinced that Hopkins came into the building, but never left. That if anything happened to him, his body was still there. That's where your list came in, Miss Prince.''

''What?'' Ginnie asked hazily. His voice was starting to seem hazy, faraway. She had to listen very hard.

Harkis went on. ''Sutherland made a list of everybody in the building that weekend and where they lived. He nosed around and noticed there was way too much dead space in the building. He started to suspect there were some kinds of passages from the basement up through the building.''

Ginnie opened her eyes and tried to sit up. She couldn't. "The list? Did you find the list?" she asked, trying to think clearly.

Harkis gave another indifferent shrug. "We found it in Prouty's stash of stuff. All Sutherland's papers, plus the ones he took from you. All kinds of strange stuff in Prouty's stash. Women's nightclothes. Even microfilm. We haven't figured that out yet. But we know what the list was—of who was in the building when Junior Hopkins disappeared, where they lived and of suspicious places in the building.''

Ginnie shut her eyes again. The dizziness was worsening. Harkis's voice was becoming even tinier in her ears, like the drone of an insect.

"Sutherland's mistake was keeping notes on all this. Prouty prowled the tower rooms regularly. He saw them. He knew he had to get Sutherland out of his way. He followed him to the mountains that weekend and killed him. Made it look like an accident. He thought he'd cleaned anything incriminating out of Sutherland's apartment. But he hadn't. You found the book and the list. The walls started closing in on him again. And that's when he started getting really desperate.''

Ginnie squeezed her eyes shut more tightly, then shivered. Nightmare images played at the edges of her mind.

"I guess that's most of the news," Harkis said, shrugging again. "Mrs. Treat says she wants Prouty's dog. Me, I wouldn't have it. I don't want to think of the things that dog's seen. One of the officers is taking the birds for his kids. Me, like I say, I wouldn't have 'em.''

Ginnie said nothing. She seemed to be having a dream while she was still awake. She was tangled up in Alfy's leash. It was almost tied around her ankles and she couldn't move. Mr. Prouty was coming toward her, smiling. "This is just between us," he said. "Just between us murderers." He drew his gun.

"I guess I should go," Harkis said, rising. "We'll be talking to you again tomorrow. Can I do anything for you?"

Ginnie's eyelids fluttered. Her lips moved, but she said nothing.

"Miss Prince?" Harkis said dubiously.

In Ginnie's fever dream, she thought she saw her father. He looked at her sadly. "Daddy," she said, delighted and relieved to see him. She tried to stretch out her arms to him.

His face was rigid with sorrow and disapproval. "You killed a man," he said. He turned his back on her.

When she touched him, he disappeared, as if her very touch were destroying.

She tried to call for him, to explain, but could not.

"Miss Prince?" Harkis repeated. He picked up her hand. It was clammy, her pulse beat erratic.

He pushed the buzzer for the nurse.

The nurse, seeing Ginnie, immediately called for a doctor.

"You've got a very sick young lady here," the doctor told Harkis. "Very sick."

IT WAS WAYNE who took her home from the hospital twelve days later. Except, thought Ginnie, it didn't feel like going home.

Wayne had taken it on himself to find her another apartment and to have her things moved. He didn't think she needed to see Hawthorne Towers again. Ginnie agreed.

He had been released a week before she had. The wound in his hand had been worse than the one between his ribs. Prouty's first bullet had miraculously missed doing serious damage other than the loss of blood. Wayne still carried himself gingerly, which made his limp a bit more pronounced. He had a bandage around the palm and back of his right hand. Otherwise he seemed fine.

He had been there for her in the hospital, dependable as always, kind as he paradoxically could be, more close-mouthed than ever. Neither of them talked much about the future. Wayne kept a kind of armor of reticence around himself. Ginnie supposed it was his way of telling her, once again, he was a man not interested in relationships.

As she recovered, mostly they argued, although it was without the old rancor.

Ginnie didn't think she should get another apartment in New Hampshire. She disliked her job, had lost her chance at the one in Maine, and she had a mountain of hospital bills. She thought she should go back to Indiana where she belonged.

Wayne argued that she was in no condition to make a major decision. "Wait," he kept saying. "Give it time. Hey, you're no quitter. Things have got to get better, right?"

In the end, he prevailed out of sheer stubbornness. Now, with Ginnie beside him, he drove toward the edge of town. It was nearly noon.

"I thought you said this apartment was on the other side of town," Ginnie said.

"I'm taking you up to this Italian restaurant in Concord first," he said. "You need to fatten up. The doctor said you need to gain ten pounds."

"Italian," Ginnie said dubiously. "I didn't think you'd eat Italian food. It's too good."

He shrugged. "I'll suffer. You've got to take better care of yourself. You're the only person I ever knew who went into the hospital and *then* got sick."

Ginnie set her mouth at a rueful angle. In addition to her other troubles, she'd turned out to be allergic to half of her medications.

She had spent Christmas Eve having hallucinations and Christmas Day with an I.V. in her arm. Wayne had brought her a funny little pine tree growing in a red pot, with red and silver bows tied all over it. He'd also brought her a large stuffed Rudolph the Red Nosed Reindeer toy.

He'd given her a new watch, as well. Hers had somehow been smashed in the confrontation with Prouty. It was a beautiful watch, and she suspected it was far more expensive than her old one. But, as usual, he'd been laconic about it. He'd simply handed her the box and walked out the door before she could open it. When she tried to thank him, all he said was a rather harsh, "Forget it."

Her problem was that she couldn't forget, not anything. She thought she'd come to terms with most of the experience, but not with how she felt about Wayne. She remembered too clearly what it was like to be held in his arms. And she remembered with equal clarity what he'd said about not making commitments. She stared down at the watch. Its gold gleamed in the weak sunlight.

Silence filled up the car. Wayne gave her a dark sideways glance. "You still bothered about killing Prouty?"

She shook her head. "Not as much. I—I try to think of it as an accident. I didn't mean to kill him. Only to stop him."

"That's good," he said.

She gazed out her window at the snowy landscape. They had passed the edges of town and pine trees lined the road. "It'll haunt me, though," she said softly. "I've killed someone." There was more to it than that, and she'd try to tell him the rest as soon as she had courage.

"He killed more than once."

Ginnie nodded, her face somber. Police had found the remains of seven men in the bog. "I know. And I wonder if anybody's ever going to want me working for gun control again. It'd look pretty hypocritical."

"You're not a hypocrite," he said. "Never think that."

The silence settled again. He pulled off onto a side road. Ginnie looked at him, wondering what he was doing. "This isn't the way to Concord."

"I'm going to take you for a walk first. You've been cooped up in that place. You could use the fresh air. I asked the doctor. He said it was okay."

She looked down at her fur-trimmed snowboots. She wondered why he had brought them to her to wear home. He'd brought her clothing warm enough, in fact, to brave Siberia.

"Besides," he said, staring at the road. "I want to talk to you."

Her glance threw him a question that he didn't choose to answer. He drove until he came to a clearing by the river.

"Come on," he said. "We'll walk along the river. There's a trail. The kids use it for snowmobiles."

He got out, came round and opened her door. He helped her out, then jammed his hands in the pockets of his leather jacket. They started down the snowy trail in silence.

The day was cloudy and snow was starting to fall. The river, edged with ice, surged grayly over the boulders in its bed.

They walked only a short way before they came to a grove of bare birches that overlooked a bend in the river. Wayne stopped and stood, gazing out.

He didn't so much as glance at Ginnie. He shifted his wide shoulders so the leather of his coat creaked softly. The wind tossed his dark hair, stirring it across his forehead. "I wanted to show you something."

She stared at him. He looked troubled, unhappy, almost angry. His regular features seemed to all be stern, bleak lines. "What?"

He took a deep breath. "This." He reached into his pocket and took out his automatic, the one Ginnie had used to shoot Prouty. She flinched at the sight of it.

He hefted its weight in his hand, then drew back his arm. As hard as he could, he threw the gun. It arced high into the air, then splashed, disappearing beneath the gray water. His face was full of bitterness.

"And this," he said, still not looking at her. He reached into his other pocket and drew out his other automatic. It, too, he pitched as high and hard as he could.

He turned to her. His eyes met hers. The set of his mouth was more severe than before. "That was for you. That was because of you. That's what I had to show you. I'll never own another gun."

"Wayne," she said, almost unable to speak. "You didn't have to do that. Your gun saved my life."

He jammed his hands in his pockets again. He looked genuinely angry now, and the wind, as if angry, too, tossed his hair harder. "Ginnie, I almost got you killed. I never should have taken you down there that night. What happened is my fault. That's one of the things I have to say. I'm sorry. I didn't tell you in the hospital because it seemed too easy a place to do it."

"Wayne," she said, putting her mittened hand on his sleeve, "you haven't really blamed yourself for this, have you?"

She took a deep breath and swallowed. "If I'd shot when you told me, he'd never have hit me. That's what bothered me most. Because every time I look into my heart, I know if I had to do it over, I'd kill him again. And next time, I wouldn't hesitate. I'd do it sooner. That's the truth."

There. She'd said it. Once, she'd never thought she could admit such a thing.

A muscle tightened in his jaw. He looked out to the river again. The corner of his mouth twitched downward slightly. He didn't say anything for a long time. "That's good to know," he said. "That's good."

He paused again before he went on. He stared up at the empty sky. "The other thing I've got to say is this. I'm the kind of guy who keeps to himself. I met you at a time in my life when I didn't want anybody close to me. Nobody."

"I know that." She took her hand away from his arm. "I understand."

He shook his head. The line of his jaw tensed and he cast her a sidelong glance. "What I'm saying is it wasn't the time for me to let somebody into my life. There wasn't any room."

He paused, then frowned out at the water. He shifted his shoulders uncomfortably again. "It wasn't the time and there wasn't any room. I met you when it was absolutely impossible for me to get involved with a woman. Impossible. Absolutely."

She looked away, biting her lip. She hoped it would be easier if she didn't look at him, but it wasn't. Every feature of his face was branded on her mind and would stay branded there, she knew.

He hunched his shoulders against the rising wind and thrust his hands more deeply into his pockets. "But," he said, "like a fool, I fell in love with you anyway. This is hard for me to say. I'm not good at saying these things."

Ginnie turned to stare at him, her lips parted. *"What?"* she said.

He grimaced slightly. His dark eyebrows drew together in a critical frown. "I said I'm not good at saying these things. Okay, I'm—extremely fond of you. But what I did to you is not—it's not forgivable. It's my fault you got hurt. It's my fault you had to shoot Prouty. I don't think I could have saved you from him. I tried, but I was too slow."

He shook his head, his mouth twisting more bitterly. His words came slowly. "I'll never be able to tell you what I felt when he shot you. Or when he put that gun to your head. Never. I guess—I guess that I understood then what hell is. Hell is seeing the person you love in pain. Hell is thinking that you're going to lose them."

He swallowed. "Hell was seeing you in that hospital and knowing it was my fault." He turned to face her. "It nearly killed me. If you'd died—" He broke off, unable to finish. He shook his head again.

Ginnie looked at him, tears burning her eyes. "Is *this* why you've been so—so tight-lipped lately? Because you blame *yourself*? Wayne, I never blamed you for a minute. Never."

He studied her face, his own solemn. He reached out and smoothed a stray curl back from her cheek. His hand lingered, his fingers warm against her jaw. "I mean it, Ginnie," he whispered, his throat tight. "For me, hell is anything that hurts you."

Her lips trembled. She felt the pulse in her throat leap. "Then what would heaven be?"

His thumb traced the outline of her lower lip. His eyes followed its motion. "Heaven is what I have no right to ask for."

Hesitantly, lightly, she placed one hand on his upper arm. "Maybe you should ask anyway."

"Ginnie—I don't have anything to offer you. A body that's got a lot of miles on it. A mind that isn't a professor's. A company that's still getting on its feet. I don't have a lot of money in the bank. Our backgrounds are different. I must seem like a rough guy to you. I put you in danger in a way that's—unforgivable." The muscle in his jaw twitched again. "But for what it's worth," he said, "I love you."

She looked at him, slightly awed. "Oh, Wayne," she breathed. "I love you, too. I don't care that you're starting over. I'm starting over, too."

He looked at her hand. He took it in his own, then looked back into her eyes. "So—what do you think? We might start again together?"

She nodded. "Together. Yes."

He gave her a long, searching glance. Then he started to smile. When he smiled, Ginnie's heart blazed with love.

He put his arms around her waist. She put her good arm around his neck, lay her other hand on his leather sleeve. He looked down at her, still smiling.

He drew her close, lowered his face to hers and kissed her. The cold wind seemed to die. The winter air no longer ached with cold. A warmth like sunshine spread through Ginnie.

His lips told her all the things he couldn't make words say. His mouth against hers was more passionate and eloquent than any poem.

The kiss deepened in intensity until it dizzied her. He drew back, holding her tight and breathing hard. "We may never get to lunch."

She sighed happily. "We may never."

"You know what kissing you is like?"

"No. What?"

He smiled. "Flying. Kissing you is like flying. A thousand miles an hour."

He kissed her again. He was right, she thought joyfully. It was like flying. She was filled with a soaring feeling of joy and rightness and wonder.

"Come on. We can't keep standing out here." He took her hand in his. Together they walked back to the car.

He leaned over from time to time to kiss her ear or brush a snowflake from her hair.

He stopped beside the car and took both her hands in his. They smiled at each other. He took her in his arms again and held her for a long time, just held her. Ginnie rested her cheek against his chest, feeling whole and happy. In his arms was excitement, but a wonderful peace was there, as well. She nestled against him, savoring it.

Behind them the river flowed on, heading homeward.

And the snow fell, making everything clean and white and unscarred again.

Harlequin Intrigue®

COMING NEXT MONTH

#153 WHEN MURDER CALLS by M. L. Gamble
Megan Summers, TV ratings coordinator and
mother of two, was just getting her life in order when
a serial killer—dubbed the Grim Reaper—caused
chaos in the cozy hamlet of Melbourne, Florida. All
became suspects except for attractive Jack Gallagher,
who despite his odd obsession and hidden agenda,
gave Megan support, shelter, love.... But could he
shield her from the Reaper's scythe, which by the
hour whispered closer and closer to home?

#154 THE JAGUAR'S EYE by Caroline Burnes
Hard work on the Maya excavation wasn't all that
distinguished Celeste Coolridge. The villagers
claimed a mystical tie to the fiery-haired stockbroker.
Archaeologist Mark Grayson's passion had been
reserved for the legendary ruby known as the
Jaguar's Eye. Now he tasted both love and fear for
Celeste as the Maya whispered of strange omens and
an ancient prophesy. Somewhere in the ruins of an
age-old civilization lay the bloodred stone that was
the key to Celeste's fate....

Harlequin Superromance®

Hamilton
H·O·U·S·E

A powerful restaurant conglomerate that draws the
best and brightest to its executive ranks. Now almost
eighty years old, Vanessa Hamilton, the founder of
Hamilton House, must choose a successor.
Who will it be?

Matt Logan: He's always been the company man, the
quintessential team player. But tragedy in his
daughter's life and a passionate love affair made him
make some hard choices....

Paula Steele: Thoroughly accomplished, with a sharp
mind, perfect breeding and looks to die for, Paula
thrives on challenges and wants to have it all . . .
but is this right for her?

Grady O'Connor: Working for Hamilton House was
his salvation after Vietnam. The war had messed him
up but good and had killed his storybook marriage.
He's been given a second chance—only he doesn't
know what the hell he's supposed to do with it....

Harlequin Superromance invites you to enjoy Barbara
Kaye's dramatic and emotionally resonant miniseries
about mature men and women making life-changing
decisions. Don't miss:

- CHOICE OF A LIFETIME—a July 1990 release.
  - CHALLENGE OF A LIFETIME
    —a December 1990 release.
- CHANCE OF A LIFETIME—an April 1991 release.

HARLEQUIN
American Romance®

RELIVE THE MEMORIES....

From New York's immigrant experience to San Francisco's great quake of 1906. From the muddy trenches of World War I's western front to the speakeasies of the Roaring Twenties. From the lost fortunes and indomitable spirit of the Thirties to life on the home front in the Fabulous Forties...**A CENTURY OF AMERICAN ROMANCE** takes you on a nostalgic journey through the twentieth century.

Glimpse the lives and loves of American men and women from the turn of the century to the dawn of the year 2000. Revel in the romance of a time gone by. And sneak a peek at romance in an exciting future.

Watch for all the **A CENTURY OF AMERICAN ROMANCE** titles coming to you one per month in Harlequin American Romance.

Don't miss a day of **A CENTURY OF AMERICAN ROMANCE**.

A CENTURY OF
AMERICAN ROMANCE
1960s

The women...the men...the passions...the memories....

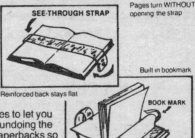

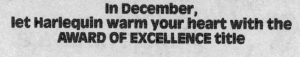

Harlequin Superromance

THEY'RE A BREED APART

The men and women of the Canadian prairies are slow to give their friendship or their love. On the prairies, such gifts can never be recalled. Friendships between families last for generations. And love, once lit, burns hot and pure and bright for a lifetime.

In honor of this special breed of men and women, Harlequin Superromance® presents:

SAGEBRUSH AND SUNSHINE
(Available in October)

and

MAGIC AND MOONBEAMS
(Available in December)

two books by Margot Dalton, featuring the Lyndons and the Burmans, prairie families joined for generations by friendship, then nearly torn apart by love.

Look for SUNSHINE in October and MOONBEAMS in December, coming to you from Harlequin.

MAG-C1R